The
Dragonstone

Lynn McInroy

First published in Great Britain in 2012

Ghostly Publishing, 34 Bakers Close, Plymouth, PL7 2GH

The moral right of the author has been asserted

Published in Great Britain by Ghostly Publishing –

Visit www.ghostlypublishing.co.uk for more information

Connect with the author at
www.ghostlypublishing.co.uk/LynnMcInroy/

The Dragonstone

To Frank, for his constant support

ACKNOWLEDGMENTS

Many thanks to all my writing friends for their encouragement, especially Imran and Zareen.

The Trouble with Pheasants

'Garramikis!'

A breathless hush fell on the hall. King Olave gaped at his distinguished guest, and round the polished tables, gleaming with gold and silver plate, the nobles of Cardevin froze. The train of servitors bearing the dishes for the main course halted, their platters held high. The baron of beef and the galleon-shaped pasty steamed gently, headed by the pièce de résistance; a brace of elegantly-dressed fowl.

'What imbecility is this? You place before me a pheasant?' The Sultan glared round the assembled diners, his mustachios quivering. 'This is an insult most vile!'

'My dear Ahmed,' King Olave of Cardevin looked bewildered, 'What troubles you?'

'What troubles me!?' The sultan's eyes glittered. 'That, you know full well. Almeina, my beloved first wife, the mother of my heir, what is her family crest?' He waved his hand at the leading servitor. 'A pheasant! This is nothing but a calculated insult. You will regret it.' His gaze swept the room and his voice rose to a shriek. 'You will all regret it!'

There was a mass indrawing of breath and then nothing. The huntsmen on the tapestries lining the walls were not more still than the nobles of Cardevin.

Spinning on his pointed toes, Ahmed stalked to the middle of the hall and turned by the large candelabrum.

'Ashkali, Maimonis, Dashiri, b'vashek malai orga meilis!' Arms outstretched, the Sultan chanted, his hands twisting in strange gestures. The incantation continued, sonorous, impressive, terrifying. A thickening aura of menace blanketed the hall and bound the diners to their seats.

'Alamma, alamma, alamma, mantaratek!' The flames of the candles leapt a foot high, then guttered. Ahmed threw his head back, the jewel in his brocade turban stabbing green fire at the King. Then he turned and swept out of the hall.

No-one moved. The standards hung from the roof fluttered in the breeze from the open door.

'What does this mean?' whispered King Olave at length.

The noble next to him leant forward. 'Your majesty, it means trouble.'

* * *

The King's Council had gathered in some haste. The council chamber had been lit with such candles as were immediately available and deep shadows flickered on the faces of long-dead kings, their portraits seeming to leer or wink as the light altered. At the head of the great table stood the king's gilded chair, cushioned in scarlet velvet. As King Olave had not yet arrived, knots of three or four Councillors were forming and reforming in agitated discussion.

'First time we've been on friendly terms for 100 years and now this!'

'Who would have believed it!? And on the last day of the state visit.'

'Never did trust those Azimantis.'

'Shame Sigid isn't still our Wizard. He'd've stuffed a toad in Ahmed's nonsense!'

'The Hereditary Wizard left in a hurry.'

'Expect he's gone to look up his books. Must be the first time he's had a practical task to do.'

'Yes, but can he? I mean, who's ever seen him perform magic?'

'Stand for the King!' The imposing figure of the Lord Chamberlain stood by the door, resplendent in his scarlet coat, his silver staff clasped in one hand. King Olave bustled in. In his hurry, his robe had become hitched up at the back, showing the gold silk lining against the purple velvet.

'Sit, sit. This is dreadful! Friendly relations with Azimantis for the first time since King Magnus I and this happens. What was my chef thinking of?' Olave fitted his rotund figure into his chair.

The Chief Minister clasped his hands on the table, the great ruby in his ring of office glinting in the candlelight. 'Your Majesty, the Royal Chef is distraught. All his efforts to produce a sumptuous banquet which would woo the Sultan into amiability are for nothing. It is a disaster. He asks why he wasn't told of this problem.'

'Well, why wasn't he?'

No-one spoke for a moment. Then the Chief Minister coughed gently and said, 'Sire, did you know about it?'

'Of course I didn't.' Olave flushed irritably.

'And nor did we. We made all the usual enquiries beforehand about the Sultan's preferences, and nothing was mentioned about pheasants.'

Olave sighed. 'We can't retract two cooked pheasants now. We'd best send an emissary after the Sultan to try to repair the damage.'

'Your Majesty, there is worse.' The Chief Minister bowed his head. 'I have consulted the Hereditary Wizard. Sultan Ahmed has cursed Cardevin.'

'Cursed Cardevin!? With what? A plague of frogs? A murrain of cattle? An epidemic?'

'Your Hereditary Wizard is searching his books at the moment, Sire. I've asked him to attend the Council as soon as he has any information. We must take advice from him.'

'Of course! Feo! He'll know what to do'. The King's face brightened, then shadowed again. Feodin Fiorson had an awe-inspiring knowledge of his extensive library, but no-one had ever seen him perform any magic.

* * *

In his study overlooking the sea, Feodin Fiorson, 34th Hereditary Wizard of Cardevin, was searching an ancient tome bound in dragonskin. The candlelight cast flickering shadows of his aquiline features on a tottering pile of volumes at the end of his desk, bound variously in hessian, snakeskin and red morocco leather. On the dark wood of the bookcases lining the walls, larger shadows danced, alternately comic and menacing.

'That's not quite right,' muttered Feo, tugging a lock of dark hair and leafing over another three pages. 'Ah, this is more like it.'

He read for a minute, then pulled a smaller book from the middle of the pile. Turning to a page near the end, he read a paragraph and compared it with the previous volume. As he read, he picked up a quill and dipped it into a curiously-worked bronze inkwell. His first sheet of notes was nearly full.

In the ten years he had held the Hereditary Wizardship, this was the first task other than ceremonial which had fallen to him. His years of research would at last be put to use. He paused, the tip of the quill against his lips. If only his uncle, Sigid, were still here, Sigid, who had taken in his small orphaned nephew and trained him to succeed to the

Hereditary Wizardship - and then died before he could complete the training. Feo sighed. He was well able, he knew, to decipher the Sultan's curse and to construct a counter-spell, but King Olave would have to find a magician who was able to perform it. Feo knew none of his magic worked.

He shook himself. He might not be able to perform magic, but he was the best theoretical magician in the continent. This was his task.

'Need more information on the ritual.' His eyes glinted green as he stooped to pick up a scroll from the floor.

He ran his fingers along the angular script, then went over to one of the bookcases, murmuring 'Aemelioranus should have something to say about that'.

The pile of books grew, until finally, with a sigh of satisfaction, he marked his place in the volume he was reading with his notes, gathered two more books and headed for the door, saying 'That should cover it'.

* * *

There was a rap on the door of the Council Chamber and the Lord Chamberlain announced, 'The Hereditary Wizard of Cardevin.'

Tall and angularly thin, Feodin Fiorson stood a moment in the doorway, then entered the Council Chamber and swept off his hat in a deep bow to King Olave. In his hatband, the phoenix feather which was his badge of office shone flame and bronze in the candlelight.

'Your Majesty!'

'Feo, is this true?' King Olave wiped his brow. 'Did Ahmed lay a curse on Cardevin? Can we lift it?'

Placing his pile of books on the table, Feo sat where the King indicated and opened the first one at his parchment of notes. He scanned the council, eyes flashing as green as the Sultan's turban jewel. 'Your Majesty, My Lords, I have searched my library and I have found the text of the curse the Sultan uttered.' Aware that the attention of everyone in the room was focussed on him, he opened the book at a page covered in fine crabbed writing. 'It is a most unusual formula, at least in this part of the world. Even in Azimantis itself this type of spell isn't common.'

'Feo, have you found out what the curse will do?' King Olave leant forward, stiff with apprehension.

'I think I have, Your Majesty. It wasn't easy to decipher. The spell is written in an archaic dialect of Kashimo and took some effort to understand. Even now, I'm not certain I have a complete grasp of it, but with some further study, I'm sure all will become clear.'

Olave stood up abruptly and barked, 'Feo, what is going to happen to us?'

'Your Majesty,' Feo said, startled, 'The Sultan's curse is a powerful one. At the next new moon, Cardevin will implode and vanish beneath the sea.'

A silence thick enough to grasp filled the chamber. It was cut by the Lord Chamberlain's staff clattering to the floor.

'...vanish beneath the sea.' King Olave's voice shook. 'What can we do? Can we persuade Ahmed to lift the curse?' He wiped the sweat from his brow, pushing the gold circlet to the back of his head.

The Chief Minister spoke. 'Ahmed has sailed for home, Your Majesty. He has a fast ship and a following wind. We have no hope of catching him.'

'Are we certain the curse will work?' A note of desperation crept into Olave's voice.

'Azimantis is renowned for its ancient magic,' said Feo, pushing the dark hair off his forehead. 'In the reign of Jazar I, Azimanti magicians raised an entire city for his wedding festivities, complete with chefs and entertainers for the wedding feast. I have all the details of the spells in Mehmet Ali's book on eastern magic. There are some very interesting techniques used.'

'FEO!' Olave's face was red with frustration. 'We need to know if the curse will work!'

'Well, that's a little difficult to say...That is, magic used to work in the West; after all, Cardevin defeated King Afram's fleet with magic, but of recent years I don't remember hearing of a single instance of an effective spell.'

'But Ahmed comes from the East, not the West.' The Chief Minister clasped his hands on the table. 'We need to know if his curse will be effective here.'

'There's no reason why it shouldn't be... And the East, the East is full of magic. I've collected many fascinating spells from there.' Feo looked round the Council. 'Magic isn't special to any one place, you know. If the casting is correct, the spell will work anywhere. Yes, I have to say I think the curse will work.'

'Then by Azert's eternal fires, what are we going to do about it, man?' The Commander of the King's Armies banged his fist on the table and Feo jumped.

'Do about it? Lord Marshal, there is a counter-spell.' Feo hastily leafed through several pages and scanned the text. 'It is a complicated ritual with an incantation in Bustani and a long list of equipment.'

'Feo, can you perform it!' The King leaned forward, a hint of hope in his eyes.

'Of course I can! Well, I can perform it but I don't know if it will work. That is, it's a very difficult ritual.

Everything must be exactly right.' Feo said suppressing a feeling of panic, then added with a hint of relief, 'And there's one item I haven't got. The dragonstone.'

'Can you get one?'

'First, you have to kill a dragon.'

'We don't have any dragons in Cardevin.'

The Chief Minister broke in, 'There are dragons in Fazimar.'

'How long will it take you to kill a dragon and bring back the dragonstone, Feo?' asked King Olave.

'Kill a dragon!? Me?' Feo rocked back in his seat. 'I can't kill a dragon!'

'Nonsense, man, you're too modest.' The Commander of the King's Armies bristled fiercely. 'You've the reputation of the finest student of magic in the continent. Of course you can kill a dragon!'

'B-but I'm not a swordsman - and you have to use weapons to kill a dragon.'

'Of course you'll have help, Feo,' the King broke in, 'I have in mind my second cousin, Horsa. He's an excellent swordsman. Between your magic and his fighting ability you should be sure to succeed.'

Mouth open, Feo tried to find something to say.

'That's settled then.' said the Chief Minister.

'Feo, join me in my library in half an hour,' said King Olave, 'I'll call Horsa and we'll plan your expedition.'

At the obvious dismissal, Feo stumbled to his feet and managed a low bow before he left.

* * *

Feo scratched on the library door and was admitted by the guard. King Olave looked up from his inlaid desk.

'Come and sit, Feo. You know my cousin, Horsa, I think.'

A stocky man in a plain dark green tunic was sitting beside the huge stone fireplace. He looked up and smiled.

'Hello, Feo. It's a long time since we retrieved your grimoire from Halli the Thief.'

'Horsa, it's good to see you. But how we're to escape from this pit of cockatrices is beyond me.' He wandered over to the cream and gilt bookshelves and absently pulled out a volume on seafaring.

Horsa stroked his auburn moustache. 'It doesn't sound easy, does it?'

'Not easy!? It's impossible,' Feo burst out. 'How can two of us slay a huge flame-throwing monster? It's certain death!' He cast a wild glance round the room. Even the cupids on the painted ceiling seemed to be jeering at him.

King Olave stood up and paced agitatedly round the desk. 'Feo, Horsa is the best swordsman in a thousand miles. And you're the finest magician in the continent. You've got to do it.'

'I'm a theoretical magician,' said Feo, 'I don't perform magic, I study it.'

Sighing, the King said, 'I know the position of Hereditary Wizard is mainly ceremonial, and there isn't normally a need for performing magic, but our situation is desperate. If you and Horsa can't do this, then Cardevin is doomed.'

There was a shocked hiatus. Then Feo whispered, 'There is no other way? You can't get the Sultan to retract the curse?'

Olave shook his head. 'By the time we caught up with him and persuaded him to retract the curse - if we could - it would be too late. Feo, you're our only hope.'

Feo sat, stunned, in his head a picture of Cardevin sinking below the waves, first the cliff with his own

Wizard's Castle, then the tall white spire of the King's Palace.

After a moment, Horsa said quietly, 'Feo, we'll do it. We've got to do it!'

Feo raised his head, a bleak look in his eyes. 'We've got to do it. But how?'

King Olave sat down with a sigh. 'We are all agreed it has to be done, so we need to make plans. You can take ship for Fazimar tomorrow. What do you need to take?'

'Fazimar?' Horsa groaned. 'A large supply of ink for forms and plenty of gold for bribes. Even with that, we'll be lucky to get out of Fazimar City within a week.'

'Has King Marcus settled his quarrel with Cardevin?' asked Feo 'We could be thrown in jail. And then how would we get our dragon?'

'Er... not exactly,' said Olave, 'so I think it would be unwise to send you as official visitors. But as private travellers...'

Feo dropped his head in his hands. 'It isn't enough that we have to fight a dragon, we have to do it with no official support. And avoid getting thrown in jail for breaches of petty regulations!'

'I'll make a prime offering to Hoaga, the goddess of heroic quests, before you leave. Her support will smooth the way.'

'Hoaga, the patron of desperate ventures. That's appropriate!', muttered Feo.

Looking contrite, King Olave said, 'I know it's not easy, Feo, but I'm sure you and Horsa will succeed.' His gaze sharpened as he turned to Feo. 'Your own uncle died in the struggle to protect Cardevin. You do know it was Ahmed's cousin who killed Sigid?'

'Killed? But he died of a seizure!' Shock made an icy lump in Feo's stomach.

'So we thought at the time.' Olave sighed. 'It wasn't until several years later we were given information about a magical attack. By that time we had succeeded in starting negotiations with Ahmed about a treaty, the one we should have signed today.'

Feo jumped up and walked to the window, staring blindly out over the darkened courtyard. His uncle, Sigid, who had taken in his small orphaned nephew and brought him up to succeed him as Hereditary Wizard, had died defending Cardevin. Suddenly he felt as if the whole weight of the island were resting on his shoulders. Sigid had given his life for it. Could the 34th Hereditary Wizard do less?

Turning back to Olave and pushing down the knot in his throat, he said, 'I'll do it. I don't know how, but I'll do it.'

Olave sighed with relief. 'All Cardevin will be grateful.'

'I can't let Sigid down,' Feo murmured to himself.

'And, of course,' King Olave continued, 'the celebrations when you return will be the biggest Cardevin has seen for years. Fireworks, banquets, a procession through the town...'

Pacing across the room, Feo remembered the hours Sigid had spent training his younger self in the most arcane branches of magic. Sigid had never doubted Feo was worthy to become the Hereditary Wizard. He must be able to do this.

'And everyone will rejoice that Cardevin has been saved once again by its Hereditary Wizard.'

Feo turned. 'Of course, the Hereditary Wizard has many times been the salvation of Cardevin. It is right and proper that it should be so again.'

'Exactly.' Olave nodded.

'Then how are we going to do it,' said Feo, sitting down beside the desk.

* * *

An hour before dawn, Feo and Horsa were boarding ship for the three day journey to Fazimar. Feo gazed up at the riding light on the mast and made a silent vow to Sigid that he would justify his faith in him.

A Familiar Kitten

'Name?'

'Feodin Fiorson.'

'Permanent residence?'

'The Street of the Lantern-Makers in Bukhat City,' replied Feo glibly. He glanced round the hall, trying to see where Horsa had got to, but his view was obstructed by a forest of stone pillars and a teaming crowd of visitors applying for papers to visit their families, or import bales of cloth, or export dragon's teeth, guaranteed genuine.

'Reason for visit?'

Turning back to the desk, Feo pulled himself up to his full height and swept his cloak over one spare shoulder. 'To kill a dragon.'

'Really?' The official looked down at his papers and smiled to himself. 'How many?'

'Just one.'

'I can only give you a visa for three weeks,' said the official, bending over his counter to scratch some marks on a slip of parchment. 'You mustn't enter the precincts of the Royal Palace and you must show this whenever asked.

You are required to report to the Office of the Town Guard every other day.'

'And how,' said Feo looking down his large nose, 'Am I supposed to do that if I'm hunting dragons?'

'That's up to you.' Then the official ran a piercing glance over Feo from dusty boots to dark hair. 'I thought it was only one dragon?'

'It is,' said Feo through his teeth. 'Now, I know I can't do anything here without a permit, so tell me, where do I go to get what I need?'

'Down there,' said the official, waving his stylus at three dark corridors without looking, 'and before you go, it's five doublards to validate the pass.'

He bit the coin that Feo tossed down and stowed it in the darker recesses of his tunic before stamping the parchment with a large seal. By the time Feo had picked it up, he was already arguing with the next man about whether his cartload of dormice should be classified as food or exotic pets.

Feo turned on his heel and stalked off, peering over the heads of the crowd for Horsa's auburn hair. Everywhere he looked, knots of traders were disputing with bored officials. The babble mixed with the squeals of restless animals and rebounded from the low roof, assaulting his ears with a ferocious din. Feo strode on, cursing the square stone pillars which blocked his view. On the third circuit of the hall he spotted his partner leaning against the wall, stroking his moustache with one finger. A pair of buxom young women were vanishing down a nearby corridor, giggling. Feo's eyes flashed emerald with irritation as he strode up.

'Where have you been? I've been looking everywhere for you!'

'I know,' said Horsa with a grin, 'I couldn't catch your eye so I just stayed here. I was sure you'd find me in the end.'

'And the two young ladies?'

'Those two?' Horsa glanced towards the corridor entrance 'They were asking me the way to the Parcel Collection Office. I had to tell them I didn't know.'

'But - ' Then Feo laughed. 'This place is execrable. Come on, Horsa, we've got to find the office for hunting licences.'

They strode down the first corridor side by side, their heavy boots thudding on the stone flags. Feo's midnight-coloured cloak swept his heels and the phoenix-plume, which was the badge of the Hereditary Wizards of Cardevin, drooped from his hat. Horsa, whose tastes and lack of height prohibited such impressive garb, wore the plain brown tunic and trousers of the traveller.

The corridor started to slope down, and at the same time grew steadily darker and lower. Patches of damp infected the walls and a slick of green trickled into a puddle. They stopped and looked at each other.

'This can't be right,' said Feo impatiently. 'At this rate we'll be down to the dungeons before we find an office.'

Horsa shivered. 'No official would work in this area. Their sense of self-importance wouldn't allow it. We'd better try the next passage.'

The third corridor turned out to be the right one. A few yards down they found a heavy wooden door labelled "Keeper of the King's Game". They knocked.

There was a long pause before a voice said 'Enter'. Bent over a dark desk was a heavily-bearded figure. He blinked behind his spectacles and announced, 'I'm Snorkin.' He paused and then added impatiently 'Keeper of the King's Game. What are you here for?'

Feo stepped forward and said smoothly, 'We regret disturbing your labours, Seigneur Snorkin, but we wish to acquire a Dragon Permit.'

'What sort of permit? If you want permission to import dragons you're in the wrong office. You want the Royal Customs.'

'We want a permit to hunt, Seigneur.'

'Oh, in that case I suppose you've come to the right place.' He leant forward. 'And what makes you think you're entitled to a Dragon Licence.'

Feo's jaw dropped. 'But the King encourages dragon-hunting! They're classified as vermin.'

'Quite so, quite so, but we can't let just anyone have a Dragon Licence. Oh, dear me, no!'

Feo gathered his wits and pinned an ingratiating smile on his face.

'Of course, Seigneur. I quite see that. But you wouldn't have any hesitation in granting one to,' he drew himself up and fingered his cloak-clasp significantly, 'the High Wizard of Bukhat, would you?'

'Of course not! The High Wizard of Bukhat.' Snorkin scrabbled through the papers on his desk, visions of Snorkin-frogs and Snorkin-rats palpably hanging over his head.

'Ah! I have it! Now, how many dragons is it you want to kill?'

'Just one.'

'Only one? I can give you a good rate for five.'

'No, thank you. One will be fine.'

Snorkin scribbled busily for a moment, then looked up. 'You know you'll have to travel to a restricted area to find dragons?'

'What do we do about that?'

'You need a Travel Pass. Do you intend to carry weapons?'

'I'm not planning on strangling a dragon with my bare hands!'

Snorkin looked at him disapprovingly. 'There's no need to be facetious. You want an Arms Permit, then. What about your friend here?' He jerked his head at Horsa, who was fingering his moustache in bemused silence.

'The same for him.'

'Why didn't you tell me that at the beginning,' said Snorkin petulantly. 'I'll have to do it all over again now.'

There was silence for several minutes while Snorkin shuffled papers. Then he leant back in his chair and picked up his tablet.

'Now let me see,' he said, licking his stylus, 'You want a Dragon Licence, a pass to travel to the Upper Negus Reserve, a permit to carry weapons, same for companion...' He scribbled furiously on his tablet. 'That will be thirty-five doublards and seven minims.'

'Thirty-five doublards?' Feo looked outraged.

'Oh! I'd forgotten,' said Snorkin hastily, 'since it's the King's third cousin's birthday I can offer you a small discount. Shall we say eighteen doublards all told?'

Feo counted the eighteen coins onto the desk. He watched from the corner of his eye as Snorkin, still talking, put the money away and noted that more than half of it slid into Snorkin's purse.

'There's a sub-licence attached to the Dragon Licence which entitles you to kill two wyverns. The Licence must be taken to the Reserve Officer at Upper Negus for validation. Be sure to keep a copy. You must get the Weapons Permit and the Travel Pass stamped by the Chief of the Town Guard before you leave and the Travel Pass counter-stamped at each waystation on the route.'

Feo wondered what on earth he was going to do with a Wyvern Licence. It was enough to have to kill a dragon, let alone adding a poison-dripping scaly bird.

'Is that all?'

'Yes - oh, there's one more thing. You must hire an official guide to accompany the hunt.'

'And where do I find one of them?'

'That's not my department. Try the Parks Reserves and Outlands Agency.'

* * *

Emerging from the big wooden doors of the port offices into the square beyond was a relief. Although there was just as much bustle and noise as inside, in the open air it dissipated more quickly.

Feo cast an eye over the lowering clouds and pulled his cloak closer round him. Carts, loaded with every variety of saleable goods, moved in all directions. Between them, dodging impact at the carters' curses, walked people in wildly different styles of dress, from sailors in rough blue trousers and shirts through merchants in dark, well-cut coats to the odd nobleman in bright silks.

He turned to Horsa. 'Where are we going from here?'

'We'll find an inn before it gets dark. We'll have to leave the Parks Reserves and Outlands Agency until tomorrow. By the time we'd manage to find it tonight, it'd be bound to be closed.'

They headed for the nearest street out of the square, dodging carts and pushing through knots of pedestrians. A cart travelling diagonally passed so close in front that if Feo hadn't taken a step backwards, it would have run over his boots.' As it was, he was near enough to smell every one of the half dozen spices it seemed to be carrying. He started to turn to Horsa and realised he could feel a hand at his belt. Spinning round, he grabbed and found himself with a fistful of dirty brown shirt. 'What...' The wearer of the shirt, not able to pull free, groped at his waist. A moment later he was waving a very sharp knife in Feo's face. Another moment, and a sword swung up from behind Feo and the knife went flying.

'Now, what exactly are you doing with my friend here?' Horsa's sword point hovered between the shirt's collar and the straggly beard.

The thief looked wildly round and then yelled, 'Guards! Guards!' Pushing through the crowds towards them, Feo saw two men in grubby red coats with an anchor on the collar.

'What's this, then?' The first guard reached them and eyed Horsa'a drawn sword with disapproval. 'You can't threaten people with an open weapon in Fazimar City!'

'This man has just tried to rob my friend.' Horsa kept his sword point steady.

The second guard appeared beside the first. 'I don't care what you say he's done, you can't threaten anyone with a weapon. Let him go!'

'He's just threatened my friend with a knife!'

The first guard looked round ostentatiously. 'I don't see any knife. Let him go, or it's a month's hard labour for you!'

Reluctantly, Horsa sheathed his sword and the thief vanished into the crowd.

'I shall have to report this.' The first guard made a show of extracting a tablet. 'And you'll have to stay in the port cells until we've sorted this out. Both of you.'

Feo looked desperately at Horsa. 'We can't do that. It could be weeks.'

The second guard looked Feo up and down. 'Have you checked your money yet?'

Horsa stepped forward quickly. 'Can I make a small donation to your widows' fund?'

The two guards looked at each other.

'Say, 20 doublards? To help your charitable work?'

'We-ell. Thirty doublards would help a needy widow.' The first guard looked at Horsa. 'And we look very kindly on those who support charity.'

The thirty doublards vanished rapidly into the first guard's belt pouch and they turned towards the other side of the square. Feo and Horsa headed for a street out of the port area as quickly as they could.

Just before they turned up it, Feo looked back towards the port. 'Horsa, look over there!' On the other side of the square, the red coats of the two guards stood out beside a bearded man in a brown shirt. 'They're arresting him!'

Horsa turned. 'No they're not,' he said, 'They're just sharing the proceeds.'

* * *

'Are you sure we've got all the permits we need?' Horsa stepped carefully over the gutter in the centre of the cobbled street. A trickle of dark liquid flowed down it, carrying the detritus of the market to the river.

'So far as I can tell,' grunted Feo. He hunched his shoulders under the cloak, glowering at the unfairness of a life which had set him up in a comfortable house with time to pursue his research, and then ripped him out of it to send him on a Wild Dragon Chase.

His brooding was shattered by a bloodcurdling screech. A small black blur shot out of an alley on the left and hit his legs. Feo stumbled. He caught himself and bent to pick up the missile. A dazed kitten sat on his hand, blinking with shock.

'Where did that come from?' Horsa peered up the alley.

'I don't know. She isn't hurt.' Feo scratched the kitten's ears with an absent finger.

'It's a pretty scruffy beast,' said Horsa, eying the unkempt fur. 'If you put it down, I expect it'll find its way home.'

'Home!' exclaimed Feo. 'She isn't even properly fed. I can feel her ribs.'

'Feo, you can't keep it! We're on a dragon hunt!'

'Every wizard needs a familiar,' said Feo loftily.

'You've never had one before.'

'Well, I have now!' Feo tucked the kitten into the top pocket of his cloak. She squeaked once and curled up, drowsy in the unaccustomed shelter. 'Hoaga, who guides our quest, sent her, so she must be needed.'

The street was deserted. As they continued on their way, Feo wondered if the market odour, trapped by the narrow stone canyon, had driven the people indoors. Why was he walking down this dirty road when he could be sitting in his comfortable library researching the uses of cockatrices? Then a rumble in his stomach reminded him it was time to eat.

The two rounded a corner and were confronted by a long, low building with an open door at one end. Its whitewashed walls were topped by a moss-grown thatch which swept down to overhang the ground-floor windows.

The upper casements peered through the thatch. A board swung over the door, showing a sinister-looking traveller devouring a large joint of meat. The road beyond narrowed still further and turned sharply to the right.

Horsa sniffed. 'Smells like venison to me. Let's book a room and get some food. I'm famished.'

Feo headed for the door without a word. It had started to rain and the phoenix-plume drooped even lower, dropping a steady trickle of water down his neck.

'Good afternoon, gentlemen! How may I serve you?' A round man in a white apron appeared, rubbing his hands and beaming, as they ducked through the door.

'Good afternoon. A room for two if you please. And dinner.' Feo shook the water from his hat with an impatient hand and regarded the bedraggled feather with disfavour. 'Does it always rain here?'

'No, no. Most unusual. You'll find your stay at the Wyvern's Head quite comfortable, I do assure you.' The innkeeper was talking very fast and his two eyes had parted company in an unnerving fashion, one peering over Feo's shoulder while the other looked directly at Horsa.

'I'm glad to hear it! What about this room?'

The innkeeper vanished behind the counter and reappeared holding a large book. His eyes had rejoined each other. 'I have a very nice room available, two beds, looks out over the front of the building. If I can just have your details?'

He filled in the columns across the page of the register and then said, 'Can I see your papers, please?'

Feo passed over the sheaf of documents.

'High Wizard of Bukhat!' remarked the innkeeper, his eyes showing a tendency to wander again. 'What brings you to Fazimar?'

'I've come to kill a dragon.' Feo looked at the man, daring him to comment.

'A very good place to come for that. Yes, these seem to be in order.' He handed the papers back to Feo who watched, fascinated, as he pulled his eyes back together. 'Let me show you to your room, sir.'

The front of Feo's cloak started to twitch and heave. A black head emerged and regarded the innkeeper's gyrating eyes with astonishment.

'Ah, yes,' said Feo, 'I nearly forgot. A bowl of milk and another of meat for my friend.'

'B-but animals are not... The regulations don't allow... But I'm sure in the case of a High Wizard of Bukhat...' The innkeeper gave up the attempt to keep his eyes in order and led them upstairs.

The room was whitewashed and neatly, if sparsely furnished with a pair of wooden beds, two oak chairs and a table and a large cupboard. Over the beds hung a small sampler. It read, "Order in all things". Feo flung his bag at a chair and extracted the kitten from his cloak.

'Now, what is a proper name for a Wizard's familiar?' He held the small black body level with his nose. A pair of emerald eyes gazed calmly into his own larger ones, and a faint rumble vibrated the whole body.

'At least it looks the part.' Horsa stood beside him examining the kitten with amusement. 'A black cat without a hair of white.'

'Of course she does.' Feo looked down his nose at Horsa. 'Hoaga sent her.'

Of course she did!' remarked Horsa wryly, 'It's an invaluable aid for a desperate quest.'

Feo ignored him and examined the kitten again.

'Kirrin. That's your name, Kirrin.' Kirrin opened her mouth in a gargantuan yawn, then jumped at a tap on the door.

The door opened, and an elderly woman with a wrinkled peach of a face bobbed a curtsy.

'The food for the little cat, sir,' she murmured, crossing the room to place a small tray on the floor. She fished a piece of parchment from her pocket and handed it to Feo. 'Would you mind filling this in, sir? It has to go to the Town Guard in the morning.'

Feo scanned the page and scribbled a few lines on it before handing it back. The round face wrinkled a little more in a soft smile, remarking, 'These regulations do go on a bit, sir, don't they?' as she went out.

Feo dropped onto the bed, propping his boots on the bottom rail. 'Why, in the name of Hoaga, have I come here? I've written more just to enter this city than I write in a week of work at home.'

'So that you can go back and spend the rest of your life at home, researching magic.' Horsa prodded the door-latch with a questing finger. 'This door won't lock.'

'Never mind that. We haven't anything to steal.'

Horsa glanced at Kirrin, now licking the bottom of the milk-bowl, and crossed the room. He bounced on the side of his bed. 'Straw mattresses. Hope there aren't any bugs. When do we find this guide?'

'We go to the Parks Reserves and Outlands Agency tomorrow to hire one.' Feo hauled himself upright. 'It's getting dark. Let's see what the kitchen has to offer. Kirrin can sleep off her meal while we eat.'

The inn's common-room was long and black-beamed. As yet, there was only a sprinkling of customers, most clutching a leather tankard. Feo and Horsa sat near the blazing log fire.

'What would you like, sirs?' The serving-wench's smile beamed from a chubby face dusted with freckles. She couldn't have been more than thirteen.

'Dinner for two hungry travellers and a couple of mugs of your local ale while we're waiting.' Feo watched with surprise as the girl's face dropped.

'Oh, sir, I'm sorry, but we haven't had any ale these six months. It's the new regulations, you see. The King's Inspector of Beverages has to check and seal every barrel, and he's that slow, by the time he gets to it, it's gone off.' Her face brightened slightly. 'We've got some very nice Rasculian wine, though.'

'Give us two mugs of that, then,' replied Feo with resignation.

'Pretty little thing,' said Horsa lazily as the girl bustled off, 'Shame she's not a bit older.'

Feo snorted. 'I might have known you'd be sizing up the local girls. If this one's too young, what about the lady who brought the form up?'

'Now, be serious, Feo. She's old enough to be my grandmother! I like my women old enough to be interesting, but not that old.' He looked round the room and sighed. 'And no ale to drink! You know, if you got your books out, you could transform that wine into beer in the twinkling of an eye!'

I'm sure can find a spell for it somewhere," said Feo, his shoulders drooping, 'and the wizards a hundred, two hundred years ago could have done it in the click of a finger. But I've never managed to make any of it work.'

'For a man who collects old spells, you're a terrible sceptic. For a Hereditary Wizard, it's unbelievable!'

'The Hereditary Wizardship has been a ceremonial position for generations. There's been no need for a major piece of magic since the storm that sank the galleons of King Afram. I never saw Uncle Sigid do more than unsour the milk or jiggle King Olave into amending a law. And I can't even do that! I'm not even convinced magic still works,' replied Feo bitterly.

'So you don't believe the Sultan's curse will work?'

'Well... "Cardevin will implode and vanish to the depths of the sea...".' Feo shuddered. 'It's different in the East... more mysterious... they haven't lost their powers like us... But I don't see what I can do to stop it.'

'If you can't, we're sunk... Literally. ' Horsa leant forward and stabbed his finger at the table. 'You've got to, Feo. You're our only hope.'

Feo stared at him in dismay, then jumped as two mugs of best Rasculian arrived with a bang.

'Dinner in two minutes,' called the girl over her shoulder as she vanished into the rear of the inn.

The Town Guard Strikes Again

Feo passed a miserable night. The room certainly looked out over the front of the inn, but it was also directly over the common-room. The guests down there were enjoying themselves so much that they carried on well into the small hours and made sure that the whole street knew what a good time they were having.

Whenever Feo did start to drift, pictures of the implosion of Cardevin forced their way into his mind. Would its square towers topple to the centre before vanishing under the waves, or would it go so quickly that nothing could be seen but the vortex of water filling the hole where it had been.

He tossed and turned, cursing the prickly mattress for adding to his discomfort. Horsa slept soundly in the other bed. But then, Horsa would sleep through an earthquake.

At last, a grey light straggled through the window. Feo felt a firm hand shaking him out of his restless doze.

'G'way,' he mumbled.

'Come on, Feo. If we're to hire a guide we'd better get moving.'

Feo rolled over and looked out of the casement. The cobbles sulked with a flat, oily sheen. It was still raining.

'If we go now, we'll be back for a late breakfast.' Horsa nodded at the foot of Feo's bed. 'Kirrin'll sleep until then.'

Feo looked down and saw the small black form sprawled beside his feet. Her still-bulging stomach was fluttering rhythmically.

In the hall they met the serving wench, her hair tied up in a blue kerchief, carrying a leather bucket of ashes from the fire. She bobbed a curtsy.

'Good morning, sirs.'

'Is it?' uttered Feo.

The innkeeper followed her out of the common room, wiping his hands on his apron.

'Good morning, Sirs, good morning. I trust you slept well?'

'No!' said Feo and stalked out of the door.

Conditions outside were as uninviting as they had looked from the window. The rain was falling in a fine soaking sheet which soon penetrated every crevice in their clothing. Horsa pulled his cloak closer round his shoulders but Feo just strode on, glowering at the world.

They passed down the street which ran to the port, heading for the big square which fronted the Customs buildings. Either side, the small dark houses refused to look at them, their windows still lidded with dark curtains or ancient ragged blankets. The sole improvement on the previous day was that the rain had washed the gutter clean, removing the market debris.

Reaching the square, they found it deserted. The only remnants of yesterday's crowds were the heaps of rubbish at the corners, from which the rain leached an unsavoury fluid. The splintered wood doors in the stone hall which housed the port offices were barred and chained. Above the roof they could see the bare masts of the ships at anchor, their riding lights glimmering in the faint dawn. The only sign of life was the night watchman's lamp in his shelter, but there was no sign of the watchman himself.

'Where is everyone?' Feo roused from his brown study to look round in amazement.

Horsa looked vexed. 'I was banking on finding someone in the port area to direct us. I should have realised. The officials won't start work this early.'

'But what about all the other people?'

'No ship movements allowed until the officials are there to regulate them.'

'What about the winds and tides?'

Horsa shrugged. 'Everyone has to wait for the winds, the tides and the officials.'

'So what do we do now?' asked Feo, hunching his shoulders deeper into the wet collar of his cloak.

'There's supposed to be a Town Guard office in the square,' said Horsa. 'They should know where the Park Reserves and Outlands Agency is. If they're there.'

They walked round the square, peering at the shuttered shops which in the daytime sold everything from hot soup to wyvern's claws (guaranteed to keep you safe from robbers). Above the shops rose the weathered stone facades of the merchant offices, their grimy windows giving no hint of the wealth that changed hands behind them.

'That looks like the Town Guard's office.' Horsa walked across to a door which had once been painted red. Over the top swung a sign with a sword and shield. This door, too, was chained and locked.

Horsa peered at the collection of notes pinned to the worn wood. 'No information about when they're open,' he said in disgust, 'Just a lot of regulations about stuff you can import and export.'

Feo turned his back on the notice and looked round the still-deserted square. 'So what now?' he asked.

Horsa swivelled, scanning the roads out of the area. 'That street's going up the hill, and it's wider than the rest.

I'll wager that's the route to the town centre.' He led the way to a gap between one shop advertising the best smoked carp in town and another offering to negotiate between any citizen unfortunate enough to breach the regulations and the government department concerned.

As they climbed the hill, the buildings lining the street changed from squat brick warehouses to shuttered shops and finally to an area of solid stone houses. The soaking rain had moderated to a fine drizzle, allowing the changing scents of the districts to pull Feo from his melancholy - the strange medley of yesterday's food and imported animals round the port square, the more intriguing mixture of spices, leather and distilled liquor in the warehouse area and the tantalising aroma of fresh coffee from the homes. Feo realised he was hungry.

The ground levelled off and the road started to wind between groups of trim cottages, their doorsteps' gleam polished by the rain. At least the streets were quiet at this hour, which made it easier to walk. Unfortunately, the supply of people to direct them to the Parks Reserves and Outlands Agency was also severely limited. Eventually, Horsa managed to stop a matron in a red cloak, who was bound for the market by the basket she was carrying.

'Are you sure you want the Parks Reserves and Outlands Agency?' queried the lady, simpering up at Feo's large nose. 'I've never heard of that one. I know where the Parks, Gardens and Cemeteries Office is - three streets down, turn left and then second right. It's just on the corner.'

'No,' said Feo, a dangerous glitter in his eye, 'It's the Parks Reserves and Outlands Agency I want.'

'Thank you very much, Madam,' broke in Horsa, spotting a short man two blocks away and dragging Feo towards the distant figure. 'Feo, you can't lose your temper with her. She was only trying to help.'

'She's an idiot,' said Feo, his lip curling with disgust. 'I know perfectly well where I want to go. I just don't know how to get there.'

Horsa looked round. The man had vanished and the street was empty. Ahead, the ground started to rise again towards the King's Hill and high above, the spires of the palace soared over the town, reflecting a watery ray of sun. He stared, amazed. Turrets were piled on battlements, spires on towers, cupolas rested precariously on roof ridges, the whole executed in a creamy marble which magnified the warmth of the sun.

'Does that really belong here, Feo?' he asked in disbelief.

'So that's the King's palace,' said Feo. 'It looks as if the temple of Miktel at Isiphus has crashed into the Akron Fortress.' He straightened his hat. 'Appalling taste in this climate.'

Horsa shivered and pulled his cloak round his stocky figure. The struggling shaft of sun had been defeated and the thin drizzle which had plagued them for the last hour was turning back to serious rain.

'Let's head for the palace,' he suggested, 'There're bound to be lots of offices in the area.'

'Why not,' said Feo despondently, 'We've nothing better to try.'

The road to the King's Hill rose gently at first, then steeper and steeper until Feo's and Horsa's feet slipped on the slick cobbles. Then it started to turn this way and that, while the crumbling grey stone of the ancient houses on either side leaned closer and closer, almost, Feo thought, as if they were trying to engulf the travellers.

'Look.' Horsa pointed to a corner a little way ahead. A bent black figure was turning into the street towards them. 'She looks as if she knows the place.'

Feo looked up and then turned away, a grey fog of hopelessness filling him. 'Why should she know where the Parks Reserves and Outlands Agency is?'

The old woman hobbled slowly nearer, leaning on a rough stick. Horsa stepped out as she approached, and she turned towards him, tilting her face up to look at him. One eye was totally white, the other black and piercing.

'Excuse me, Madam, do you know the way to the Parks Reserves and Outlands Agency?'

She clasped a hand round a gold amulet half hidden by her shawl, and then her head turned to Feo. He had the queasy feeling that she was looking at him with the white eye rather than the black.

'Ah, you've a long way to travel, you two.'

Horsa looked bewildered. 'The Agency's in the city. It can't be that far.'

She cackled quietly. 'You want to find a dragon? You'll be sorry. One of you will be sore wounded, the other consumed with guilt. And the dragon will win!'

Feo stepped closer, fear fluttering his stomach. 'We won't get the dragonstone? But we must.'

'Must? Must? Have you ever seen a dragon? The great claws and the fiery breath? They're hard to kill, mortal hard. And you're not prepared, not yet you're not.'

'I have my books with me. They'll tell me what I need.'

'Yes, the books are good, but what about the spells?' Her black eye closed entirely, leaving the white one glaring at Feo. 'I say, you most of all have a long way to travel and by a dangerous road. And if you do not take the right path, you will fail.'

'We must get the dragonstone. We have no choice. And how would you know our fate?' Feo turned away.

'My blind eye sees more than your two. I know what I know.' The old woman's jaw snapped shut and she limped down the hill, her stick tapping on the cobbles.

Shivering, Feo turned to Horsa. 'Do you believe her? How did she know we were hunting a dragon? There can't be many with the need and even fewer wild enough to do it.'

Horsa's jaw was set as he stared after the diminishing figure in black. 'It had the ring of truth,' he said slowly, 'but we must go on. We have no choice.'

'We have no choice.' Feo laughed without conviction. 'We have no choice.' He turned and tramped upwards. 'Horsa, I can't do magic like Sigid did. I don't think I can do this.'

'We can do it. We can do it, because we must.' Horsa caught up with him and grasped his arm. 'Feo, we can't give up now. We're just beginning.'

'Just beginning.' Feo's shoulders slumped as if the whole of Cardevin were resting on them. 'Yes, she was right. We've got a long way to go. And we still don't know where the agency is.' He looked round, but there was no-one to ask, and he carried on upwards.

The stone houses crowded in until there was only a thin slit of sky between them. Feo had a moment of vertigo when he really felt they were moving to crush him. A few pedestrians passed them, hurrying down the hill, their drab tunics and trousers marked with damp patches of darker brown. None would stop to give them any directions. At last, they broke out of the maze and emerged into the broad square where only an intricate tracery of iron separated them from the marble towers.

The palace seemed like a mirage, unreal beside the ancient warren they had traversed. They turned and looked back down a slope of tumbled slates, wet and leaden.

'Is that all the distance we've covered?' said Feo, resting against a gatepost. 'It felt as if we'd crossed the whole city.'

'Yes, but there's hardly three yards of straight road in the whole area.'

Horsa turned and scanned the empty square. 'I did expect to find someone here, or maybe some signs for the offices.' He looked at the gatepost where Feo was leaning. 'You're covering a notice.'

They scanned the curling piece of parchment, which contained a somewhat weather-faded list of prohibitions on the palace square. 'It's forbidden to set up a stall to sell any kind of merchandise, conduct public entertainments, advertise...I can't read this bit....loiter in view of the palace...'

Feo's gaze slid over the open space. It came to rest on a file of men in red cloaks which was just entering the square. 'Bura's thunder! This looks like trouble.'

The file veered sharp left and marched straight for the two companions. When it was three yards away the leader threw up his arm and shouted, 'Halt!' He took two paces forward. Feo eyed him in dismay. A large dark moustache conspired with a black hat to hide his expression. His cloak was three inches longer than his followers' and boasted a frog of tarnished braid at the throat.

'Captain Ghosham of the 3rd Patrol of the Town Guard. Papers, please.'

Feo fished in his pocket and handed over a sheaf of parchment. He didn't know what to expect, but Ghosham just leafed through the heap and gave it back.

'These seem to be in order. However, I must warn you not to loiter in the vicinity of the palace. Do you realise you must report to the Central Office of the Town Guard by midday?'

'But we only got here yesterday. We were told to report every two days,' said Feo with a glare of exasperation.

'That is correct. You must report on the day after arrival and every second day after that. You have three hours.' Ghosham pulled his moustache irritably.

Feo groaned. 'Where is the Central Office?'

The Captain pointed off to the left. 'It's over there, by the city wall and next to the Merchants' Gate.'

'But that's not in the centre,' protested Feo, 'this is the centre of the city.'

'It's central to the Town Guard,' retorted Ghosham. He wheeled his men and marched off.

* * *

Two hours later, Feo and Horsa emerged from a dark tunnel where two buildings bridged the street and found themselves facing the Merchants' Gate. Its twin stone arches, high enough to pass a laden camel, framed the dusty road away from Fazimar. Two guards in faded red tunics slouched either side, leaning against the walls in the shelter of the gate. Feo gazed longingly at the open road for a moment and then turned away.

'Where now?' he said helplessly.

Horsa looked round for someone to ask for directions. A string of half a dozen laden mules was passing through the gate, but the driver was dressed in a turban and ankle length robe - definitely not Fazimari garb. He tried to stop a tall man in a tailored black tunic and trousers, but he brushed Horsa off, muttering 'No time, my good man, King's business.' Several other characters in less reputable garb veered off when Horsa approached them, a distinctly guilty air to their gait.

'It's no good,' said Feo, a resigned look on his face. 'You'll have to try the gate guards.'

Horsa strode over and queried the guards. One jerked a thumb towards the right side of the gate. The other didn't even deign to break his half-doze.

To the right of the gate a motley assortment of buildings leaned heavily on the wall. The first two were barely more than shacks, their walls crumbling and their roofs badly in need of rethatching. The third house was larger than the preceding hovels and had an open door. Feo peered in cautiously. The last thing he wanted was to finish the day in jail for burglary.

A man with a red military tunic and grizzled beard was sitting at the table which occupied the centre of the room cleaning his nails with a dagger. Two buttons on his shoulder marked him as a sergeant. Feo heaved a sigh of relief. Their luck had changed at last.

'Yes, this is the Central Office,' growled the sergeant. 'What do you want?'

He thumbed through the pile of parchments slowly until he found the entry permit. Rubbing a grimy thumb over the seal, he traced the writing with one finger, mouthing each word as he deciphered it.

'Seems to be in order. Report in again, day after tomorrow.' He turned away and picked up the dagger.

'Ah - Lieutenant?' asked Feo.

'I've told you it's OK,' he said without glancing up.

'Yes I know, Captain, but can you tell me where the Parks Reserves and Outlands Agency is?'

'How should I know? I'm not a guide.' He turned his back on them and propped his boots on the table, which showed signs of much previous use.

* * *

'According to our last set of directions, the Office should be in a street off to the left,' said Horsa, frowning as he mentally checked their progress. Feo looked round at the rows of undistinguished houses which lined the street , their faded doors painted in the same shades of blue and brown as the hundreds of other houses they had passed that afternoon. 'It'd better be,' he said. He glanced at the dropping sun, trying to estimate how long before they had to start back to the inn. At least the rain had stopped, but he felt as if he'd spent at least a week tramping the streets of Fazimar, looking for offices which were hidden in the most unlikely places. His whole body ached. What was he doing, chasing permits and licences and other useless bits of parchment, when Cardevin was in deadly danger? He'd abandoned a comfortable life doing what he did best to rescue his homeland and where was he? Standing in a strange part of a strange town, looking for yet another office. It wasn't long to sunset and he was exhausted. The thought of trying to find their way back in the dark appalled him.

'This is it,' said Horsa, 'We turn left at the iron pump, then it's about six doors down on the right.'

They skirted an ornate water-pump in the middle of the cross-roads and turned into the narrow street. Coming towards them was a Town Guard Patrol.

'Azert's eternal fires!' said Feo, 'They're bound to inspect our papers and if we get delayed any more we'll have to find this place again tomorrow.'

'Let's hope they're quick about it,' muttered Horsa. 'It's taken us all day to get this far.'

The file marched up and the Captain bawled, 'Halt!' The guards formed a ragged line, scuffling to get as far from the Captain's eye as possible.

'Papers,' barked the Captain.

Feo pulled out the handful of parchment and watched the Captain leaf through it. They're getting so worn, he thought, if they inspect them much more they won't be readable by the end of the three weeks. Absently, he pulled back his sleeve and scratched his arm. The Captain looked up at the movement and then leaned forward, his gaze riveted on Feo's wrist.

'What's that?' he snapped.

'What's what?' said Feo, bemused.

'On your arm.'

Feo looked down. Where he had scratched, a small red spot was visible. 'I don't know.'

'Pull your sleeve up... Higher!'

Along Feo's exposed arm the spots clustered as tight as the patches on an Aurelian giraffe.

'What disease have you got?'

'I haven't got any disease!'

'Yes, you have. There's the evidence.'

Behind the Captain the file of guards was stealthily backing off. Sensing this, he turned and screamed, 'Halt! Stand to your positions!'

Swinging on Feo, he shouted, 'It's a serious offence, you know, bringing infection into Fazimar. How long have you had it?'

'I haven't got any disease,' Feo yelled. 'This has only just happened. And if it is a disease,' his voice rose an octave in frustration, 'I caught it in your salubrious city!'

'Guards! Seize him!'

The guards shuffled uncomfortably for a moment, each angling for the back of the file. At a furious glare from their Captain, they stumbled forward and reluctantly grabbed Feo's arms.

'Feodin Fiorson, I'm detaining you on suspicion of knowingly bringing disease to this realm, of not declaring said disease on entry and of wilfully spreading infection abroad.'

'It's not true! There's nothing wrong with me!' Feo struggled to break the guards' grip. 'Horsa, you've got to get me out of this.' He was vaguely aware of Horsa vanishing round the corner as the Captain said, 'What about the other one? Has he got it too?' Then his cloak was pulled over his face and he was swung round and dragged forward at a trot.

The Curse at the Wyvern's Head

Feo rolled over, wondering how the mattress which had been prickly but well-filled the night before had become so hard. He opened one eye and stared blankly round.

Where was Horsa? Even his bed was gone. There wasn't space for it anyway. The clean white walls had aged to a dirty brown. The windows had crawled up the wall and transmuted themselves into a small barred opening near the ceiling.

A demonic howl shot Feo to a sitting position on the side of the bed. The hairs on his neck vibrated with shock and his mind cleared. He dropped his head in his hands, groaning as he remembered yesterday's arrest.

Distant sounds of life percolated into his consciousness; the faint clatter of a bucket, the bang of a door, the tramp of marching feet. He raised his head, pushing the dark hair out of his eyes and wrinkling his nostrils at the pervasive scent of ancient cabbage soup and unwashed bodies. This was not going to be a good day.

'Hey, you. Breakfast.'

Feo turned to the array of bars which made up the fourth wall of his cell. A face hung there. Below a grimy eyepatch, several days growth of whiskers speckled the jowls.

'You deaf or something? I said breakfast.'

Feo rose and made to walk to the bars.

'No, back, right back against the wall. I know what you're in for and I don't want no Zampel-cursed foreign disease.'

As Feo moved to stand under the tiny window, the jailor opened a hatch and slid a plate onto the cell floor. He turned to go.

'Wait a minute.' Feo took an instinctive step forward.

'Eh? What's that?'

'How do I get out of here?'

'What d'you say?'

Feo's heart sank to his boots as he realised the jailor was deaf as a post.

* * *

Raised voices in the distance aroused Feo from a depressed doze. Words started to emerge as the argument drew closer, and with a spark of interest, Feo recognised Horsa's tones.

'I'M - HERE - TO - SEE - FEODIN - FIORSON.'

'All right, all right, don't shout. I can hear, you know. Veeling Foursome? We've no-one here by that name.'

'I - HAVE - A - PERMIT.'

'Vermin? Vermin? No vermin in here. I keep a clean jail, I'll have you know.'

'PERMIT!'

'Don't wave papers at me, you Azert-sent young devil. Can't read anyway - never could.'

'HERE - HE - IS. THIS - IS - THE - MAN. FEO - Feo!'

Feo sat up in hope at the sight of Horsa's face, nearly as red as his hair with the effort of bellowing.

'Have you come to get me out?'

'Well, not exactly... Not yet anyway. It's taken me all day to get the permit to visit.'

'You mean,' said Feo with a bitter look, 'I'm going to spend another day in this benighted hole, locked up by an idiot in the company of lunatics?' His voice rose to a screech. A despairing howl echoed him from the far end of the building.

'Now, you'll have to be patient, Feo. I'll get you out of here, but I need a bit longer, that's all. I've got an appointment with the Lieutenant in charge of the jail in the morning. I'm sure he'll see reason.' Horsa winked broadly at Feo.

'Morning? I'll probably have a knife in my back by then.'

'Everyone here is securely locked up except the old man and I slipped him a doublard to look after you. You'll be fine.'

'He probably thinks you gave him the doublard to poison me.' Feo rubbed his eyes with a despondent hand. 'Just get me out as soon as you can.'

* * *

'Psst! Hey, you.'

Feo opened one eye. Where was the voice coming from? A look at the small barred opening confirmed it was the middle of the night. Everyone should be fast asleep, dreaming of lost freedom. A sudden thought struck him. Had Horsa hit some insurmountable problem in organising his release and resorted to a jailbreak? Feo rolled off the bed and pressed his face to the bars.

The voice came again. 'Hey, you. What's your name?'

Peering across the dingy passage in the dim night lighting, Feo could see a tubby figure against the bars of the opposite cell. A pair of bare feet and grimy ankles protruded from beneath the brownish prison blanket wrapped round it.

'Feo. Feodin Fiorson. Who are you?'

The round face emitted a high-pitched giggle. 'Oh, my name doesn't matter. What are you in for?'

'They've accused me of spreading disease.' Feo glared at him, realising that Horsa and escape were not involved.. 'What about you?'

The face folded secretively round pursed lips. 'Now, that would be telling, wouldn't it?'

'If all you're going to do is ask questions, I'm going back to sleep,' said Feo in exasperation.

'No, no, don't do that.' The bloodshot eye drooped in a sly wink and the voice lowered to a confidential whisper. 'I can see by your clothes you're an outlander. If you tell me why you've come to Fazimar, I might be able to help you. And then, you could help me.'

'I've come,' said Feo loudly, 'to kill a dragon. And how could you help me with that?'

'HUSH! Not so loud!' The face peered down the dark corridors and turned back, satisfied. 'If you shout like that, they'll hear you.'

'Who will hear?'

The tubby figure pressed tighter to the bars and breathed the words to Feo. 'If I say their name, they'll hear for sure. Better not.'

'All right,' said Feo impatiently, 'forget it.' He sat on his bed and folded his knees into his chest. 'But how could you help me to kill the dragon? How can anyone help me?'

'Ah, now you're asking. You'd be surprised what I can do. Did you know that dragons have two brains?'

'Two? How can they have two brains?'

'Never you mind. They do. The second one is at the base of the tail.'

Feo's chin sank to his knees. 'That just makes it even harder.'

'Do you know which brain controls the flame?'

'Do they really breath fire?'

'Of course they do. They wouldn't be dragons otherwise.' The tubby figure started to turn away. 'If all you do is ask silly questions, I'm not talking.' Then the round face looked at Feo and hissed, 'You're not one of them, are you?'

'Of course not. I don't even know who they are.' Feo straightened up and looked at the little man hard. 'Which brain does control the flame?'

'The rear one, of course.'

Feo rubbed his chin thoughtfully. 'That's going to be difficult. It means we'll have to attack from both ends at once.'

'Yes, yes. That's right.' The round face was abstracted, the ears straining in each direction in turn. Then he whirled round and spat out, 'Back to bed and pretend to be asleep. They're coming.' He vanished under his blanket.

Feo looked both ways down the corridor but could detect nothing. He cast one more glance at the vague mound in the opposite cell and rolled back into bed. The first grey light of dawn was hazing the window-bars when he finally fell asleep.

* * *

'Feo! FEO! Wake up!'

What was wrong? Steffi knew better than to wake him like this. It must be urgent. Of course. The Sultan's curse. Cardevin was imploding and the King's Belltower was about to topple and crush him.

'FEO! I've got the answer!'

He opened one eye without comprehension. Then Horsa's words fell into place, but they still made no sense.

'The answer to what?'

'The spots, Feo.'

Feo looked at the arm thrust through the bars. It was speckled with the familiar red bumps.

'You've got it too?' Feo's shoulders sagged as the full weight of despair fell on them. If Horsa were jailed too, they'd never get out.

'Yes, and I know how.' Horsa opened the lid of the basket he was carrying and a small black head popped up.

'Kirrin? What's she got to do with it?'

'Look.' Horsa turned the kitten over and stroked her fur up. Feo leaned closer. He could see nothing odd to begin with, and then he spotted a rapid movement in the depths of the fur.

'Fleas.'

'Yes, she's crawling with them. And she slept on your bed that night.'

Feo stared at Kirrin for a moment, green eyes to green eyes, and then he sat back. He felt a little light-headed. All this trouble for a few flea-bites, and from a Fazimari animal to boot. He burst out laughing.

Horsa grinned and then jumped as the madman in the distance loosed another shriek.

'Importing disease to Fazimar, indeed. Call the jailor,' said Feo, wiping his eyes, 'I want to see the Lieutenant now.'

* * *

The Lieutenant's office was in the tower at the entrance to the prison. As they climbed the crumbling steps, Feo concluded that the position of Prison Commander was not a prestigious one. It was obvious that no repair work had been done for a very long time.

Despite the jailor's care, the door screeched on its single hinge. The man inside looked up.

'Wait outside,' he said, waving, and the jailor obediently shut the door behind him.

The room was in no better repair than the staircase, but it was well swept and neat. One wall had a cluster of parchments pinned to it. The others were unadorned grey stone. On one side, the single window looked out over the prison quadrangle.

Behind a battered wooden desk sat a dark-haired man in a faded red tunic, its braid and buttons glinting in the sunlight. He was regarding Feo with an air of interest.

'You are the High Wizard of Bukhat, I believe?'

'Lieutenant?' queried Feo.

'Lieutenant Affali.' He rubbed his hand over his short hair, blinking a little tiredly. 'I understand you want to speak to me.'

Feo drew himself up to his full height and swept his cloak back over one shoulder. 'I, the Hered... the High Wizard of Bukhat, come to your country on a mission of some importance. I go about my business, keeping carefully to your laws and regulations, and what happens?

I'm arrested on a ridiculous charge and thrown into prison.'

Horsa stroked his moustache, hiding a grin behind his hand.

'Yes, yes. I see you were arrested for spreading disease.' Curiosity lit the dark eyes as they examined Feo. 'You don't look ill to me.'

'Of course I don't look ill. I'm not ill. I was arrested for this.' Feo pulled his sleeve up and waved his arm, thick with the now-fading red blotches, at the lieutenant. 'And, to add to the insult, I acquired these in Fazimar!'

Lieutenant Affali leant forward on his desk. 'Really? And can you prove that?'

Feo waved Horsa and the basket forward. 'We have found the source of the spots. They're flea bites. And the fleas came from a Fazimari cat.'

Horsa pulled an indignant Kirrin from her basket and stroked back her underfur until Affali nodded that he could see the vermin. He turned to Feo.

'Let me see your arm. Yes, it's possible they are flea-bites. And how did you come in contact with these fleas? There are too many spots to be the result of stroking a cat.'

'I have adopted her as my familiar. As the High Wizard of Bukhat it is only proper that I should have a familiar.' Feo looked down his nose at the Lieutenant.

'Ah, yes, a wizard's familiar.' Affali leant back with a smile. 'She has been a little too familiar, wouldn't you say?'

'I suppose you might say that.' said Feo, a little disconcerted by Affali's lack of response to his assumed title.

'So where did you acquire your familiar?'

'I found her when I arrived in Fazimar. She came to me as we were walking up from the port, and it was obvious she was meant to be with me. As you can see, she is black without a hair of white.'

'And why,' said Affali, straightening in his chair, 'did you not have a familiar before then?'

'My previous familiar was most unfortunately lost in a duel with the Sublime Magician of Islia.' Feo replied without hesitation. 'I was still mourning her when I was tasked with my current mission.'

Horsa was looking at Feo with unabashed admiration. Affali glanced at him and then returned to Feo.

'So, you come to Fazimar in perfect health, pick up a stray mongrel cat on your way through the city, and then associate so closely with it that you are clothed with bites from its fleas.'

'Just so.' said Feo, looking him in the eye.

'And then the Town Guard arrest you and throw you in prison for importing and spreading disease.' Lieutenant Affali shook his head and sighed. 'It's so improbable it might actually be true.'

'Of course it's true.' said Feo. 'I've been arrested on a false charge and I should be released immediately.'

'I will have to consider your case.'

Feo's heart sank. Surely he couldn't be kept here any longer? Then a thought struck him and he motioned to Horsa. 'If your Honour would care to accept...'

'I hope you're not attempting to bribe me. I'm not a petty bureaucrat on the make.' He looked irritated for a moment, then sank into thought. 'Yes, I think we'll do it this way.' He turned back to Feo briskly. 'I accept your story, improbable though it may seem. No-one could present such a ridiculous tale unless it was true. I'll sign you off as fit and well, with a countersignature from your jailor. Then I'll send a reprimand to the Town Guard for being too officious.'

'This is all very well,' broke in Feo, 'But how much longer am I going to have to stay here?'

'I'll sign the papers now and you can leave at once. I have enough trouble keeping the lunatics off the streets and safe without cluttering my prison up with foreign wizards.'

Feo, lost for words, allowed Affali to escort him and Horsa to the door. The lieutenant called for the jailor and then turned to Feo.

'I hope you're not offering bribes to everyone you deal with,' he said severely. 'Not everyone is corrupt enough to accept them.' Then he smiled. 'Anyway, my religion won't permit it. I'm a Dhavian.'

Feo and Horsa looked at him in bewilderment.

'We're not allowed to accept bribes, to lie - or to take life. Funny, isn't it? I've been trying just as hard as you to get out of this place.'

'Then how did you get here in the first place?' asked Horsa, pulling his moustache.

'That's a long story. To put it briefly, I was conscripted in mistake for another Affali and I've spent the last five years trying to convince the authorities of their mistake.' He sighed. 'I've a nice little farm in the foothills...'

Feo shook the lieutenant's hand vigorously. 'I hope you get back there soon.' Then a sudden thought struck him. 'The Town Guard won't make a complaint to your Commander, will they?'

'I doubt it.' He laughed. 'And if they do, he can always cashier me.'

* * *

'Be quiet, Kirrin,' snapped Feo as they mounted the wooden staircase to their room at the inn. 'Stop scratching.'

'That's odd,' said Horsa. 'It's been very well behaved in the basket till now.'

Feo flung open the door and stopped dead. A cloud of feathers swirled up, landing on his cloak. He batted an arm at the shower, pulling more feathers into the vortex. 'What's happened?' he yelled.

Horsa stepped in beside him. 'We've been turned over,' he said, surveying the chaos with disgust.

The cupboard door hung drunkenly from one hinge, its contents making an untidy waterfall to the floor. Near it, the table and chairs lay on their sides. The beds were upside down, their mattresses slit from top to bottom and oozing yellow-brown straw onto a rustling heap. On top of them lay the source of the feathers - the pillows, slit like the mattresses and turned inside-out. Above them, the sampler read at a steep downhill slope, "Order in all things".

Feo picked up a chair and sat down heavily. 'What now?' he asked.

Footsteps pounded up the stairs, heralding the arrival of the innkeeper. He appeared in the doorway, apron hanging from his neck and eyes nearly meeting at the back of his head. 'What's wrong?' he gasped, 'I heard a scream.'

'See for yourself,' said Feo, rising to his feet, 'and what sort of place is this anyway?' His voice rose to a bellow. 'I'm away for a few hours...'

'Two days,' murmured Horsa.

'...on important business...'

'In prison.'

'...and my room is destroyed.' He glared at the innkeeper, an angry pulse throbbing in his temple.

'M-m-my dear sir,' stuttered the innkeeper, his face pasty and his eyes rigidly fixed, one on each corner of the room, 'I'm so sorry for the inconvenience, we've never had such goings on here, not in all my born days. Just sit still, we'll have it all sorted in no time, perhaps a glass of wine?' Without waiting for an answer, he turned and yelled down the stairs.

A trio of domestics appeared and set about the room, aprons flying. Feo started coughing as the straw and feathers flew.

'Come, dear sir, please' begged the innkeeper, 'my private parlour's next door. Sit in there until the room's in order.' He danced round Feo, trying to brush the litter from the midnight-coloured cloak.

'Come on,' urged Horsa, 'you can't do anything here.'

* * *

Half an hour later and well-plied with good wine, the two returned to the room, the innkeeper hovering at their elbows. All traces of debris had vanished, the cupboard door was propped shut and the sampler sat at its habitual horizontal.

'Now, if you would like to check your bags, by the time you've had dinner, you won't know anything has happened.' The innkeeper's eyes had unfrozen and were wandering vaguely above a nervous smile.

Feo turned over the contents of the table as Horsa pulled open the cupboard door. His notebook and writing-case were both there. Everything seemed to be in order.

'Feo?' Horsa's muffled voice emerged from the depths of the cupboard. 'Is your bookbag over there?'

'No. It should be in there.'

Horsa withdrew from the cupboard. 'It isn't.'

Feo felt the fury rise inside him and his eyes glittered greenly. 'Do you know what was in it? My spellbooks. What is a Wizard without his spells?' His voice dropped an octave as he turned on the innkeeper. 'I come, an innocent traveller, to your misbegotten establishment, I pay my bills, I bother nobody and what happens? My property is desecrated. My belongings are stolen. What Azert-cursed son of a one-eyed whore did this?'

'N-no one here.' quavered the innkeeper.

'Quiet, lackwit.'

Feo pulled himself up to his full height, his eyes snapping green fire. His cloak billowed like a storm cloud as he stretched his arms wide, fingers spread taut.

'In the name of Hoaga, the great one, the giver of Justice.

'By the power of Zampel, the Commander, by the sword of Miktel, by the magic orb of Adana, may this work be done.

'Though you flee to the bowels of the earth: you will not escape my wrath.

'Though you sink to the depths of the sea: my just anger will find you.

'Woe to you, the thief of my treasure: woe to you, who stole more than you knew.

'In the dust will you walk, and none will recognise you.

'In the midden will you search for food, and none will take pity on you.

'On withered wing will you fly: the power of speech will leave you.

'Tremble, oh fool, at your fate: as I have said, so will it be.

'So will it be, so will it continue: until you restore what is mine.

'Hoaga, hear my words. Let Justice be done.'

Feo finished and stood, arms outstretched. A smothering silence filled the room.

A Guide from the Chalice

Feo staggered slightly and let his arms drop to his side. A grey mist filled his vision and he felt chilled to the bone.

'Feo, you're white as a leper's ghost.'

He felt Horsa's hand steadying him as he dropped onto a chair. The mists began to clear, and as he raised his arm to wipe his forehead, he was puzzled to see a sprinkling of snowflakes on the sleeve.

'Feo, are you all right?'

Horsa's worried face appeared in his field of vision. He made a determined effort and shook the rest of the fog away.

'I'm fine. It's very cold in here. Can't we have a fire?'

'Of course. I'll see to it at once.' The innkeeper fled through the door, his teeth chattering.

Horsa pulled the other chair beside Feo and sat down.

'You frightened the innkeeper out of ten years of his life. What were you doing?'

'That was Ibin's spell to turn a man into a fly. At least I think it was.' Feo sighed. 'It won't work anyway.'

'Feo, you're still shivering. You've not picked up jail-fever, have you? We've got to leave in a couple of days.'

Pulling himself upright in the chair, Feo said firmly, 'There's nothing wrong with me that a good night's sleep won't cure. That jail was impossible.' He nearly believed it himself, except for the leaden weights which were dragging all his limbs down.

Horsa eyed him suspiciously and then said, 'Come on. We'll get some dinner and have an early night. We've got to find our guide tomorrow.'

* * *

The inn's common-room was quiet that evening. A couple of locals sat by the window playing an obscure game with coloured discs. It seemed to involve a lot of swearing and regular lubrication with mugs of the local wine. Apart from them, the only other customer was the resident drunk, who sat in the corner near the servery lining up his empty mugs in front of him and raising his voice every so often to remark that his wife didn't appreciate him.

Feo and Horsa sat in the inglenook fireplace. Even though a pile of logs roared flame up the chimney, Feo couldn't seem to get warm. He knew he needed a good meal, but all he really wanted was to crawl into his bed.

The serving wench appeared and Feo let Horsa order for him. They were served rapidly with plates of steaming venison stew and bread still warm from the oven. Feo started to eat but soon let his attention drift to the rest of the room.

A man in a blue tunic and black trousers came in and ordered a drink. He settled down near the game-players, but when he spotted Feo's phoenix plume and blue cloak, he rapidly finished his drink and left. A buxom young woman came in next, accompanied by a man old enough to be her father. Her giggles stopped abruptly when she glanced towards the fireplace and they left without even ordering. Several other people straggled in after that, but no-one seemed to want to linger. Word had obviously got round about Feo's performance that afternoon.

By this time, Horsa had finished his food and was leaning back in his chair with a contented look. 'Haven't you finished yet?' he asked with surprise. 'I thought we'd start planning our journey.'

'Carry on, then,' said Feo. 'I'll eat while we talk.'

Horsa fished in his pocket and pulled out a scrap of parchment and some charcoal. 'We'll arrange for our guide first thing in the morning and have a talk with him about what we'll need. Then we'll have to buy the food and equipment and hire some horses before we can leave.' Horsa made some notes on the parchment.

'Oh, I expect the guide will take care of that,' said Feo, pushing a piece of venison round his plate.

'I have my doubts. I'll settle for a guide who can guide, and I'm not even too sure of getting that.'

'What's the point of worrying? I'm a failed wizard without a spell-book. I'm going to get eaten by a dragon and Cardevin will vanish beneath the waves.' Feo prodded the meat to the other side of the plate. 'Nothing we can do is going to change anything.'

'Feo, you can't give up now. King Olave and all the citizens of Cardevin are relying on you. We've got to press on and make things come right. Cardevin is the special care of Hoaga, Lady of Justice. She wouldn't allow a terrible thing like that to happen to her people.'

'Hoaga. I suppose not.' Feo speared the venison and put it in his mouth. He thought of King Olave, trusting his Hereditary Wizard to lift the curse, and all the innocent folk of Cardevin, going about their daily lives in the belief that he would succeed. Horsa was right. He couldn't give up now. It was the Hereditary Wizard's duty to protect his country. And if he died in the attempt, at least they would honour his name in the short time they had left. And if he succeeded... 'What are we going to need for the journey?'

'Provisions for a couple of weeks of course. I'm not sure if we'll be able to supplement them by hunting. Waterskins. Weapons to attack the dragon and also to protect ourselves. We'll ask the guide what's best to take. Horses to carry them and ourselves.'

'The innkeeper hires horses. We could look at them after dinner. How many do we need? Three? Four?'

'We'll have to find out if the guide brings his own, but we can look in the stables tonight, at least.'

Feo looked down at his plate. It was empty.

* * *

The sun was dropping fast when they entered the stable-yard. It was deserted. A litter of old straw covered the cobbles but they could hear a contented champing from the stalls.

'Hello? Anybody here?' The call echoed from the walls. There was a long silence before a boy in a leather jerkin appeared.

'Your pardon, sirs. Have you been waiting long? I'm fair run off my feet today, what with Jem being off to see his family.'

'Jem?'

'He's the ostler, sir. I'm just the stable boy. I can do anything he can, though. I knows all the horses.'

'Then you're just the person we want.' Horsa led the boy towards the stalls. 'Can you recommend us three or four sound horses to hire for a couple of weeks? We'll need two to ride and one or two for baggage.'

'Yes, Sir. My name's Kimmi. You'll tell the innkeeper it was me as sorted you out?'

Feo watched Horsa examine a succession of animals. He hoped that whatever horse was chosen for him to ride, it was a nice quiet one. By the time Horsa and Kimmi had picked a glossy black, a couple of bays and a chestnut, he and the boy seemed to be in fair agreement. The horses were returned to their stalls and Horsa joined Feo at the gate.

'That boy's after the ostler's job. He'll give us a sound set of horses in the hope we'll put in a word for him.'

'The ostler doesn't keep a very clean yard,' said Feo, nodding at the dungheap. 'There's a good week's litter there.'

'Even so, that pigeon must be getting lean pickings. I'd have thought it would have done better at the back of the kitchen.'

The bedraggled bird jumped away at the sound of voices, made clumsy by a twisted foot.

'That's why. A crippled animal's bad luck. It'll turn the milk sour and burn the roast. The cooks'll chase it off.' Feo turned towards the inn. 'So you think we're all right for horses. That leaves the provisions and weapons.'

'We'll leave those until we've hired our guide. He should be able to tell us the best places to go. If he's not taking a backhander, that is.' Horsa made a face of disgust.

'Who isn't in this place,' muttered Feo.

* * *

'I'll just have a word with the innkeeper before we leave.' Horsa left Feo at the doorway and headed for the round white-aproned figure who was beaming behind the desk.

'Good morning, sir. A lovely day to be out.' The man waved an arm at the sunshine streaming in through the door. 'I trust you slept well?'

'Indeed. However, we will sleep even sounder when my friend's book bag is returned,' Horsa said with a spurt of irritation.

'Ah, yes. The theft.' The innkeeper's face clouded and his eyes started to quiver sideways. 'M-most distressing. We're doing everything we can to find the thief.'

'Have you informed the Town Guard?'

'Oh, you wouldn't want me to do that. There'd be forms to fill in, statements to make. And you might find yourselves detained until it's all sorted out. It could be months. Not to mention the expense.'

'Expense?'

'Of course. A few doublards here, a few doublards there. Payments for informers, payments for witnesses, rewards for return of the goods, a payment to the judge.'

Horsa looked shaken. 'Detained for months? We can't do that. We'll have to rely on you, then.'

'I'm sure we'll find the book bag for you.' The innkeeper's eyes veered abruptly to opposite sides of the hall before he pulled them back to Horsa. 'Can I do anything else for you?'

'Yes, we're going on a trip of about two weeks, so we need to hire some horses - three or four - I'm not sure yet. Your boy Kimmi helped us to pick some out last night. Can you reserve them for us - he knows which.'

'Certainly, certainly. A pleasure to oblige. I'll get Kimmi to clean the saddles for you. Do you want pack bags as well?' He stopped suddenly. 'When are you leaving? We're short-handed in the stables. Our ostler hasn't returned - he should have been back last night.'

'Not for a couple of days at least.'

The innkeeper's face cleared. 'That's all right, then. Everything will be ready for you.'

'Good. I'll tell you exactly what we need tonight.'

* * *

The phoenix-plume in Feo's hat sparkled a fiery orange in the sun as the pair approached the iron pump. He looked round nervously as they turned left, but the red cloaks of the Town Guard were not in evidence. The sixth door on the right was painted a bright green and boasted a brass plaque which read, 'Parks Reserves and Outlands Agency'. It was firmly shut.

'Where are they?' said Horsa, trying the door. 'This is supposed to be office hours.'

'Probably on indefinite leave,' grunted Feo. He stooped and picked up a grubby fragment of parchment with a broken string. 'Look at this.'

They peered at the wobbly letters and deciphered, 'At The Chalice if wanted urgently.'

'The Chalice?' Feo looked at Horsa.

'Sounds like a tavern.' He stared both ways down the street. 'No sign of it.'

'We'll have to find someone to ask.' Feo kicked the door with venom. 'Why are the only efficient parts of this place the ones which obstruct you?'

'I think we'd better go back to the pump. There should be a few people going through the crossroads.' Horsa set off towards the iron pump.

Feo trailed behind him. Yet another obstacle in their path. They were never going to get out of Fazimar.

At the crossroads, they peered down the streets. A group of women were walking, baskets on arms, along the street Feo and Horsa had come up to reach the pump, but they were heading away towards the market. A man in drab labourer's clothing was slouching down the road in the opposite direction. Then Feo spotted a middle-aged woman in a blue dress and yellow shawl walking in their direction.

Feo smiled at her and doffed his hat. 'Excuse me, madam, can you direct us to The Chalice?'

'The Chalice? You wouldn't want to go there,' said the woman, talking to Feo but peering sideways through her lashes at Horsa's flourishing moustache. 'I know several much nicer places.' She blushed and pulled her shawl more tightly round her shoulders.

'Madam,' said Horsa, forestalling Feo's explosion, 'We have to go there to meet a friend.'

The woman looked doubtful. The Chalice was obviously not the sort of place you would meet anyone respectable.

'How do we get there,' pressed Horsa.

The directions, when disentangled, led them to a narrow alley a few houses away from the green door. Looking down the dark slot, his nose wrinkling at the stench of the rubbish piled against either wall, Feo drew back in dismay.

'Are you sure this is the right place?'

'As sure as I can be.' Horsa picked his way past the first pile and walked a little further. 'I can see it from here,' he called.

Feo jumped as a brown blur shot past his legs. He watched as a dog with a bald back vanished down the street at the run.

Half a carved wooden chalice still clinging to a few flecks of its original gilding swung over a battered door. Feo peered doubtfully over Horsa's shoulder.

'Is it open?'

'Let's see.' Horsa pressed the latch and pushed. The door juddered into the tavern.

Inside, the thick dark was barely broken by a lantern over the bar. Feo stumbled over a chair-leg as they moved forward, but slowly, as his eyes adjusted to the light, he was able to make out a small room with three empty tables and a fourth occupied by two men.

'Heggi? Heggi, bring me another drink' bawled the bigger of the two.

There was a long pause before a shuffle was heard in the passage behind the bar. An ancient woman appeared carrying a leather jug. Feo noticed that, by the dark stains down her skirt, she was as unsteady of hand as of leg.

'Hurry it up, Heggi. I'm dying of thirst.'

'Argh! You and your thirst. It would take Zillim and all his disciples to keep you supplied.' She banged the jug down and turned.

'Mistress. We're looking for a man.' Horsa stepped forward.

'Looking for a man? You're in the wrong place here. Nothing but these two wineskins.' She spat in the dust. 'Now if you come back tonight, that's different.' She peered up at Horsa slyly. 'You want a strongbox moved? Or someone removed? Or just a pass to the palace? You'd never tell it from the real thing. But come back tonight.' She made a move towards the bar.

'No, Mistress. You mistake me. I'm looking for a particular man, the officer of the Parks Reserves and Outlands Agency.'

'Oh, him.' She sniffed and jerked a thumb at the occupied table where the two drinkers were listening with somewhat addled attention. 'He's the bigger of the two beer-barrels. I wish you luck of him.' As she shuffled back towards the passage, Feo just caught the muttered words, 'But you'd be better coming back tonight.'

The big man at the table was struggling to fasten the top button of his tunic. 'Office very quiet this morning.

Just popped in here to get a little something for my cold.' He coughed unconvincingly. 'What can I do for you?'

'I would prefer,' said Horsa with decision, 'to discuss business in the office.'

'Much more comfortable in here,' said the man, attempting to stand up.

'The office will be quite comfortable for what we need.'

Horsa led the way along the alley with the big man stumbling behind, muttering about his gammy leg. Feo brought up the rear. At the green door, Horsa rescued the key before it was dropped in the gutter and opened up.

The small room was littered with heaps of discoloured parchment. The official swept a pile from the chair and sat down heavily. 'Now,' he said, 'we have a number of vacancies for guards in the... in the...' He tried to focus on a sheet of writing with no success.

'We're not here for a job, we want a guide for the Upper Negus,' stated Feo. 'We are going to kill a dragon.'

'Dragon-hunters? I know just the guide. Ne-, Ne-, Nello, that's right.' He shook his head from side to side. 'No, no good, he died last year. Who else have we got?' He sat swaying for a moment, focused on the middle distance. 'Shallon. It'll have to be Shallon. If you come back tomorrow morning, we'll fix it all up.'

Horsa stepped forward and planted his hands on the table. 'We are not moving until we have our guide.'

'But I can't do it as quickly as that. It takes time. First I've got to send a message to Shallon, then - '

'You send the message to Shallon. We'll wait.'

The big man sighed and fumbled round his table for writing material. 'You foreigners. You're all the same. Always in a rush.' He picked up his pen, dropping it twice, and located a piece of reasonable parchment from the middle of one of the piles.

'Write that we want to meet here at midday.'

'But we can't arrange things that quickly.' He looked at Horsa's set features. 'All right, all right.' Finishing the note with a crossing out and several blots, he went to the door and yelled, 'Boy!' A young lad with a dirty face appeared after a few minutes and ran off with the message.

'Now, if you want to wait in comfort, there's a very pleasant hostelry called The Chalice. You go out, turn right and - '

'Don't bother,' said Horsa, 'We'll be back at midday.'

* * *

Feo and Horsa arrived back at the office as the palace clock was chiming. The green door was ajar, and Feo could detect the murmur of voices. As they entered, the big official wavered to his feet and beamed.

'Ah, there you are. Bang on time. I like people who don't waste time. Here's Shallon, your guide for the trip.'

A stocky, thirtyish woman with curly hair stepped forward. 'Pleased to meet you. I'm Shallon. What ails you?'

* * *

Feo watched Horsa and Shallon listing provisions for the journey. Their elbows were resting on a polished wood table in a small room with black beams and whitewashed walls, and in front of each of them was a beaker of good wine. Stroking his moustache, Horsa was discussing the weapons they would need and casting the odd appreciative glance at Shallon. Trust Horsa to land up on an expedition with an attractive female guide.

At least Shallon's taste in inns was good, thought Feo. No suggestions about repairing to The Chalice from her. She'd taken them to a small inn in the next street which, she maintained, served the best wine in the city. Taking a sip from his beaker, he thought she might be right.

He was still not entirely happy with the guide. She admitted she had never run a Dragon-hunt before, but insisted she knew more than all the other guides put together. Her late husband, Nello, had been the best dragon guide in all Fazimar.

'Feo, Shallon says she can be ready to leave in two days.'

'Two days? Don't we need any more permits or anything?'

'No, just the supplies. She'll buy those tomorrow and pack them the day after. All we have to do is hire the horses.'

Feo's heart sank. Somehow, he'd never believed they'd get this far. The vision of a fiery dragon towering over him started to loom very large indeed.

The Ostler's Return

'We'd better see the innkeeper now about the horses.' Horsa strode towards the inn door.

Feo followed, shoulders hunched. Not only did he have to slay a terrifying beast, he had to get the right bits back to Cardevin and make an ancient and convoluted ritual work. His phoenix-plume drooped over his collar, its vivid colours mocking his mood.

'Innkeeper?' Horsa banged his fist on the desk.

The innkeeper hurried out of the back, wiping his hands on his apron. His eyes quivered as he greeted them.

'Good evening, sirs. Please excuse the delay. We're at our wit's end. A party of horsemen just arrived and no ostler to deal with them.'

'Isn't he back yet?' Horsa looked concerned. 'What about our horses?'

'Kimmi will manage your horses, but how we'll cope with the rest I just don't know. Old Jem has a twisted foot, but he keeps the stables running.'

'I shouldn't have thought a lame ostler was much use, but no doubt Kimmi does his running round. Can we settle the hire of the horses now?'

'Of course. Just go right through. Kimmi was expecting you tonight.'

* * *

The dungheap had vanished from the corner of the stableyard and Kimmi was busy with half a dozen dusty mounts. He turned as Feo and Horsa entered the yard, greeting them with a beaming smile.

'Good evenin', Sirs. Your gear's all ready. Lucky this lot didn't come in before I was done'. He smacked the chestnut he'd groomed on the rump and it clopped into a stall.

Feo wandered round the yard while Horsa completed arrangements. He could find no enthusiasm for preparations which were rolling inexorably towards his probable death. Visions of the dragon kept flashing into his mind, its scaly head, its huge eyes, its sulphurous breath. Shuddering, he pushed them from his thoughts and straightened up. He could see that Horsa was still occupied with Kimmi, but there was something odd in the corner which had housed the dungheap. Walking over, he looked closer. A pigeon was hunched there.

'That's all settled.' Horsa's voice behind him made him jump. 'That's the bird we saw yesterday, isn't it? You can tell it by the twisted foot. It and the ostler must make a good pair.'

The pigeon turned its head and shook its feathers into some sort of order. Then it sidled up to Feo's feet and looked at him.

'That's odd,' said Horsa. 'Why doesn't it fly away?'

'Perhaps Kimmi's been feeding it,' muttered Feo.

The bird pecked at Feo's toe and started to hobble across the yard. Every few feet he turned round to look at Feo before struggling on. Feo stared. He'd never seen a bird behave like this before. Then Horsa jumped to Feo's side. 'Follow him,' he said urgently, thumping Feo on the back.

Feo stumbled round. The pigeon moved faster than he expected, and he was only just in time to see it vanish through the door at the end of the stables. He stepped through the opening with Horsa at his heels. The bird was pecking at a pile of straw in a disused stall.

Horsa fell on his knees beside the heap and started to scatter it. The pigeon flapped up, perching on the sidewall. As Horsa reached the centre of the pile, a corner of blue velvet appeared.

Feo started forward. 'My bag!' he exclaimed.

A gust of icy wind swept in from the yard, swirling the straw into a blinding blizzard. Feo and Horsa swung their arms round, trying to keep the hail from their eyes. When it settled, a small dark man was kneeling beside them.

Staring at the little man in astonishment, Feo stammered, 'It's the ostler.'

'Oh sirs, I didn't mean no harm.' He wrung his hands, half-sobbing. 'I'm just a poor man, and my mother, she's behind with her tax. I didn't think a few books would make all this trouble.'

Horsa looked at the man sternly. 'You took what wasn't yours. The deed returned on the doer.'

'I'll never do anything like that again. I swear by...'

'Just you make sure you never do, and remember, the next Wizard may not be so merciful. Now go.'

Jem stumbled out of the door, his twisted foot dragging.

Feo stood holding the blue bag as if it contained the Crown Jewels. 'My books... I've got my books back!'

Horsa shook him, his face alight. 'Feo, do you realise, your spell worked!'

'No, it didn't. I tried to turn him into a fly.'

'Yes, it did. Think of your words. "On the midden will you search for food, and none will recognise you. On withered wing will you fly; the power of speech will leave you." He became a pigeon. That's it. That's it!'

'You're right. My spells work. They really do work. I'm a real Wizard!' Feo felt a bubble of hope rise in his throat. Maybe, just maybe, he could save his homeland.

* * *

Feo's phoenix-plume burned gold in the sunlight as he strode back to the inn. Horsa beside him was scarcely less excited. If Feo's spells were working, maybe they really did have a chance.

Feo's step slowed. 'If I... ' he started, 'If I really can work magic, I should be able to turn that daisy into a rose.'

Horsa came to a halt. 'Should you?'

Feo delved in the bag and leafed through a small, dusty volume. 'Here it is - in here.' He drew himself up and stretched one hand out towards the flower, muttering a short incantation under his breath.

The daisy sat there, looking like a flower enjoying the cool of the evening.

'It doesn't look any different.' Horsa prodded it doubtfully.

Feo's heart sank and his shoulders drooped. 'It hasn't worked.'

'Maybe the time of day is wrong. Or it's not in the right place.'

'This spell doesn't depend on that. It shouldn't make any difference. It just didn't work.'

'There has to be a reason. The other spell worked.'

'It couldn't have. Someone else must have done it. Someone whose magic really does work.' Feo sat down on a stone and dropped his face into his hands. The vision of Cardevin vanishing beneath the waves returned with terrible realism.

'Feo, it was your spell. It did work.' Horsa shook Feo roughly by the shoulder. 'You turned a man into a pigeon.'

'Then why didn't the daisy turn into a rose?'

'I don't know, but there has to be a reason. We've got to find out why. We need your magic.'

Behind them, a disembodied eye appeared. It blinked and stared after them with an expression of malign satisfaction before disappearing with a soft plop.

* * *

Dinner was a subdued meal. Feo kept muttering odd spells which popped into his mind, to no effect but to drive the few occupants of the common-room nearer to the door. The food seemed to have no flavour. He glanced at Horsa. He was eating with a fair appetite, but by his expression was probably two days out from Fazimar on the road to Upper Negus.

Feo sighed. Horsa at least had no more to worry about at the moment than to remember everything they needed. Feo had to fathom how to make his spells work. Why wouldn't the daisy turn into a rose? Why hadn't any of the small spells he had tried over dinner done anything? He had turned a man into a pigeon, hadn't he? Yes, he had! That spell had worked; it had definitely worked. He could do it. All he had to do was find out how.

There had to be a reason. Feo could feel it. He remembered the feeling of power flowing when he cast the spell on the ostler. And the terrible exhaustion afterwards. There'd been none of that with the other attempts.

But he'd done it once. He still had a little time before their confrontation with the dragon. And now he knew where he should be looking for answers. He would work it out. After all, he was the Hereditary Wizard.

'Ahem!' ventured Feo.

'Eh? Oh, sorry.' Horsa sat up. 'I was running over the route Shallon suggested.'

'How are we going to travel Kirrin?'

'Kirrin.' Horsa stared at Feo. 'You're surely not taking the kitten with us.'

'Of course. She's my familiar. What else would we do with her?'

'We could leave it with the innkeeper.'

'How could I be sure she'd be looked after? Remember the state we found her in.'

Horsa sighed. 'I suppose you won't be happy unless we take it. We'd better find a suitable basket for it to travel in. We've got one or two other things to find tomorrow. We can do it then.'

'And when do we start?'

'Shallon will bring the supplies tomorrow night. She'll check the horses and stow everything in the packs the next day, and we leave the following dawn.' Horsa stroked his moustache. 'Very efficient woman, that.'

Feo suppressed a shudder. Events were moving much faster than he liked.

* * *

Shallon arrived with a loaded cart as the smoky rim of the sun kissed the horizon. Feo and Horsa were already in the stableyard examining the horses and packs with Kimmi. Jem was nowhere in sight. As they entered the yard, they had seen his back hobbling rapidly out of the other gate.

'Good even, gentlemen. How went it today?'

'I think we have it all. Including this.' Horsa pointed to a wicker basket from under whose lid Kirrin's black face was peering.

'A cat! In Bura's name, what want you with a cat on a dragon-hunt!'

Feo drew himself up and looked down his nose at Shallon.

'She is not just any cat. She is my familiar.'

He caught Kirrin as she jumped out of the basket and rubbed her ears, listening to the contented purr.

'Well, you're the hunter. But in all my born days I've never been on an expedition with a cat.' Shallon moved over to examine the horses, shaking her head. Feo caught a mutter of 'Wizards surely are strange folk.'

By the time the horses had been checked, the long shadow from the inn was touching the far wall of the yard and the pile of clean straw was tinted with rose.

'I think that's enough for tonight. The horses look fine and the tack is sound. Kimmi here has done you proud.' Shallon nodded to him and Kimmi beamed broadly.

'The cart can stay here tonight. I'll trust Kimmi will see it comes to no harm. I'll be packing at first light, so you bring anything else down early.'

Horsa nodded and said, 'I wanted to check with you about reporting to the Town Guard. We went in today to show our papers and asked about exemption while we were away. They weren't interested. I don't want to default because we have to come back through here after.'

Shallon grinned. 'That's no problem. That is, assuming you have a doublard or two to spare?'

'We can find some money.'

'We'll just pay a couple of friends of mine to report for you while you're away.'

Horsa's jaw dropped. 'Won't they notice? It was the same guard again today. He must know us quite well by now.'

Shallon roared with laughter. 'By the King's beard, if we kept to the rules, nothing would ever get done. The guard won't worry so long as someone shows him the papers. And maybe slips him a coin or two at the same time.'

Feo wrapped his cloak tighter around his shoulders and shivered in the grey light of dawn. Yesterday's clear sunset had been replaced by racing clouds, which he eyed with foreboding. They echoed too closely the dark of the near future.

'Here's the rest of the baggage.' Horsa came through the gate of the yard and added a couple of bundles to the pile by Feo's feet. 'I've made sure Kirrin's securely shut in our room. We don't want a kitten packed with the food.'

'Where's Shallon?'

'I expect she'll be here any minute.' Horsa looked at Feo's huddled form. 'I told you we'd need those clothes we got yesterday. You should have worn the lined cloak as well.'

Feo sniffed with scorn. 'I will accept the wool tunic and leggings if I must, but the Hereditary Wizard of Cardevin cannot be seen without his cloak and hat.' He turned away from the bags and peered through the gate. 'Here's Shallon. Now we can get started with the packing.'

The day travelled swiftly from lowering dawn to a sunset barred with black clouds. Feo concentrated on the mundane demands of organising their equipment to keep his forebodings at bay. Even so, at odd moments, a scaly head with slitted yellow eyes would appear to him so vividly that he was surprised that it vanished when he blinked. Finally, he looked round and could see nothing else on the ground.

'Right. We're done,' said Shallon, standing up and stretching her back. 'We all need a good night's sleep. We saddle up at dawn and leave within the hour.'

* * *

Feo slept uneasily, plagued all night by vivid dreams of which he could remember little in the morning. The only image he retained was of Cardevin sinking slowly beneath the sea. His uncle, Sigid, the preceding Hereditary Wizard, was standing on the top of his tower, calling faintly, 'Feo, Feo, you failed! The Hereditary Wizard has disgraced his line. I cast you out from the annals of Cardevin.'

The feeling of despair clung to him as he stumbled downstairs carrying Kirrin's basket. He had so little time to unravel the secret of his magic. If only Sigid had not died so suddenly and had had the opportunity to complete his successor's training. Things would not have reached this dreadful pass where Feo was being flung quite unprepared into the struggle to save his country. How could he possibly complete his commission in the short time he had. He was doomed to fail. Perhaps it didn't matter if he perished in the fight with the dragon. If he did survive, he would be a homeless wanderer.

He moved through the final preparations in a trance, barely conscious of anyone else. It was a shock when he found someone tugging at his sleeve.

'Sir, Sir!'

Feo's eyes pulled reluctantly into focus.

'Sir! Can I come with you?'

Feo looked at Kimmi in surprise. 'What? Come on the dragon hunt?'

'Sir, there's nothing for me here now Jem's back. I'll just be the stable boy, taking orders like before. And Jem beats me when he takes the fancy.'

'But it's dangerous. You might be killed!'

Kimmi's eyes sparkled. 'It'd be exciting! I've never been out of Fazimar before. I'll make myself useful. I can cook and look after the horses and pack up the camps.' He looked up at Feo, his body taut with suspense.

Feo looked at Shallon helplessly. 'We can't take a boy with us!'

Shallon thought for a minute and then said slowly, 'I don't see why not. Kimmi's a good lad. We could do with some help on the journey and he doesn't have to fight the dragon.'

Kimmi's face broke into an expression of amazement and delight. 'I'll tell Jem I'm going on a dragon hunt!' and he raced into the stable to fetch another horse.

* * *

They passed through the Merchant's Gate an hour after sunrise. The two guards barely stirred from their half-doze as the line of horses passed under the stone arches. Turning in his saddle, Feo looked back at the grim grey stone walls of the city, and was thankful to be out of that madhouse of regulations and officials.

Beyond the midden-heaps which bracketed the gate, the market gardens which supplied the city stretched for some distance before petering out into open countryside. A succession of low hills appeared ahead, their sides clothed with woods where the occasional deer could be seen in a clearing.

The road north from Fazimar was winding and ill-kept. As Feo's horse stumbled for the tenth time, he muttered, 'I should have thought all those officials could have organised some road repair.'

Shallon caught the remark and laughed. 'By the King's beard, you don't expect those layabouts to get anything done? Anyway, there are so many officials issuing rules and checking they're obeyed, there's no-one left to do a bit of honest digging.'

Feo grunted and pulled his cloak round him to keep out the morning chill.

* * *

By midday, they had left the city behind and were starting to enter the foothills. Feo shifted uncomfortably in the saddle and looked with envy at Horsa who was riding easily a few yards ahead. He sighed with relief when Shallon called back, 'We'll halt here.'

Kirrin was scratching at her basket as Feo dismounted, so he released her before tethering his horse. When he turned round, he found her having her ears rubbed by Kimmi.

'She's a knowing one, this cat.' Kimmi picked her up and looked into her eyes. 'My grandmother had a black cat. She always said he knew more than he would tell.'

'She's a magic cat,' said Feo with conviction. 'There's not a hair of white on her.'

Kirrin climbed from one lap to another while they ate, accepting scraps of dried meat until she was stuffed. Then she curled up until they were ready to leave.

Feo picked her up to put her in the basket, but she mewed and struggled so much that he offered her his pocket instead. As they rode out on the road again, he could feel a warm purr against his chest.

The further they rode from the city, the wilder the landscape grew. The rolling foothills clothed with grass and areas of low woodland gave way to a more rugged vista of rocky outcrops, ravines and valleys of dense forest. Overhead, kites circled, searching for movement in the rough terrain, and every so often a thurill would bolt from the grass verge as the horses approached and vanish into the scrub.

The sun was a handsbreadth from the horizon when Kirrin began to struggle again. Feo pulled his cloak open to allow her head to peep out but she wouldn't settle. They halted for a moment at some crossroads to check the route and she was out of Feo's pocket and balancing on the saddle before leaping to the ground and racing into the bushes. Feo yelled 'Kirrin!' and (falling off the horse), ran after her. His stiff muscles hobbled him, but he pressed on, trying to trace the black shape in the shadows.

He pushed through scrub and circled trees, following a wisp of black fur or a gleam of emerald eyes. Horsa was behind, keeping a sharp eye out in case Kirrin doubled back.

Feo slowed and stopped. He hadn't seen a glimpse of the kitten for several minutes. 'Kirrin, Kirrin,' he called. The echo came back after a moment, but there was no trace of a small black kitten. He called again. There was no response. Horsa came up and laid a hand on his shoulder. 'I'm afraid we've lost her,' he said gently. 'We can't stop any longer. We have to make camp before dark.'

A leaden mass filled Feo's stomach as he turned back. 'A wizard doesn't lose his familiar,' he said, 'It just doesn't happen.' He walked beside Horsa in silence, thinking of a small kitten in the wild at night.

As they drew near the road, they started to hear Shallon and Kimmi calling. They quickened their steps as they made out the words.

'Feo, Horsa! Come back.'

Feo dodged around the bushes before the road, holding his breath in suspense. The voices sounded eager. He didn't dare believe that a kitten could have circled back so far in such a short time.

He burst out onto the verge. Shallon and Kimmi had the horses reins looped around their arms, and on Kimmi's shoulder was Kirrin. Horsa caught up with Feo and stopped short.

'Look,' said Kimmi, showing a grimy red neckerchief, 'she brought this back with her. I've never knowed a cat who fetched things before.'

'That animal is trouble,' said Horsa, and stalked off to his mount.

The party travelled on in a stony silence, with Feo and Kirrin bringing up the rear. Kirrin seemed unaware of her disgrace. She curled up in Feo's pocket and settled down for a nap after her exertions.

Daylight was thinning when Kirrin awoke and started to struggle. With a wary eye on his companions, Feo tried to calm her, but it was no use. She wriggled until her head was out of his cloak. At that very moment, a party of men on unkempt horses burst out of a clump of trees and headed for them at a gallop.

Where Is Feo?

The horsemen were among the party before they could close up for protection. Three of them cut Feo off from the rest of the group, who were too engaged with the other four to rescue him. Feo saw the glint of swords in the fading light. Then he was whirling his horse round to try to dodge the bandits. His stiff muscles protested and he nearly fell off.

The three horses bore down on him, leaving no way to escape. He saw the leader approach with his sword flourishing above his head. The blade glinted red in the setting sun as it descended. He felt the thwack on the side of his head and everything went dark. After that, there was a confusion of jostling and pushing, mixed with more blows from all sides. His horse bunched its muscles and then he was hanging on at a wild gallop, urged on by shouts surrounding him.

* * *

Three dejected figures stood by the side of the road. Five horses nibbled the grass on the verge, one limping as it walked.

'We can't follow them today. It's already dark.' Horsa looked at Shallon in despair.

'No. We'll have to track them in the morning.' Shallon laid a hand on Horsa's arm. 'Don't give up hope yet. I've got friends in these parts. They'll likely know who the bandits are.'

'Yes, but how long is it going to take to find Feo – if we find him. They might have killed him first.'

She squeezed and released his arm. 'Don't worry. They won't do that. They want him for ransom. You saw how they broke away as soon as they had him.'

'That's true.' Horsa had a vivid picture of the bandits galloping behind a hill, Feo in their midst with his hat tipped over his eyes. At least they had a little time to find him, but this was not the sort of situation Feo was good at. He was alone in a company of violent men without the ability to fight his way free, even if the odds had not been seven to one, and without the dependable skill to cast a spell.

Kimmi was twisting the red neckerchief Kirrin had found between his hands. 'See this,' he said, 'isn't this like the scarves those bandits were wearing? Cats don't fetch things, do they? I reckon Kirrin knew they were round. She was trying to warn us.'

Horsa looked at the scarf with sudden interest. It was like the ones the bandits had worn, now he came to think about it. He'd never seen a cat retrieve anything, any more than Kimmi. Kirrin had been trying to warn them. Perhaps Feo was right and she really was his familiar and not just a stray. So at least Feo wasn't quite alone in captivity.

'I think you're right,' he said.

He turned to Shallon. 'Where can we camp for tonight? We'll have to be ahorse by first light tomorrow.'

They made camp just out of sight of the road in a small hollow. A stream ran down one side, providing water for themselves and the horses and in this sheltered dip there was enough grass for grazing. Taking stock of their state, Horsa was thankful the bandits had not been too serious about the fight. They had come off very lightly considering how they had been outnumbered; just a graze on one of the horses' legs and a cut on Kimmi's arm.

Horsa slept restlessly, pricked by confused dreams of bandits circling Cardevin on seahorses while Feo stood on the highest point of the island watching the waves lap at the hem of his robe. He woke well before dawn and found that the others were stirring too.

After a hasty bite, they set off towards the spot they had last seen the bandits, hoping it would be light enough to search for tracks by the time they reached it. In the event, they had to hang back for half an hour to avoid spoiling the traces before there was light to see them.

Kimmi was first to venture forward, squatting down and sniffing the tracks like a dog.

'Their horses were tired. They won't have gone far last night.'

Horsa was surprised. 'How can you tell?'

'I know.' Kimmi looked at him sideways.

'Kimmi's a good tracker,' said Shallon. 'Happen he's right.'

They swung back onto the horses and followed the trail. Horsa tried to suppress hopes of finding Feo quickly. It all seemed too easy.

It was. A few miles down the traces, they petered out in rocky ground. Kimmi cast round the area in wider and wider circles, but eventually had to admit defeat.

'What do we do now?' asked Horsa, trying to ignore the leaden lump in his stomach.

'We have a break and some food and think,' said Shallon firmly. 'If we can't outguess a bunch of ragamuffin outlaws then we're not worth a clipped minim.'

It was a subdued meal. No-one felt much like talking and they couldn't delay long enough to light a fire. Horsa ate without knowing what he was swallowing, his fears rising as he thought of Feo, alone among enemies except for a kitten. Then he looked across at Shallon, her brow drawn in a frown of concentration, and he began to believe that she might just be able to work out where Feo was.

Shallon finished the last piece of waybread and crossed to squat between Horsa and Kimmi, smoothing the earth in front of her.

'Now,' she said, 'the lie of the country is like this.'

She sketched in the dust with a twig.

'We are here, right next to the hills. To the Southwest, here, is a bunch of villages. It's very rich land, heavily farmed, so the bandits aren't likely to go this way. Here, to the East, the Great River runs only a mile from the road, and it's impossible to cross until at least twenty miles upstream. I think the bandits have gone Northwest, deeper into the hills. Not many people live up there and it's easy to hide in the valleys. I reckon we should head this way and keep a sharp eye to pick up the tracks again. They can't have hidden them travelling at that speed in the dark.'

They set out at a modest pace, scanning the undergrowth for signs of disturbance. The terrain grew rockier and the vegetation changed from grass and trees to scrub as they penetrated deeper and higher into the hills. Hardly a word passed between them until mid-afternoon, when Horsa pulled his horse up.

'It's no good,' he said in despair. 'We'd have seen signs if there were any. We've lost them.'

Bandits Are Too Familiar

Feo clung onto his horse grimly as it raced out of all control. He had lost the reins in the melee, and couldn't spare a hand to grope for them. Nor could he straighten his hat which was jammed firmly over his eyes.

The ground must have been smooth, as his horse ran freely until there was a sudden jerk in its motion. Its pace slowed to something more reasonable and Feo realised that someone had caught the flying reins. He risked a hand to push his hat straight, hoping it was Horsa or Shallon. It wasn't.

Surrounding him were seven rough-looking men on shaggy ponies. Both men and animals looked as if they could do with a good bath and a square meal. Feo raked his eyes round the terrain. There was no sign of the rest of his party, only a maze of hills and narrow valleys.

'Come on, you!' The bandit holding Feo's reins tugged as the horse slowed a little.

'Give me my reins,' demanded Feo. 'I will not be dragged round the country like a parcel. I am the Hereditary Wizard of Cardevin!'

'Hear that, friends?' The bandit laughed, his straggling black beard wagging against the red neckerchief which was the only spot of colour in his drab clothes. 'He's the Hereditary Whatever of Nowhere! That should be worth a few doublards.'

'Ay, at least twice what we were thinking of asking,' said another.

'What d'you think, Chief?'

The man at the front turned and glared. 'Less noise from you! And keep the pace up. We've still a few miles to go.'

'I demand to be released!' said Feo, 'You'll regret it if you don't.'

Guffawing so hard he nearly fell off his pony, the bandit holding Feo's reins gasped, 'Do you hear that, lads? We'll regret it!' Turning to Feo, he said, 'What're you going to do, then? Turn us all into daisies?'

There was general laughter before the Chief turned again and shut them up. Feo muttered an incantation under his breath. Nothing happened except the bandit leading him turned to see what he was up to.

Feo slumped in the saddle. The magic on which he had thought he was gaining a tenuous grasp had deserted him again. What use was he going to be against a dragon? They would all be killed and Cardevin would be annihilated. And all of it would be on his head.

The ride continued for some time longer, winding down narrow valleys and turning along unsuspected paths. Feo moved automatically with the motion of his horse, his ears full of the sound of the waves breaking over the Cardevin countryside, sweeping all before them. When the ride ended, he dismounted and sat where he was put.

By the last shreds of daylight, he watched the bandits make a crude camp in the rocky bowl where they had halted. Its steep sides were dotted with small bushes, clinging to a precarious existence, and Feo could see no break in them except the narrow crack where they had entered. He sat immobile, wondering desperately what to do. There was a movement against his chest, and he realised that Kirrin was still with him. He pulled her out of his pocket and she sat on his knee looking unconcerned.

'A cat!' Black Beard had approached without Feo hearing. 'How did that get here?'

'She's my familiar,' said Feo. 'She's always with me.'

'Your familiar!' Black Beard laughed. 'Of course, the Hereditary Whatever of Nowhere must have a familiar, mustn't he?' He dropped a packet of bread and cheese and a flask of water by Feo. 'See if the pair of you can turn this into a banquet. We can't have you falling off your horse before we get our money.'

Feo fed Kirrin cheese until she would take no more. It was some comfort that she seemed unworried. It implied that there was at least no immediate threat.

Kirrin retreated to his pocket to sleep and Feo wrapped himself in his cloak. He was surprised to realise in the morning that he had dreamed no nightmares of Cardevin's destruction.

The bandits woke just after sunrise and seemed to have little to do after the Chief sent one of them off on horseback. Feo fed Kirrin, still without any plan in mind. He knew they were watching him and there was no way he could reach the crack where the path was without being caught.

Even if he did escape, where could he go? He hadn't the faintest idea where they had brought him and he had even less knowledge of the surrounding country.

He knew his friends would be searching for him, but how would they follow the tortuous path he had taken the day before? His mind went round and round like a prisoner in a treadmill, but he got no further.

In a nearby crevice in the rocks, a disembodied eye appeared. It watched Feo for a few minutes, blinked with content and vanished.

By a couple of hours after sunrise the bandits were plainly getting restless. The seventh bandit reappeared from his trip and shook his head at the rest before reporting to the chief. The mood started to turn rougher and one or two of the bandits drifted over to the rock where Feo sat and started making jokes about the "Hereditary Whatever of Nowhere". He ignored them but they seemed to find it very amusing. Several more came over to share the fun.

Kirrin was wriggling in Feo's pocket, so he lifted her out and set her by his feet. She sniffed at the rock and decided it wasn't interesting, so she started exploring the ground around it. Feo noted that she was restless and experienced a stab of fear. Every time that had happened so far, trouble had followed.

She made a slightly longer sally from the rock and came within reach of one of the bandits. He scooped her up and held her aloft in one hand.

'Ho, friends! Look what I've got here. It's the Whatever of Nowhere's familiar.'

There was general laughter as he tossed her like a ball to a companion. Kirrin squealed with terror. Feo stood up and strode forward.

'Give her to me!' he demanded.

The bandit holding her tossed her to the next.

'You'll have to catch it first!'

Feo dodged after Kirrin, and again, and again. Then the next bandit caught her clumsily and she hissed and sank her claws in him. He yelled and looked at his wrist.

'Look! It's drawn blood!'

He whipped out his knife. Feo drew himself up to his full height and spread his arms, his cloak flowing back in the breeze.

'You shall not harm her!

'By Mika, by Raxos, by Azert, let all evil thinkers beware.

'On the ground shall you hop, on the dusty ground.

'Lower than the lowest shall you be...'

The words flowed from his mind, through his mouth and hung in the morning air. The bandits were silent, with expressions that ranged from plain fear to terror. The very air seemed to crackle with static.

'So may it be! By Azert, by Raxos, by Mika!'

Kirrin , suddenly on the ground, scampered away towards the entrance to the bowl. The clearing was empty. No, not quite empty. Round Feo's feet he could see a group of brightly-coloured toads. Another couple were hopping over from the other side of the clearing.

Feo was exhausted. Shivering with cold, he sank down heavily on the rock and stared at the gaudy beasts. He didn't remember seeing them before. And where was Kirrin? She'd completely vanished. He thought about going to look for her, but he hadn't the energy to stand.

He was all alone. Everything was wrong. He wasn't much of a wizard after all. Even his familiar had deserted him.

* * *

Horsa stared at the flames of the campfire. They flickered, pale and attenuated in the late afternoon sunlight. He could see in his mind the picture of Feo being bundled off at the gallop, just a piece of goods to be exchanged for money. So much hung on his freedom, the fate of the whole of Cardevin and all its people, and besides, he didn't deserve this. For all his eccentricities, he was a good friend and Horsa could not imagine anyone he would rather have beside him. How were they going to find him? Would anyone know where to find the bandits? Or would they be able to get in touch with them to arrange a ransom? Could they manage all the arrangements in the short time they had? And worst of all, would the bandits just take the ransom and murder Feo?

He shook himself and stood up. Where was Shallon? They had to decide what to do next.

Shallon and Kimmi appeared on the small path from the stream. The five horses followed, still dripping water from their noses and looking considerably perkier. While Kimmi tethered and fed them, Shallon picked up a sack and came to the fire.

'Any signs of the bandits?' asked Horsa without hope.

'No signs of people near the water. We'll have to tackle this another way. Not Zillim and all his disciples could find the bandits without tracks to follow. There's a village about an hour's ride from here where I have friends. I reckon we should make for there and start enquiries. It's the only village for miles and if there's a band of outlaws in the region someone must know something about them.'

Horsa sighed. 'I hate to abandon the search, but we don't have any option.' He paused for a moment and then burst out, 'What use am I if I can't even protect Feo? Even Kirrin's done a better job of warning him than I have.'

'Peace,' said Shallon, laying a hand on his arm, 'You can't foresee every danger. We need to concentrate on getting Feo back.' She gave his arm a gentle squeeze and released it.

'Of course.' Horsa forced himself to think clearly. 'You think Feo's been taken for ransom? How will they demand the money? They don't know where to find us.'

'That's something else we can fix at the village. While we're seeking news, we'll also spread some. We can make sure they know how to find us.'

Horsa turned to douse the fire. 'Let's get going. We should reach the village well before dark.'

'Hold on. We all need a hot meal. We'll have time enough after that to reach the village by sunset. I'll need most of the evening to talk to all the people who can help and the word wouldn't be spread till next morning anyway.'

'I suppose we're in no danger from the bandits. If they capture us as well, there'll be no-one to pay a ransom for Feo.'

'True - but then they'll know that. We don't have to fear them. We'll only have trouble if there's another lot.'

Horsa looked at her in horror.

'No, no, I don't think it. This is the first I've heard of outlaws in this district. The pickings are too thin.'

The group round the campfire was subdued, but as the warm food started to take effect, the gloom lifted a trifle.

'We'll have to stick closer to Feo after this,' Horsa said, 'I hadn't thought how conspicuous that blue cloak makes him. And we'll never get him to change it.'

'And the phoenix-plume,' added Kimmi, 'I've never seen anything like that before.' He pushed some scraps into a small parcel. 'Kirrin will be hungry when we find them.' His face crumpled with worry. 'They will be all right, won't they?'

Horsa and Shallon exchanged glances. Horsa looked away.

'We'll find them, Kimmi, never you fear. They'll be right as the King's tithe.' Shallon patted him on the back.

Kimmi looked a little doubtful, but accepted the reassurance. Horsa thought of an impractical half-fledged magician and a part-grown cat in the charge of a bunch of ruffians with nothing to lose, but kept his worries to himself. Upsetting Kimmi would do nothing to help them.

Packing up after the meal took little time. The horses were watered and Horsa reckoned that they looked fresh enough to manage the ride to the village, though they would be better for a quiet night. They strapped the last packs on and prepared to mount.

'What's that!' Kimmi whirled round and half-drew his dagger. The faint scuffling in the undergrowth grew louder and he crouched, searching for a direction. A black blur raced from the bushes and leapt at him. He was about to strike when Horsa grabbed his wrist.

'Stop! It's Kirrin!'

Horsa dropped to his knees and picked up the cat. He looked her over in wonder. How had she found them? She'd obviously travelled long and fast. Her pads were scraped and her fur matted with thorns.

'Here.' Kimmi offered her a scrap of meat. Her panting slowed and she sniffed it hungrily. Horsa let her finish the packet of food before he voiced the question in all their minds.

'Where has she come from? And how do we backtrack her?'

Kimmi looked doubtful. 'I don't think I can follow the traces of such a small creature, even in broad daylight. For sure there's not enough light left today.'

Shallon shook her head. 'Such a little thing and so lithe. You'll never track her.'

Horsa looked at Kirrin in despair. She knew what they all wanted to know, but how could she tell them - or even understand that they needed her to?

Kirrin finished the small bowl of water which Shallon set before her and made a half-hearted attempt to tidy the fur on her chest. Then she turned to Horsa, looked him straight in the eye, and then turned and trotted across the clearing before he realised what she was doing.

'Kirrin! Come back!' Horsa ran after her and scooped her up.

'She's trying to lead us,' said Kimmi, bouncing with excitement.

'Yes, but she can't walk all that distance again,' said Horsa, 'She's exhausted.'

Shallon came up and thumped Horsa on the back. 'She's given us a path! We'll carry her on horseback. I'm sure she'll let us know if we stray.'

They trotted eagerly forward in the evening light, all tiredness forgotten. Kirrin's path lead them winding into the hills, round shoulders of rough grey stone and through shallow valleys of wild thyme. When they tried the wrong branch at a fork, Kirrin struggled and mewed until they took the other way.

The sun was an hour lower in the sky when they entered a sheer canyon. Horsa glanced up at the vertical walls a trifle nervously. It would be all too easy to roll a boulder or two down from those heights, but there were no signs of life up there. Horsa could see the larks circling freely at the top. Surely they would show alarm if there were any intruder?

The canyon appeared to be coming to a dead end. Horsa looked at Kirrin.

'What now?'

Kirrin struggled free of Horsa's arms and leapt down. Her sore legs nearly gave under her, but she recovered her balance and raced ahead round a massive boulder. Horsa followed her and stopped, jumping off his horse. In the middle of a dusty hollow, he recognised a midnight-blue cloak. He ran forward. Feo was sitting on a stone, looking in bewilderment at a group of brightly-coloured toads. They hopped all round him, crimson and gold, green and azure.

Horsa shook his shoulder. 'Feo! Are you all right? Where are the outlaws?'

Feo gestured vaguely round. 'Here. There. They were going to kill Kirrin.'

Horsa looked round wildly. 'The toads? You turned them into toads?'

'I did? Must've. There's nothing else.'

A golden one hopped close to Horsa's feet. He stooped to pick it up. It shot sideways, its eyes sparkling with alarm, but kept near Feo's legs. Horsa realised that all the toads were jumping in a tight circle round the Hereditary Wizard.

'Is he all right?.' Shallon came up beside Horsa. 'And where are the bandits?' She looked round the empty area warily.

'I think these must be them.' Horsa gestured wildly at the toads. 'But I can't believe he's done this.'

'He turned them into toads! Who'd credit it?' She looked at the group with wonder. 'But you don't get toads in this country. Too dry. And I've never seen fancy coloured ones.'

'Then his magic is working.'

'That's why they're all keeping close. They know the only body who can help them.' Shallon shook her head in amazement.

Horsa turned to Feo and realised he was gazing into the distance, aware of nothing round him.

'We'd better get him to that village, Shallon. He's much worse than he was after transforming the ostler. But then, I suppose he's had seven times the work to do.'

Shallon and Kimmi cornered the seven toads and scooped them into a bag. The bandit's horses were found penned into a cave and they strung their reins together, tying them to the saddles with the pack horses. Feo's horse was with them, complete with his precious book bag. They set a fast pace back along the canyon. Horsa rode beside Feo, steadying him when he seemed likely to fall off, and worrying about reaching the village by nightfall.

Dusk had gone, and it was by moonlight that they topped the last rise and saw lights below. Shallon urged the tired horses to a trot. As they passed the first thatched cottage at the edge of the village, a bearded man stepped into the road and flashed a lantern in her face.

'You know me, Berek. Where's Aisu? I've a bunch of weary travellers who need a bed and maybe some help.'

'Shallon! We haven't seen you in a gryphon's age. Aisu's at her house. She'll be glad to see you. There've been nobbut a few visitors since the King started issuing Travel Passes.'

Horsa steadied Feo with a sense of relief. Hot food and warm beds were close, and perhaps some useful advice. If Feo was to learn to control this wild talent in time, they needed that more than anything.

They rode on into the village and halted by a square two storey house with a stone roof. Two carved sphinxes guarded the entrance and a lantern glimmered on the wall outside.

Shallon banged on the heavy door. As it opened, the light from inside reflected across intricate carvings. Horsa wondered what manner of person would live in this isolated village and boast such an exotic door.

He soon found out. The door swung wide, and framed in the light stood a thin woman, so tall that her head nearly touched the doorframe. Slipping the dark shawl from her head, she stepped forward and embraced Shallon.

'My dear, it's long and long since you were here.'

Her voice was deep and somewhat husky. Although her height was commanding, it was her eyes, dark and full of knowledge, which gripped attention. It seemed to Horsa that she was of middle years, but it was hard to be sure.

'Aisu, it's good to see you. I bring friends to make up for my absence.'

'They are most welcome.' She turned to the others. 'My house is open to you. I have expected you these several days. You have a long way to travel, in many senses. You have come to the right place, but your paths from here may be very different from what you expect. But the time for this is tomorrow. Come in. There is fire and food, and that is all you want tonight.'

Time for Papers

Feo woke. The sun, now at its zenith, was flooding into the room, turning the air golden and making the dust motes dance in its path. He rolled over. He was lying in a bed tucked close to the big chimney from downstairs.

Downstairs? He rubbed his eyes. He remembered standing in a dusty canyon with the sun sweeping almost horizontally along it. His shadow stretched right across to the other side, right over those scruffy bandits who were... who were...

They were going to kill Kirrin! Feo's eyes flashed green lightening. No scabby outlaw was going to murder his wizard's cat! He stood tall and straight, spreading his arms wide to gather power and then swinging them in, pointing all ten fingers at the evil-doers. Half-forgotten words jumped into his mind and he repeated them, hardly aware of their meaning. He felt a surge, first of heat, then of cold. He looked, but there was no-one there.

His mind fogged over and he sat down heavily on a rock. He was just aware that Kirrin had deserted him. After that, he had no idea how long he sat.

Horsa's voice broke through for a bit, and Shallon's. Later, there was a long period of jogging up and down, and feeling cold - so very cold. Of course - he must have ridden here - wherever here was. Then there was a warm fire, a lot of bustling round him and a vile herbal drink. Finally, he remembered the softness of the bed under his aching muscles.

Feo sat up. He felt warm again and he was as hungry as a bandersnatch. His mind had cleared and all the pieces of the puzzle had slid into their proper places, but he still couldn't work out what had happened to those bandits.

Half an hour later, washed and dressed, he traversed several corridors before he discovered the way downstairs. Rounding the last turn of the staircase, he found himself in the great hall. The sunlight was flooding in from deep windows, giving the glossy dark panelling an extra warmth. A wood fire was blazing in the ample hearth and three people were sitting at the table in front of it. Kimmi was at the end, intent on a bowl of stew, and with their backs to him sat Horsa and Shallon, his arm easily draped round her shoulders. Feo smiled to himself. He should have seen this coming.

As he approached, Horsa turned round and sprang up when he saw him.

'Feo! You're awake at last. Come and eat.'

Shallon nodded a greeting, looking pleased to see Feo back to normal. Kimmi just stared at him, a grin splitting his face.

'Where's Kirrin? Is she all right?'

'She's here, by the fire.' Horsa pointed to a small basket. Peering in, Feo could see a black shape, its sides heaving in a gentle rhythm.

'She's just very tired,' Horsa continued. 'She fetched us to rescue you. She had a huge meal last night and she's been sleeping ever since.'

Feo looked at Horsa with a tinge of triumph. 'I told you she's a magical cat.'

'Yes, you did. And you were right.' Horsa threw up his hands in mock surrender. 'I still don't know how she covered the distance in such a short time. She was exhausted when she found us.'

Feo sat down. 'Where are we?'

'This is Aisu's house,' said Shallon. 'She's an old friend and sees more than most. She's out this morning, but when she comes back, I think she'll be able to give us some good advice.'

'Right now, I'm more interested in food than advice.' Feo picked up a spoon and gave the bowl which had appeared before him his full attention.

'When do you plan on leaving?' asked Horsa, turning to Shallon.

'Feo looks well recovered. We'll rest a day and leave the day after tomorrow. That will give us time to have a talk with Aisu.'

Feo looked up. 'How can she help us?'

'If she is willing, she can direct us along the most hopeful path to complete your quest.'

'But what does she know about killing dragons?'

'She knows many things.' said Shallon firmly. 'You will have to ask her.'

Feo looked at her doubtfully and then turned towards the door. There was a voice outside, a deep half-remembered voice, but he couldn't tell where he had heard it.

A tall figure dressed in black paused in the doorway. Her aquiline features were shadowed by the fine shawl over her head and her piercing eyes took in the whole room at a glance.

'Children, I'm pleased to see you well today.' She swept across the room, the skirts of her robe just swinging clear of the flagged floor. 'You've all eaten? Good, then I think it's time to talk.'

Aisu sat herself in the big carved chair at the head of the table. Shallon leant forward and asked, 'What has become of the toads?'

'They are headed over the pass towards the Meiklin Wastes.' She gave a throaty laugh. 'I don't think they'd come back here for a king's ransom.'

'The toads?' Feo broke in, 'What do you mean?'

'I restored them to human shape first, of course.' Aisu broke off and looked at Feo sharply. 'You turned the bandits into toads. You don't remember?'

Feo's head ached with the effort of recall. 'I remember some toads,' he said slowly, 'They were hopping round, very strange colours. I've never seen coloured toads before.'

Aisu sucked in her breath sharply. 'This is worse than I thought.' She gave Feo a stern glance and spoke with emphasis. 'We cannot have an untrained wizard running round. It is too dangerous.'

Feo stiffened. 'I may be untrained, but I have given many years of study to the Hereditary Wizardship. And it runs in my blood. My family have provided Hereditary Wizards to the Kings of Cardevin for 500 years.'

'Feo, you have the talent. There is no doubt about that, but that is what makes it dangerous.' Aisu laid a hand on his arm. 'You must stay here a while and learn to use your gift. Otherwise you will never gain control of it.'

'I think you should take Aisu's advice.' Feo looked up and saw Shallon's concerned face. He hesitated, seeing on one side his unpredictable talent facing the razor claws and furnace-breath and on the other, Cardevin sinking into the sea before he had even reached the hunting-grounds. He turned to Aisu and opened his mouth to ask her how long the training would take, but before he could speak there were raised voices outside the door and an ungainly figure burst in and teetered to a halt in the middle of the hall.

'I come in the name of the King!' The spherical body rocked slightly as the words rushed out.

'Grem! It's some time since we had the pleasure...' Aisu looked at the fat man with distaste. His brown jerkin barely spanned his middle and greasy black curls shadowed his puffy face.

Grem tugged his jerkin down and fastened on an ingratiating smile. 'Indeed, Aisu, it's been too long. I really should have an assistant. There's far too much work for one pair of hands.' He pulled out a large red handkerchief and mopped his brow before continuing. 'But this is a business visit. I hear you have guests, and foreign ones at that.' He put the handkerchief away and drew himself up. 'In the King's name, I demand to see their papers.'

Feo looked at the speaker with horror. 'This can't happen now,' he muttered to Horsa, 'We're all going to land in jail this time.' The vision of drowning Cardevin grew sharper and larger in his mind. He heard Horsa's whispered reply, 'Don't worry, I'm sure Aisu can deal with him,' and was aware of Horsa rising and crossing the room.

'Honourable Sir,' said Horsa smoothly, 'These are our travel documents.'

Grem took the proffered parchments and scanned them intently. Horsa was not reassured when he noticed Grem had one of them upside down.

'These seem to be in order,' said Grem, handing them back with reluctance. His face brightened. 'But where are your entrance visas?'

Horsa's heart sank. Those vital documents were currently being stamped by the Town Guard on alternate days.

'They're in our baggage. May I have the honour of presenting them to you when I locate them?'

'Why have you not got them with you? I will expect them tomorrow,' retorted Grem. Puffing up his chest, he added, 'The King's business will not brook delay.' He turned and bowed stiffly to Aisu. 'I will receive your guest in the morning.'

As Grem went through the door, Aisu turned to Horsa.

'That was well done. Don't worry about Grem. I can see he makes no trouble for you.'

'Trouble!' Feo stood up, pale with rage. 'We've escaped the clutches of the Town Guard, dealt with the local bandits, and now we're pulled up by this illiterate bumpkin. We're never going to get clear of this tangle in time.' He turned and strode out of the house.

'He'll be back in a while,' said Horsa with an apologetic look at Aisu, 'He needs some time to think.'

It was dusk when Feo returned. His boots were caked with mud and his face was grim. He asked for a gathering to make plans, but refused to talk before dinner.

They ate at the table before the fire by the light of several large candelabra. The meal was silent, oppressed by Feo's preoccupation. When the remnants were cleared away and the party seated round the table, he refused to speak until the rest had had their say.

Aisu nodded to Horsa. 'As Feo prefers to speak last, perhaps you should begin.'

Horsa stroked his moustache as he decided where to start. 'As you know, Feo and I have been given the task of killing a dragon and obtaining the Dragonstone so that the curse on Cardevin can be lifted. The curse must be lifted by the next new moon or Cardevin will implode and vanish under the waves.'

Aisu's dark eyes were thoughtful as she looked at Horsa. 'Indeed, you have not so very long to accomplish your task.'

'No, it will take three days to return to Cardevin after killing the dragon - that is,' he interjected with some bitterness, 'if we don't get delayed by any more of the King's servants.'

'That is the wild card,' said Shallon, rubbing a hand through her curls 'although a little gold goes a long way with those.'

'So, allowing time to find the dragon and kill it, that leaves us about a week at the most,' finished Horsa.

Aisu nodded to Shallon. 'And the organisation?' she asked.

'We have the necessary weapons and all the supplies we need. I know the route to a suitable dragon's lair. But,' she looked hard at Feo, who was sitting with his head sunk on his chest, 'we must have Feo's magic to have any chance of success.'

'Aisu, how long do you need with Feo,' asked Horsa. 'We have a little time in hand.'

'It's hard to tell. Perhaps three days, perhaps a week. I can set aside my other tasks for that time and work with him all day. There is another, quicker way to achieve this, by sending Feo on the road under the mountain, but I do not wish to do this. He must go alone and the way is very hard, and dangerous, too. He might never come back.' She looked at Feo's bowed head, and then round the gathered company. 'If he works with me for some days, by the end, I believe he will have enough command of his magic to offer a chance of success. But he won't succeed unless he does, and he may not even survive.' Aisu's dark eyes were sombre.

'Then we have time - just,' said Shallon with relief. 'Feo, what say you?'

Feo stood up slowly, the weight of the whole of Cardevin bowing his shoulders.

'I can't do it,' he said painfully. 'The risk is too great. If Grem decides to throw us in jail, then Cardevin is lost. I leave at dawn.' He paused and swept a glance over the group, his eyes laurel-dark. 'I can't ask any of you to come with me. The fate is mine alone. With my magic so unpredictable, it is far too dangerous for anyone to face the dragon with me. I will not imperil your lives as well.'

The log fire crackled in the stunned silence, making Feo jump. He sat down. Leaning his head on his hands, he forced the welling fear down.

Horsa leaped up, his normally ruddy face pale with alarm. 'You can't do this, Feo. You can't go alone. It's certain death, and then Cardevin is lost indeed. If you go, then so must I.'

Shallon strode round the table and laid a hand on Feo's shoulder. 'You mustn't do it. You need all the help you can get to come through this alive. Do you know how long it is since a dragon was killed? It's nearly three hundred years.'

Feo's head rocked back with shock. 'Three hundred years! Why didn't you tell us this before?'

'Many people set out on dragon hunts, but few keep on after their first glimpse. As for the rest,' Shallon shrugged. 'with help, most get back alive.' She rubbed a hand over her curly head. 'When I took you on, I didn't realise you were truly in earnest.'

No-one uttered a word. Even with the blazing fire, the room was cold with shock.

Feo slowly stood up. His body was numb but his mind was crystal-clear. 'All this makes no difference. I leave at dawn.'

'Then so do I.'

'And I.'

'And I.'

Horsa, Shallon and Kimmi ranged themselves round Feo.

'Children, this is a rash choice.' Aisu's brow was creased with worry. 'The speed of the gladiator did not win the race. You must use your heads if you are to come through this alive.' She glanced at Feo's set face and stood up with a sigh. 'I will not argue where I cannot change. At least let me scry your future. I may yet be able to help you.'

She crossed the room to a heavy cupboard and unlocking it, she withdrew several items before coming back to the group.

Motioning the others to sit down, she spread a dark velvet cloth over the end of the table. On it she placed a shallow silver dish with dragons twined round the rim and a matching pitcher. Lastly, just beyond the cloth, she placed a tripod with a dish of charcoal and a small box.

'You must keep silent until I give you leave to speak again. Shallon, note what I say. The smallest detail may be important.'

She picked up a pair of tongs from the hearth and held one of the pieces of charcoal over a glowing log until it glowed in turn. Restoring it to its dish on the tripod, she opened the box and cast a large pinch of its coarsely-ground contents onto the burning charcoal. A cloud of blue-grey smoke hissed up and a pungent smell drifted across the table. Feo sniffed cautiously. He detected hints of resins mixed with laurel and other herbs. As Aisu cast on another pinch, he took a deeper breath than he intended and his head began to swim.

'Hoaga, anhix astromen, agati ecolon.' Aisu stood tall at the end of the table, her head thrown back and her hands stretched out, palms down, over the tripod. She whispered a few more words and, casting more powder on the charcoal, she seated herself and took up the pitcher. Pouring a stream of inky liquid into the silver dish, she bent her head over it.

Feo's head was clearing now as the plume of smoke flowed steadily towards Aisu. He watched her, still and dark as an icon, her hands loosely cupped round the dish.

Aisu raised her head slightly, keeping her eyes fixed on the bottomless pool of liquid. Shallon bent forward to catch the muttered words which came from her. Slowly, they grew clearer and more coherent.

'The dragons are nesting low this year... the great golden eggs are already breaking... the shards fall to the ground, the fledgling staggers. Beneath its translucent skin the muscles flicker. It turns. Something is coming. There is a man behind a boulder. A screech, a jet of fire. Out of the smoke a vast protective head bends over the fledgling.'

Aisu's head dropped and she fell silent. The aromatic smoke continued to flow round her. Presently she raised her head and the words flowed again.

'A small group is riding towards the mountain. They reach its feet and start to ascend. The path is steep and rocky. They wind between the yellow boulders. Their horses' feet slip and loose small slides of scree.

'The path grows steeper. They tether the horses and proceed on foot. There is black among the yellow rock - smoke black, fire black. The way levels and opens into a dusty hollow. Golden shards lie among the rocks, thick as a redfruit rind, hard as diamond.

'One man picks up a golden fragment and turns it over in his hands. It glitters in the sunlight. Another points to a finger of rock just above. The yellow stone is streaked with rust and black.

'Tendrils of dingy fog drift down the path from above. The party turns as one man. A huge figure descends, grey-green, monstrous. They draw together. Smoke billows from the dragon, shot with lurid fire. The humans appear and disappear in the fog. All is confusion.

'The fog parts for a moment. A desperate battle is in progress. Bursts of crimson fire outline the humans. They stagger back. An enormous eye, amber and slit-pupilled, emerges for a moment. The little party stumbles towards the path. All are singed and one nurses an arm.

'Below, the horses roll their eyes in terror, but the tethers hold. The humans scramble into the saddle and start the downward path.'

Aisu fell silent. The listeners sat stunned. Above the tripod, the last wisps of smoke dissolved into the still air.

Feo's head rested on his hands in black despair. His quest seemed doomed before he had even found a dragon. Then a small spark of defiance rose. He must succeed. He must succeed, or Cardevin would perish. And after all, what was a Hereditary Wizard if he could not set prophecy at naught?

He stood up slowly, pushing the weight of fear up with him.

'Nevertheless, I leave at dawn.'

With a firm tread but leaden heart, he left the room.

The Pointing Finger

The sun was an hour from rising when Feo emerged from the house. The night chill was still in the air and he shivered convulsively, uncertain if it was caused by the cold or what lay ahead. No-one else was about, and he was unsure whether to feel disappointed or relieved at this. He was reluctant to involve his companions in so dangerous an exploit, but they had all seemed so sure last night that they were coming. For a moment, he allowed himself to feel how much their comradeship meant to him.

A solitary bird ventured a few notes and Feo glanced at the horizon. Dawn was approaching and it was time he got moving. At least if he took no companions he could injure no-one but himself. Slinging his bag over his shoulder, he turned towards the stables.

He had thought that the rest of the house was asleep, but as he turned through the arch, he was surprised to hear voices.

'This one on the packhorse and that behind my saddle.'

'Shallon! What are you doing here?'

'I said I would come and I meant it.' She rubbed a hand over her curls. 'Someone has to see you make it as far as the dragon.'

'And I wouldn't miss a dragon hunt for all the gold in the king's treasury.' Kimmi appeared from behind the packhorse.

Horsa came out of the stable leading a second packhorse. 'I'd rather be killed by a dragon than skinned alive by the King for deserting you,' he remarked as he passed.

Feo could think of nothing to say. He looked round the yard at the bustle of preparation and wondered why these people were following him on such a hopeless mission. Then he straightened his back and squared his shoulders. The Hereditary Wizard of Cardevin would ride on his quest with a proper entourage.

Swinging his cloak back over his arm, he stepped up to his horse.

'Is the company ready to leave?' he asked, 'It's nearly dawn.'

The horses turned out of the yard in line astern and trotted to the front of the house. The heavily-carved door swung open and a tall figure in a dark cloak stepped out and raised a hand.

Shallon pulled the party to a halt. 'Aisu! I didn't wish to disturb you at this hour.'

'You must not leave without a word. I have a little - a very little - advice to offer.'

Feo pushed his horse to the front. 'Aisu, I am grateful for any advice you can offer, but I will not be deflected. I must go.'

Aisu smiled a trifle sadly. 'Child, that I know. However, the little I have to offer may save you from disaster. When you see the finger-rock, watch for danger. I can help you no more at present, but remember, I am always your friend. You may return whenever you wish.'

'I thank you for your advice and your hospitality. If I am able, I will return.' Feo swung his horse back into the line while Shallon bade Aisu farewell.

The party trotted down the village street, horses hooves thudding on the packed earth. The first thin light of dawn glanced off the shuttered windows of the neatly-tended cottages. No-one was abroad.

As they passed the last house, Feo heard a sound and looked back. He could just see a round head in a grubby nightcap leaning out of a window. It was Grem, shaking a fist. Feo doffed his hat to him and then turned back to the road.

They kept a fast pace, stopping only when they had to. The road, quiet enough at all times, was deserted at this hour. Cultivated fields hedged with thorn flanked the way on either side. Lifting their heads from the morning's grazing, a few sleepy animals paused to stare at them before returning to their business. Rabbits and thurills scuttered from under the horses' hooves and high in the sky, a hawk hovered watchfully.

By noon, the rich cultivated land had petered out to be replaced by heath. A few remnants of early blossom still clung to the bushes which dotted the short grass. In the distance, the foothills of the mountains were inscribed on the sky.

The midday meal was silent, taken standing while the horses cropped a few mouthfuls of grass. Kirrin drank a saucer of water but would not eat. When they started out again, Feo noticed that the country was changing once more. Rocky outcrops broke the rough grass and there seemed to be fewer animals about. Even the hawks had deserted them.

As the day drew on, the mountains loomed larger on the horizon. The rocky areas grew wider and the whole land seemed to hold its breath.

They made uneasy camp in the foothills right at the base of the mountains. Kirrin prowled the area, unable to settle. No-one spoke much during the spartan meal and afterwards they separated to their different tasks.

Shallon went over the horses with meticulous care. She checked that none of the harness was rubbing and lifted each hoof to examine it for stones. Then she proceeded to the packs, making sure that the contents had not shifted during the journey and they were still securely strapped.

Kimmi had elected to help Horsa with the weapons and they had unpacked the big leather bag for the first time. Kimmi polished the hide shields with an oily cloth while Horsa sharpened and burnished the swords and spears until the firelight gleamed from them.

Satisfied with the horses and supplies, Shallon came over and sat with Horsa.

'Look at you, Kimmi. If you yawn any harder your head will fall off!' Shallon waved at the other side of the fire. 'Go find your blankets, now. We're not carrying you up the mountain tomorrow.'

Kimmi stifled another yawn and stumbled over to his pack.

Shallon picked up the rag and started polishing the last shield. 'How do you think we'll do tomorrow?'

'I don't know.' Horsa looked worried. 'I've not fought a dragon before and Feo's magic...'

'Aye, it's wicked that Grem came when he did. Else I think Feo would have taken Aisu's teaching.' She oiled the cloth again and started on the other side of the shield. 'Now, don't you fret any more. We're two good fighters. And I'll tell you another thing.' She looked at him and smiled. 'Dragons are none so bright. Just you make sure and stay away from the hot end.'

Horsa put an arm round her shoulders and hugged her. With Shallon beside him, he had magic enough.

Feo sat hunched on his blankets trying to ignore the murmur of voices and the steady 'whfft, whfft' of Horsa's whetstone. One of his precious books lay on his lap and he was doggedly trying to memorise its contents and make sense of it at the same time. Kirrin seemed to sense his mood and lay still against the ancient vellum.

The cramped script started to dance in front of Feo's eyes and he must have dozed. He woke with a start to find the camp in total darkness. Three shadowy humps were visible in the cold circle, and when he found Kirrin curled into a tight ball, he rolled himself up in his blankets and waited for sleep. It was long coming (and full of disturbing dreams when it did), but when he woke to the first touch of daylight, he could remember nothing of them.

The wary party started the long ascent. The way wound to and fro between huge boulders and along the edge of sheer drops. Everywhere, the yellow rock had chipped away and left a thick carpet over the track. No birds or animals were to be seen here, and very little vegetation; an eerie silence hung over the mountain.

Feo pulled his cloak tightly round him and tried not to shiver. The early morning air was cold, but inside he was colder still. All too quickly, the time was coming when his magic would be put to the test. This time, it had to work.

Zigzagging along the steep slope, the track took them inexorably upwards. The horses frequently stumbled on the loose stones and several times they dismounted to lead them.

As the sun rose higher and reflected from the yellow rocks, the air heated and danced. Every occasional breath of chill wind was welcome. The horses began to flag on the steepening path and Shallon called a halt in the shade of a small hollow, where they tethered the animals and shouldered the packs with weapons and water before continuing on foot.

Feo climbed in a daze. The sweat was trickling into his eyes and the words of Aisu's reading threaded so persistently through his thoughts that he was often unaware if he was stumbling on the rocks.

As the path neared the summit, it closed in on both sides and then opened out into a small arena with a floor of yellowish sand. Jagged walls offered a little shade where they could pause for water. Feo flopped to the ground in the shadow of an overhang and tried to order his thoughts. Kirrin scratched urgently at his pocket, so he gave her some water and put her down beside him. She prowled round him for a moment, sniffing delicately at the stones, and then ventured a few feet across the ochre dust.

'Have you ever seen anything like this?' Horsa was standing in front of him holding out a fragment of something glittering.

Feo took it and turned it over in his hands. It was a thin curve the size of his palm, polished smooth and embedded with sparkling flecks of gold.

'The sand over there is covered with them,' continued Horsa.

Kirrin came bounding back to see what was going on. Feo held out the fragment for her to smell. She sampled it carefully and sat back on her haunches with a sneeze. Washing her nose vigorously with two paws, she backed an inch at a time towards Feo until she was pressed against his side.

Feo stared at her in amazement. 'I've never seen her act like this before.' He looked round the arena and stumbled to his feet, clutching Horsa's arm. 'Look, the finger-rock! Danger! Remember Aisu's warning.'

Horsa wheeled round and followed Feo's pointing hand. A tall yellow pillar stretched upwards, its shadow nearly touching their feet. He ran for the packs and tore them open, tossing shields and weapons to each member of the group. They drew together in a protective phalanx and scanned the area for movement. There was nothing.

Kirrin mewed and Feo scooped her up from between his feet and tucked her in his pocket. She peered out warily from the front of his cloak. Her eyes were watchful and her ears twisted from side to side.

The silence stretched, and Feo started to wonder if anything was going to happen. He noticed a tendril of brown mist drifting into the area from the far side. He was puzzled. Where would mist come from on the side of a barren mountain?

Thickening and spreading, the mist poured into the rocky bowl faster and faster. The first wisps reached his nostrils and he sniffed. Sulphur? And several even less pleasant smells mixed with it.

The fog grew thicker, blanketing the whole area and muffling the occasional chink of the weapons. Horsa shifted uneasily beside him.

'We'll never see anything in this lot,' he muttered, 'What's more, we won't even hear what's coming.'

'Ssh,' said Shallon.

They all strained their ears. There was movement somewhere near. Or was there? There wasn't exactly a sound, more a deep thrum, felt through the feet. Kirrin's eyes tracked rapidly from side to side, and seeing nothing, she hid inside Feo's cloak. He could feel her heart pounding.

A thread of scent, acrid and sulphurous, tickled Feo's nostrils. He turned his head to find its source and the fog was ripped apart by a force like the clapping of a thousand demons' wings. Shreds of mist boiled round the arena, now almost revealing, now concealing a huge dark mass.

They flung their shields up and crouched, weapons ready. A sinuous shape slid into visibility and an amber eye as big as one of their shields regarded them coldly through its slit pupil.

Feo watched, fascinated, as olive tendrils writhed through the hot breath. Then the head was withdrawn and his trance broke.

The party stumbled away from the monstrous shadow and, pressing their backs to a boulder, set their spears towards the enemy. They did not have long to wait.

A blast of furnace-breath made them fling their shields up and before they had time to gather their wits, a plume of black smoke shot with fire jetted over them. A smell of scorched leather filled the air as their shields took the worst of it.

Feo dropped to one knee, coughing and gasping for breath. How were they to survive? All thoughts of killing the monster had fled.

He bowed his head and found a wisp of cleaner air. With it his mind cleared a trifle and he saw as if it were spread before his eyes a page of the book he had studied the night before. The title, bold and angular on the yellowed sheet, read 'Fireshield - Protection Against All Manner of Flames'.

He read the words out loud, pushing up with his shield as he reached the final incantation. A discontinuity appeared in the air, peaking at his raised shield and slanting away towards the ground on all sides. At the boundary, tendrils of smoke writhed and fought to enter.

The humans slowly straightened, inhaling the clearer air. The dark mass of the dragon had retreated into the fog. No doubt its tiny brain was struggling to comprehend this strange phenomenon.

'How long can you hold it?' Horsa shifted his grip on the spear.

'I don't know,' said Feo, 'I should be able to hold it as long as we need.' He peered into the murky distance. 'I can't see the dragon. Has it given up?'

The mists in front of them split. The awful head bent towards them, tendrils writhing, nostrils flared scarlet.

Feo staggered under the impact of the roaring flame. Then he slowly straightened his back, pushing his shield and the magic it carried as high as he could reach.

The dragon jerked back as the flames rebounded in its eyes and then screamed with rage as Horsa buried a spear in its wing-root. It reared up, exposing its dead-fish-white stomach, but before Horsa could send another spear in, a huge scaled foot, armed with razor-claws, swiped across the defenders.

One dirty white claw, caked with black blood, caught Feo's shield and raked a furrow up his arm. He gasped and the fireshield wavered, letting in a few shreds of black smoke. The dragon bellowed its triumph and directed a huge jet of flame at the party. It battered at Feo's unsteady barrier. He heard Horsa cry out as the flame poured through a weak point and he forced the shield up again. The dragon drew back, screaming its frustration to the sky, and then the party was stumbling with barely-controlled panic towards the downward path.

They rounded the first corner just in time to escape another blast of fire. Feo looked back, expecting annihilation to be staring at them with slit-pupilled eyes. The track was empty. Hope surged up as he realised it was too narrow for the dragon. Then, with sickening force, he remembered it was not bound to the earth as they were.

Emerging from the enclosing walls of the path into the open, Feo looked back and saw the dragon rising above the rocky bowl in a maelstrom of shredded fog. 'Faster! It's flying!'

The party scrambled down the steep slope, loosing showers of scree onto the mountainside below, expecting at any moment a dark shadow to pass overhead, and then a still darker one to descend with grim finality. As they finally reached the horses, Feo looked back again. The dragon was still hovering in the dispersing mist. He couldn't imagine why the monster hadn't finished them off.

Pulling at their tethers and eyes rolling in terror, the horses were nearly impossible to control. Shallon and Kimmi managed to get them calm enough to mount and they set off down the mountain at the fastest pace they could manage on the uncertain footing.

Behind them, a disembodied eye appeared. It blinked and stared after them with an expression of malicious pleasure.

They rode down the way to the plain in black silence. Feo was aware of the slow trickle of blood down his arm and realised, with a pang of guilt, that none of the party was unscathed. He looked back before the path levelled out. He could just see the finger-rock near the peak. and on its tip perched a bloated form, one wing dragging, shining with a soft putrescence and trumpeting its frustration to the sky. He shuddered.

Slackening pace for nothing, they ran until the hideous sight was obscured by the knee of a hill. Then they halted by a small stream whose banks were dotted with the first vestiges of grass on that barren plain. The horses had run out their panic and hung their heads, exhausted. Shallon left Kimmi to water them and turn them out to graze while the party took stock.

Feo looked round his band of hunters with anguish. He had not brought them here to flee, defeated and injured. Kimmi was relatively unscathed, with various scrapes and grazes and a bruised knee which gave him a dramatic limp. Shallon had lost one side of her curls and suffered a deep graze the length of her arm.

His glance fell on Horsa. Shallon was bending over him with a worried expression, spreading a thick yellow salve on his arm, but the paste could not disguise the severity of the burn. Horsa's normally ruddy face was white and strained. Feo could not imagine him using his right arm again.

Shallon looked up.

'This is serious, but not beyond Aisu's mending,' she said to Feo, 'and my salve will keep it reasonably comfortable until we get there.'

Guilt flooded through Feo as he turned away. 'This is all my doing,' he muttered.

'No!' Horsa sat up straight. 'It was my job to protect you while you held the shield. And I failed,' he added bitterly.

Feo sank onto a rock and buried his head in his hands. He didn't have the energy to stand up any longer.

He was roused from his lethargy by a movement against his chest. Opening his eyes, he found himself greeted by an emerald gaze. He smiled wryly. One member of his party, at least, was still sound. He stroked the black head and Kirrin purred.

'Feo?'

Shallon was standing in front of him.

'Feo, your arm needs attention.' She squatted beside him and pulled up his sleeve.

He welcomed the sting of the liquid on the jagged cut. It was at least a small atonement. But the bitter taste of defeat and the conviction that he had betrayed his friends filled his mind.

The orange flames of the campfire leapt cheerfully that evening, but the gathering round them was sombre. Shallon sat close to Horsa, keeping a sharp eye on him. Feo was abstracted. His thoughts kept circling back to his departure from Cardevin. The King had embraced him. 'Feo, you must kill a dragon. You are our only hope.'

He must kill a dragon. But the King had never seen one. He didn't know what they were like; the searing breath, the shearing claws - but above all, those huge inhuman slit-pupilled eyes.

It was impossible to kill a dragon. It was impossible.

'Feo, we must kill a dragon.' There was a note of desperation in Horsa's voice.

Feo blinked and realised he must have spoken aloud. 'It's impossible,' he repeated dully.

'We must!' Horsa was leaning forward on his good arm.

Shaking his head, Feo remembered the bloated form on the Finger Rock. It was certain death. Need chased panic through his thoughts, stirring them into a maelstrom. Slowly the chaos subsided round one solid rock. If needs be, he would give his life for his quest. But he must be certain of being able to protect any companions who were foolish enough to join him.

Feo turned to Horsa, his eyes shining clear emerald. 'Yes, we must kill a dragon, but I will not again ask anyone to come with me.'

'You do not go without me,' Horsa stated.

Kimmi wriggled in his place. 'Don't leave me behind,' he said, the break in his voice betraying his fear but his gaze locked on Horsa.

'I will finish my job,' said Shallon. 'I'm not abandoning you.' She gave Horsa a sideways glance. 'It has been done before and we will do it again.'

Feo shook his head. 'I will tell you nearer the time if I will take any companions.' He stood up. 'Aisu's advice was good. I will ask her again when we return.'

'Pray Hoaga I have enough time left,' he added.

* * *

It was well into the following night when they reached the outskirts of Aisu's village. The journey back had been slowed partially by the horses' tiredness, but principally by the humans' need for rest.

All were exhausted by the fight, and, despite his denials, Horsa's arm was obviously paining him. Shallon had kept a sharp eye on him and called halts when she felt they were needed. Now, she rode close beside him down the street, aware that he was stretched to his limit.

A bar of light sliced the street in front of them. Shallon smiled. At a walk, the horses' hooves made no sound on the soft earth; nevertheless, Aisu knew they had arrived.

As they drew closer, the dark-robed figure came out to them.

'Children, it's good to see you. A little the worse for wear, but nothing that can't be mended.'

Feo thought he could detect a note of relief in the husky voice. He slid off his horse.

'Aisu, Horsa's arm is burnt to the bone. It will be long in healing - if ever.' He swallowed, then added in a low voice, 'I should have taken your advice. This is all my doing.'

Aisu laid a hand on his arm. 'Horsa's arm will heal. I knew you wouldn't take the advice when I gave it. But I had to give it and you had to reject it. Sleep now, and in the morning we will consider the future, not what is past.'

* * *

Despite his exhaustion, Feo woke early. As he opened his eyes, he felt the burden of his quest weight his shoulders. But the weight was bearable and his sleep had been undisturbed by dreams. This house possessed an uncanny atmosphere of peace.

Downstairs nobody was stirring. He found bread and cheese laid on the big table by the hearth and a pot of ballis tea on a trivet. He ate hungrily.

Just as he was finishing, he heard a step on the stair. Aisu smiled a good morning as she crossed the room and after pouring two mugs of the tea, sat down beside him.

'Well, Feo, you have all returned from your first venture, and that itself is an achievement. You might have done much worse.'

Feo stared at Aisu. 'Worse? I have crippled my friend.' He buried his face in his hands. 'I should have listened to you.'

Aisu laid a hand on his shoulder. 'Horsa's injury is not slight, but I promise you, he will be standing beside you when you kill your dragon.'

Feo locked gazes with her. 'He will not. Even if, by some miracle, he were fit, I will not again lead companions into danger I am unable to deflect.'

'Believe me, if you do as I suggest, you will be able to protect them. And if you do not take them, you will not kill your monster and you yourself will not return.'

Shifting uneasily in his chair, Feo said, 'My life is mine, to spend as I will, but I cannot expose others to such peril.'

'No great enterprise is without risk. The stakes of this one are high and you must have help. If you do as I advise, you have a good chance of success.'

Feo leant back and shook his head. 'I cannot take my friends to face the dragon again, but I must listen to your advice. Bar that one exception, I will do as you say.'

Smiling, Aisu leant back in her chair and said, 'That is good. First we must train you to use your magic; we will consider how to tackle the dragon later. You must spend today with me, preparing for your trial. You may not eat or drink, and at sunrise tomorrow, you must take the road under the mountain.'

'Under the mountain? What does that mean? Will I take anyone with me?'

'Only Kirrin may go with you. She is your familiar and is part of you. You may take no weapons and no tools. The road under the mountain was the final task in the training of a wizard, but it is not easy, and has not been used for many years. We don't have time to choose. If - that is when you emerge, you will know what you have learnt.'

In his mind, Feo saw the towering cliffs and the dark mouth of the road. He saw himself entering that mouth, travelling into the dark with no companion except a kitten. His heart thumped.

'I will go,' he said. His face was set and white lines were graved round his mouth.

Feo Enters the Dark

The red rim of the sun broke the horizon. Hitting the cliff above Feo's head, the first rays struck sombre sparks from the black rock. The Hereditary Wizard examined the sheer rock-face, but could see no sign of an opening which would take anything larger than a mouse. He glanced sideways, glimpsing Aisu standing motionless on a weathered cube of stone. As the sun cleared the horizon, she raised her arms.

'Tigri, Miktel, Sambu, akareret mo iknu!' The solemn words of the incantation struck Feo like a whiplash. His heart pounded as he thought of the perilous roads under the mountain which he must follow. In the struggle to contain his fear, he barely heard the rest of Aisu's chant, and when he looked up, he was shocked to see a dark opening before him.

The light seemed to battle to follow the passage into the cliff, and when, a few yards in, the path turned sharp right, it gave up completely and gloom hung from the ceiling like a century of cobwebs.

Feo jumped as Aisu laid a hand on his shoulder. He turned to look at her.

'What chance do I have of emerging from this catacomb?'

She looked at him steadily. 'I cannot say. No-one has entered here for a hundred years. You must keep your head - or you will lose it. This is a dangerous path, but it is the only one which will serve your purpose.'

'I will take the path, but what will I meet under the mountain?'

'I cannot give you much advice. This you must do alone. You may take neither weapons nor tools, and you may take no companion, except Kirrin, your familiar.'

Feo's hand automatically swept the empty space where his dagger normally hung. He could feel Kirrin as a spot of sleepy warmth against his chest.

Aisu continued, 'The one piece of advice I can give you is that you should not believe all you are told.'

'Told? I thought there would be nobody there but me.'

'You will see. Now go with my blessing. I will meet you when you emerge.'

Feo looked at the entrance with apprehension. The passage seemed almost alive. He had the feeling that while he was looking away, it had given a wriggle of anticipation.

This wouldn't do. He was the Hereditary Wizard of Cardevin, on a quest to save his country from annihilation. He pulled himself to his full height, settled his cloak on his shoulders and set his hat at a suitable angle for a Hereditary Wizard. Then he bowed to Aisu and entered the passage.

The roof brushed the crown of his hat with rocky fingers, but the floor was smooth and sandy, and Feo trod the outer leg of the passage with a firm step. Then he rounded the first turn. The shadows seemed to reach out and smother the light, its last few sparks from the rock turning to sinister red glints. Feo advanced a few paces and stopped, waiting for his eyes to adjust to the gloom, but he could see nothing. He didn't know if the passage went on or turned, or even stopped. He couldn't tell if the walls were opening into a cavern or closing in. He couldn't even feel if the roof was about to hit his head. At that moment, he realised fully what it meant to take this road without tools or weapons. He was afraid.

He didn't know how long he stood there. Eventually, Kirrin stirred in his pocket and roused him, and he knew he must go on if he were to survive. He stretched his hand, groping to find the wall, then took the first tentative steps forward. The dark seemed to press on him and he found it hard to breathe, but it was a little easier if he kept moving.

The passage wound and turned like a snake. Feo had no sense of time. He could have been here for all eternity. All that mattered was to keep putting one foot before the other.

In the black of the road under the mountain, he pressed on. He could hear water trickling now, and the atmosphere was becoming damp. It smothered him like a felt blanket.

He pressed against it, forcing his feet forward one at a time. The wall pushed him left, then right and left again. Kirrin mewed and struggled her head free of the cloak, and Feo stopped. He became aware of the lapping of water and cautiously stretched out his foot. The path finished a few inches in front of him.

What now? Feo couldn't swim across an unknown width of water. Even if he could, his soaked clothes would kill him as surely as drowning. And how could he carry Kirrin safely? Feo sat on the water's edge and gave way to despair.

Time passed. The monotonous lapping of the wavelets lulled Feo into a trance. His hand, grown limp with the withdrawal of self, dropped from his lap into the water. The chill roused him. He drew his hand out and shook it, then realised he had touched rock. He felt for the bottom of the lake. It was only two inches under.

But was it like that all across? Feeling a little further, he could detect no slope. He almost laughed out loud. Was this place all smoke and mirrors? 'It's time we moved, Kirrin,' he said, getting to his feet and easing into the water.

He felt the rock walls before he set off. The passage widened only slightly at the water's edge, and as far as Feo could tell, it didn't widen any further. He ran his hand along the left wall as he went, occasionally stretching his right arm to check the other side. The water barely rose above the soles of his boots and this part of the passage was straight. After all, this journey was not supposed to kill him. He reached the far bank and felt for dry land. Shaking the water from his feet, he ran his hand along the walls to find the next part of the passage. He did it three times, but there was no mistake.

The passage branched.

'It can't do this to me!' he muttered. Kirrin stirred sleepily. 'IT CAN'T DO THIS TO ME!!' The echoes from his shout bounced away down the rocky passage towards the centre of the mountain. Smaller echoes travelled back; 'It can't, it can't, it can't!' 'Do this, Do this, Do this.' Feo's ears rang with the random pattern of sound he had awakened, until it seemed as if the whole complex of caverns was laughing at him.

The jangle slowly started to subside, but the words were becoming transmuted. Had he really said that? Was that Feo's own voice? Of course it was! Who else was there to speak?

Feo strained his ears. A sardonic note seemed to be creeping into the echoes. He couldn't distinguish any words now, just the feeling of unfriendly laughter. Then he noticed that the volume seemed to be rising instead of falling.

Kirrin was curled in a tight ball inside his pocket, and Feo could feel her tension. Pacing along the edge of the water, he tried to detect if the sound was coming from one place. The echoes assaulted his ears from all sides, but eventually he was nearly certain that the source was the left branch of the passage.

'Do I go towards it or not?' The noise was winding Feo's nerves spring-tight. 'It doesn't sound friendly. But if I go down the other branch, I might just wander under the mountain for days. I might never come out. At least there must be something along the left branch. Even if it is hostile, I might learn something useful.'

He walked the shore twice more, trying to build up enough courage to face the disturbing sounds. Then he took a deep breath and running his left hand along the passage wall, stepped forward.

The left branch sloped steeply down and then, relenting slightly, reduced to a moderate gradient. The floor coarsened from sand to grit and then to rock, making Feo stumble on the uneven surface. All the while, the sounds continued, now dropping to a mutter, now rising to a shriek. The roof lowered until Feo had to stoop double. He had a vision of the roof and walls closing in on him until he was trapped like a fly in amber, waiting for some far future miner to chip him free.

He became aware of a dim circle in the blackness ahead, and realised with relief that the tunnel was ending. Then he stopped so suddenly that Kirrin stabbed her claws for balance. Where was the light coming from?

He inched forward, careful not to disturb a grain of rock. The light circle widened, but grew no brighter. He reached the mouth of the tunnel.

Stopping in the entrance, he strained to locate the source of the light. The outlines of the cavern were just discernible, but the illumination seemed evenly spread. He realised the noises had ceased a little time before. Relaxing a trifle, he stepped into the cave.

An unearthly chuckle struck Feo's ear. He whirled round wildly, searching for the source. The cavern seemed empty until he turned back the way he had come and looked up. There, in an arch above the tunnel entrance, was a face.

Feo took an involuntary step backwards. The face was still, eyes closed. A dark beard shadowed the lower half, but the features shone with a faint greenish light. This was both the source of the illumination and of the sound.

As Feo watched, the eyes flew open, their pupils dark circles, deep as the eternal pit. The mouth gaped among the beard and another chuckle emerged, hollow and echoing. Then the head spoke.

'Feodin Fiorson, why are you come among us?'

Feo shuddered. Us? How many were there? Then he straightened, taking comfort from the small warmth of Kirrin in his pocket, and spoke.

'Who are you?'

'Who am I? I am not. I was.'

Feo peered up at the arch and realised that it was not, as he had thought, an opening. It was a niche and the head rested in it. There was no body.

He took a deep breath and asked the question.

'Who were you and why are you here?'

The head blinked. 'I was... I was...' Its mouth shut and opened again. 'I was Ghebling. And I am here to guide you.' It blinked again and the sound died to a rusty titter.

'Who was Ghebling? How did you come here?'

'Ghebling was much like you. He came here to succeed. AND HE FAILED.' The lids flew down over the eyes and the mouth closed.

'How did he fail? What advice have you to give?' Feo asked the questions repeatedly, but the features did not stir. The head was not going to talk again.

Kirrin struggled against Feo's chest and wriggled her head free of the cloak. She mewed, gazing into his eyes. Feo sighed.

'You're right, Kirrin. He's not going to help us.' Feo scanned the cavern in the scanty light. He could discern only one exit other than the way he had come. He laid his left hand against the wall and entered the passage.

The eerie light from the head did not penetrate farther than the first few paces, but Feo was glad to see it go. The new passage was broader and higher than the old. Every few paces he zigzagged across the width to check the right-hand wall. He detected no openings.

After a long straight run, the tunnel took several sharp turns. When Feo saw a faint grey circle ahead of him, he knew what to expect. As he stepped cautiously into the cavern, he scanned the walls. The head was high on the right.

Its eyes were closed and it looked as if it were asleep. Its chin was unshadowed by a beard. The blond hair framed a face of such youth that Feo exclaimed, 'What's he doing here?'

The eyes flew open. A thin rim of iris as green as Feo's own surrounded the bottomless pupils.

'Feodin Fiorson. I have been awaiting you.' The voice was deeper than Feo expected, but marred by a hollow note.

Kirrin's head appeared round the edge of Feo's cloak as he responded.

'Who are - or who were you?'

'My name under the sun was Melkin. So many years since last I saw it!'

'Why are you here?'

'I, too, trod the path under the mountain. I did not complete it. And so I stay here, to guide other travellers.'

'Have you any advice for me?' Feo thought that this head, at least, looked as if it might help him.

'Tell me first why you have come.'

'I travel the path to complete my Wizard's training.'

The head opened its mouth in a short laugh. 'A 'prentice! Happy days! I was just such a one.'

Feo thought that 'happy' was not how he would describe a dragon hunt, but he held his tongue.

'Now let me see. You will want to know the path. I can only guide you through the next three caverns. I know no further myself. Take the tunnel on the right here and do the same in the next two caves. There are no branches between.'

'I thank you for your help.' Feo looked down at Kirrin, who was staring in fascination as the head closed its eyes and appeared to sleep. She seemed more at ease this time, and Feo took it for an omen. He entered the passage to the right of the head.

The floor went downhill round a couple of long bends, the walls remaining a comfortable arms' length apart. The blanket of utter black descended after the first turn. However, the going was good and Feo proceeded with more confidence than before.

The floor levelled out and grew rocky. Feo went a little slower and then, for no reason he could think of, he stopped. Something was wrong.

He knelt down and felt before him. The path finished two feet ahead. Beyond, there was nothing.

He sat back and shook. There had been something not quite right about Melkin. When he had closed his eyes, Feo had barely noticed the tiny smile at the corners of his mouth. He should have been warned.

Feo sped back to the cavern, reckless of tripping on unseen rocks. As he stepped into it, the head's eyes flicked open and he yelled, 'Why did you do it? You must have been like me once!'

A sly chuckle emerged as the mouth opened. 'Yes, I was like you. I failed. And in the end, so will you.'

As Feo fled down the other exit, peals of laughter followed him, fighting with the returning echoes.

This tunnel was by no means as easy as the last. It twisted and turned like a living thing and Feo kept stumbling on the rocky path. Kirrin protested and dug in her claws for balance.

Feo was exhausted by the time the passage straightened out. He sat down with his back to the wall and closed his eyes. Then he opened them again. The dark was just as thick either way. Suddenly, he became aware of the mass of the mountain above him, pressing down and compressing the blackness into something tangible.

His mind started to spiral into panic and he pulled himself to his feet, realising that unless he started moving again he would be lost. He paused long enough to remind himself of the direction he was travelling and carried on.

The tunnel went on and on. Blind as a mole, Feo lost all sense of time. He just put one foot before the other. And then he could not.

Shocked out of his stupor, he felt round for the opening he was sure must be there. He found rock, rough-hewn and dusty. Only the way he had come was open.

It wasn't possible. There had to be a route out of the last cavern and there were only three openings, the one he had arrived from, the one with the pit and this. There had been no branches on any of them, he was positive. The pit, then - there must be a route across it. It would mean travelling back the long miles to the cavern, and braving Melkin's laughter again, but it would have to be done. He wasn't going to finish as another head.

But there hadn't been any way across the pit, he was certain. He had felt all round and stretched out as far as he dared to find a far side. There was none. Nor was there a ledge round the side of the tunnel. The pit had filled it from side to side.

In desperation Feo felt all round again. There was no exit.

He pulled his hat off, rubbing a hand across his dusty forehead. At least he didn't have to bend double here; the roof was quite high.

How high? Electrified, Feo groped above his head. He could find no roof as high as he could reach. Tucking Kirrin down into his pocket, he felt his way to the roughest wall and started to climb.

As he ascended, he felt the rock close in on him until it brushed his back. First he clawed his way up vertically, then the tunnel shook itself and he was crawling on his stomach. Twisting and turning as if in the bowels of a snake, he wriggled his way through. At times, the passage constricted so much that it scraped him on all four sides as he squeezed past.

At last, the way took three sharp turns and Feo could see a faint grey circle ahead. Another few yards and he found his head projecting from a hole one jump above a cavern floor.

He peered round cautiously and located the head high on his right. It had deep lines graven in long cheeks and did not look happy, even in sleep. As the thought passed through his mind, the head's eyes flew open and it spoke.

'Feodin Fiorson, you are come. What do you want of me.'

'Who were you?'

'You want to know my name? No harm now.' The lips emitted a short laugh. 'No-one can harm me now. I was Ankhar under the sun. Under the mountain, I am nothing.'

The head's fathomless pupils regarded Feo as he extracted himself from the narrow opening and got to his feet.

'You have come a long way,' it remarked.

Feo settled Kirrin comfortably in his pocket and looked up.

'I have come far, and still have far to go.'

'That is true. You are not yet at the end.'

'Come now, Ankhar, he's come a long way down the path.'

Feo jumped and whirled round. This voice was different and it had come from behind him. It took a minute to locate the speaker. Another head rested in a niche in the corner. Its broad cheeks nearly touched the rock and the folds of a double chin concealed the shoulderless neck.

The head chuckled. 'Greetings, Feodin Fiorson. I did not intend to startle you. You have indeed come far, and you must go further. There still remains a little distance between you and the sun.' It closed its eyes before continuing.

'Ah yes, the sun, the warmth on your face, the light piercing your eyelids.' The eyes opened again, their black pits fixed on Feo.

Feo looked at the round features. 'Who were you? And how did you come here?'

'My name was Pinchip. I failed in the last stage of my journey under the mountain and so they set me here to help others.' He looked sad. 'I have helped many through their trial, but there have been few of recent years.'

'Aye, and fewer have emerged.' Ankhar's harsh voice broke in.

Feo turned. 'What advice can you give me?'

'I can tell you little except to trust your instincts.' The head grinned wolfishly. 'You are enough of a wizard to have instincts, aren't you?'

'Don't believe all you are told,' added Pinchip. 'You must use your judgement. And when you meet them, you must insist they give you what you ask for.'

'Them? Who are they?' Feo asked.

'You will know when you see them. I can tell you no more of what is to come.' Ankhar's mouth shut like a trap.

'Can you tell me where the path lies?'

'Take the passage to my right,' said Ankhar. 'That I am permitted to say.'

'I know a quicker way,' started Pinchip.

'No you don't,' said Ankhar.

Pinchip's fleshy features folded tightly round his mouth and his eyes closed. Feo looked from one head to the other, but Ankhar's eyes, too, were closed and he knew he would get no more from them. He swept his gaze over the half-dozen exits from the cavern and started down the one Ankhar had indicated.

Which Way Now?

Feo entered the passage with caution. Ankhar and Pinchip had disagreed about the way to take and even if they had concurred, he would have been suspicious. However, the tunnel was broad, but not too broad, smooth underfoot, but not slippery. Feo's pace gradually increased.

The darkness seemed to have lost its stifling quality. It was almost preferable to the eerie illumination provided by the Heads, Feo thought. That light, which should have provided comfort in the pitch-black caverns, was tainted with too many overtones of frustration and hatred, anger and regret. He wondered if it was these emotions which had caused their owners to fail. With all the intensity of his being, he hoped he would not become one of them.

Feo's foot stopped. He pitched forward, banging his head on rock and drawing a protesting mew from Kirrin. The passage had ended.

He felt over his head. The roof was as smooth and level as the floor and a scant two inches above his hat. He traced the end wall from side to side and top to bottom. There was no break, not even a minor roughness that might suggest a hidden catch. The right side was similar to the end. Feo ran his hands over the left side, hoping with desperation for a way to continue. At waist height, his fingers encountered a void.

Feo explored the cavity carefully. It was large enough to admit a person, but only just. What was more worrying was that the hole took a sharp downward turn after the first few inches. He ran his hands down it as far as he could reach. The slope steepened and the surface had a greasy feel, almost like a slide.

Kirrin stirred and made a questioning noise. Feo said 'Hush!' and thought hard.

Had he come down the right passage? It was the one Ankhar had told him to take. Pinchip had said there was an easier way, but he hadn't said this way was wrong.

Could they both be lying? It was possible, but Feo felt inclined to trust Ankhar. He wasn't so sure about Pinchip. By the standards of the other heads he had encountered, Pinchip was far too cheerful to be genuine.

Had he missed a turning? He didn't think so. The tunnel had been just the right width to run a hand down each side as he went.

It seemed he had come to the right place. Only one question remained. How could he return to this point if he found the slide was a mistake?

He couldn't.

Feo shut his eyes and stared into the same darkness he had seen with them open. He strained his mind to encompass his dilemma and then asked it the question. Should he take the opening?

From deep inside, the answer rose. He must take the shaft. There would be no going back, but he had no choice.

Feo felt for Kirrin and asked, 'What do you think?' Kirrin licked his finger and settled back in the pocket. Feo sighed.

'I know, it's my decision.'

Feeling round the opening once more, he decided he could enter either head first or feet first. Which was it to be? Feet, he thought. He might not see where he was going, but the idea of being decanted head first onto a cavern floor did not appeal.

Feo settled Kirrin, jammed his hat on his head and wrapped his cloak tightly round. Then he scrambled into the opening, put his feet down the shaft and let go.

The shaft steepened over the first section and Feo plummeted faster and faster. He crooked an arm round his pocket to protect Kirrin. Then the gradient flattened, but before he had time to draw a breath of relief, the tunnel wound itself into a succession of corkscrew turns. His speed pushed him halfway up the side of the shaft and he wondered what would happen if he did a complete circle over the roof.

He gasped for breath, the wind of passage snatching the air from his nostrils. Why had he done this? The likeliest result was to be tipped into an abyss. Even to be a head in the deserted caverns was preferable to total oblivion.

His boots were scraping on the walls and he could see gashes in the heavy leather.

See?

The tunnel was ending.

Feo emerged into free air and dropped vertically, landing on the rock floor with a jolt that rattled the brain in his skull.

He sat, head on knees, trying to get his breath. Gradually, he became aware of a continual murmur. As his wits returned, he realised that he was surrounded by voices in quiet conversation.

Who could be down here? He was still under the mountain, wasn't he?

Raising his head slowly, he opened his eyes to the brightest illumination he had seen since he entered the passages. He blinked, eyes adjusting to the comparative brilliance. Surely he couldn't be back in the real world already.

As he stood up, his gaze swept round a huge cavern, a cathedral of a cave decked with stalactites and stalagmites, sparkling with encrusted crystals; glittering with a green light.

He looked beyond the swags of rocky lace. Round the walls, in niches beyond counting, rested more heads than he would have thought possible and the whole cavern was lit by their effluence.

'Feodin Fiorson, why are you come here?' The voice was deep and resonated with authority. Feo located the speaker high on the wall. The head was darkly bearded, the fathomless eyes shaded by heavy brows. The face bore the stamp of one used to command.

He pulled himself together and replied in as steady a voice as he could manage, 'I am come to complete my training.'

'Who will stand sponsor for you?'

'Aisu is my sponsor.'

'Brothers and sisters, is Aisu acceptable?'

The many mouths stretched and uttered, 'Aye.'

'Your sponsor is accepted.'

Silence fell in the cavern. Feo swept his gaze round the walls. Heads of every age and type stared back, empty pupils surrounded by thin bands of colour. With a shudder, he turned back to the speaker.

'What may I call you?'

'Under the mountain, you may call me Dominus. Under the sun - but that is long gone.' The eyes closed briefly. 'Why do you take this path?'

'I take this path because my need is urgent and vital.'

'I must tell you that this is not an easy path, nor a safe one. You risk eternity in the caverns, or even oblivion. If you will not face these dangers, then say now.'

'I take this path of my free will.'

'Brothers and sisters, do we accept this candidate?'

Feo felt the gazes of all the heads weigh on him as they formed the word, 'Aye.'

'Feodin Fiorson, you have been accepted to enter the trial. It yet remains for you to prove your worth.'

'How may I do that?'

You must conjure a light to guide you.'

'And if I cannot?'

The head's gaze was pitiless. 'You may not proceed.'

'What will happen to me?'

'You have accepted and been accepted. If you fail now, you will join our company.'

Feo stood, fighting down the cold wash of fear that engulfed him. His mind ranged over the many times he had attempted this spell and others with no success. His final fate as a disembodied head in caverns which never saw the sun seemed certain.

Then he forced himself to think of his recent achievements - erratic and unreliable, but achievements nevertheless. The ostler turned into a pigeon, the bandits turned into toads. When he really needed it, the power was there.

Feo straightened. Need! That was the key! When he felt need, his spells worked. He swept his cloak back over one shoulder and tilted his hat, the phoenix-plume transmuting the pallid green light to burning gold. He was, after all, the Hereditary Wizard of Cardevin.

Stretching out his cupped hands, Feo searched his heart until he felt his burning need for light. He uttered the short spell and a white flower of light opened between his fingers. Wavering at first, then steadying, it cast a small globe of normality in this sickly underground world. He gazed at it, entranced.

'Well done!'

Dominus' voice broke Feo's concentration and the light dipped for a moment before he caught it. It was becoming easier to control. A separate corner of his mind was taking over its maintenance while his attention returned to the cavern.

'You have passed the first test. Now the real trial begins. Approach me!'

Feo stepped forward until he was two paces from the wall. From this point, he was looking up under Dominus' chin, but the bottomless eyes still seemed to follow him.

'Hold forth your light.'

Feo raised his hand towards the wall, the frail glow balanced on his fingertips.

'You see the alcove. In it, there are two phials.'

Feo leaned closer and examined the two small glass bottles with foreboding. Each contained a dark liquid.

'You must choose one,' Dominus continued, 'and drink it.'

'What is in them?'

'One contains a potion which is necessary to your trial.'

'And the other?'

'The other contains a slow poison.'

Feo took a deep breath and laid a hand on the pocket where Kirrin was struggling to escape. 'May I have the help of my familiar?'

'You may.'

He helped Kirrin to emerge from the cloak and held her in one hand. Green eyes gazed into green eyes as he said, 'Kirrin, now you must prove you are worthy to be my familiar. Choose, and I will drink.'

Kirrin sniffed delicately at the right phial, nostrils quivering. Then she sneezed and backed away. She sniffed the left phial, looked at Feo and mewed. He picked it up.

'Drink now,' said the voice of Dominus above his head.

With a steady hand, Feo uncorked the phial and drank its contents.

The liquid burned his throat and left a strange metallic taste in his mouth. His head swam and only cleared when Kirrin's claws bit into his shoulder for balance.

Dominus' voice penetrated the fizzing in his ears. 'Walk right.'

Feo moved like a zombie.

'Stop now.'

Feo stood staring blankly into a rectangular pit. With a shock, he realised what it was.

'Step into the grave.'

Feo half turned. 'Dominus - '

'Step into the grave. I know no more than you what you have drunk.'

Numbly, Feo stepped down.

'Lie down.'

Feo lay down full length, folding his hands on his chest. The light detached itself and settled just above his head, while Kirrin crouched like a couchant lion in the curve of his hands and stared into his eyes.

The rock surface was cold and smelt damp, but the burning heat of the potion in Feo's veins kept the chill at bay. He closed his eyes, unsure if he would ever open them again.

With no vision to hold them steady, his senses spun into the dark. He was suspended in nothing, a tiny point of consciousness in an empty universe. Then, unsure how he could sense it in such a formless emptiness, he realised he was moving.

The pace quickened, growing ever faster. A blinding light flashed by on his left and vanished before his senses registered it. More appeared, and more and more and Feo began to be pulled towards them, tugged this way and that until he felt like a cork in a maelstrom.

When he felt he would be torn apart and flung to the eight corners of the universe, the motion changed and he was falling, dropping into a depth so great he could sense no bottom. Certain of an eventual crash, his mind shut down and it was with surprise that he realised he was floating gently in a comfortable warmth.

Extending his senses, he found himself hovering in mid-air. Below him, the sea sparkled in the sun and just ahead, an island spread out like a picture-map.

The land looked tantalisingly familiar, and Feo strained, trying to identify it. Then he realised he was moving again. The island was getting closer.

Soon he was over it, the sea behind him, and he found he could move at will by concentrating on the area he wanted to see. He slid down an airy slope to take a closer look at a stone tower where a river met the sea. It clung to the low cliff, its foot mossy with age, and its gates, guarded by a phoenix on each post, were open.

Feo knew those phoenixes well. It was his home.

He alighted at the gates and passed through. Beyond, a low stone house extended from the tower, its mullioned windows glinting in the sun. As he crossed the courtyard, a woman in a brown dress emerged from the door beside the tower. He stretched out a hand and said 'Nella!', but she walked by as if he didn't exist. Feo shook his head, bewildered. Nella had looked after him since he had come to the house as a small orphaned boy.

Puzzling over Nella, Feo entered the open door. His hall spread before him, its high timbered roof hidden in shadow. On the opposite wall hung a tapestry, all the colours faded with age except the burning orange-gold of the triumphant phoenix. He crossed to the small bookcase by the fire. Nella had returned the book he had been reading to its place and he searched the shelves for it. He stretched a hand to pull it out, but somehow, he couldn't make contact with it.

The book and Nella... What was happening? The only answer was that he wasn't there. His body was still in the grave under the mountain. His mind, freed by the drug, had sped home.

He recrossed the room, but instead of returning outside, he went through a narrow stone arch and up a spiral stair. Not bothering to tread the steps, he circled the stair until he reached the top. There he paused for a moment, looking at the locked door, and then he was inside.

The study at the top of the tower was as he had left it, save a thin film of dust. Three walls were lined with bookcases full of volumes bound in ancient skins. In the fourth, two windows divided shelves full of bowls and pitchers, compasses, retorts and alembics and jar upon jar of powders and liquids.

Turning, he scanned the open book on the desk, but its yellowed parchment contained nothing of interest and he couldn't turn the page. Disconsolate, he swung round and stared out of the window at the shimmering sea. What use was it to be able to travel like this if he could do nothing?

'Good morning, dear boy.'

Startled, Feo swung back and stared at the figure behind his desk. An old man sat there, his white beard trailing down his chest. He wore a midnight blue cloak and a hat with a phoenix plume.

'You shouldn't be so surprised to see me here. It is, after all, my home.' A sly smile emerged from the beard.

'Uncle Sigid! But you're dead - you died ten years ago!'

'Quite so, dear boy, quite so, but how alive are you at this moment?'

Feo's mind slammed back to the dank grave in the cavern and fear gripped his throat.

The phoenix plume in Sigid's hat bobbed as he shook with laughter. 'Don't turn that unpleasant green. It's only temporary, dear boy, I do assure you.'

Feo straightened and glared at his uncle.

'Sigid, I know you always laughed at me when I was a boy, but let me remind you that I am now Hereditary Wizard of Cardevin!'

Sigid sobered. 'I apologise. I never could resist teasing you. You were such a solemn boy. I know you have a heavy load to carry now.' He sighed. 'And if I hadn't been so untimely killed by Ahmed, the Sultan of the East, I would have had the time to train you and you would not have needed to take this dangerous path.'

Rising, he continued, 'Come, it's time we proceeded. Kirrin is looking after your body, but it's best you are not away too long.'

Feo stared. 'How do you know about Kirrin? And all the rest?'

'I've been watching you, dear boy, every step of the way.'

A flush rose to Feo's cheeks as he thought of his various attempts at spells.

'You've done quite well, considering, but you'll never bag that dragon unless you finish your training. Come here by me.'

Feo moved over to stand beside Sigid, looking out of one of the windows. As he gazed at the rocky mouth of the river and the sea beyond, the light started to fade. It grew darker and darker, until he could no longer distinguish the cliffs. Hazy clouds of moving sparks filled the sky. A huge light appeared from the Western horizon and travelled rapidly across the sky, so fast that it had disappeared in the East before Feo realised it was the moon. But it couldn't be the moon, he thought. It was moving in the wrong direction.

While he was puzzling over this, the sky grew light again, and then dark, flashing alternately. Feo gazed at it, mesmerised, as the pace quickened, until the flashes merged into a grey blur.

He tore his mind away from the formlessness and tried to look round the study. He could see nothing. He and Sigid hung suspended in a dull mist.

Every detail of Sigid's person was visible with preternatural clarity. He examined his uncle's face with fascination. It was quite unchanged from his memory, but it bore an expression of serenity he did not recall. Sigid seemed quite unconscious of his presence.

Feo's attention was drawn back in the direction of the window. A barely perceptible flicker had started. As he watched, the flicker became more pronounced. The strange night sky reappeared and the great light travelled it from West to East. The sky lightened and the sun shot up from the Western horizon, travelling ever more slowly over half the sky before coming to a halt.

He looked behind him. The mist had vanished and the study was as it had been with one exception. Behind the desk was seated a boy.

Feo stared. Visitors were not encouraged in the Hereditary Wizard's study, and certainly not children. Yet the boy looked quite at home, studying the old folio which lay open on the desk. Beside him lay Feo's hat.

The boy looked up, his gaze unfocussed. Feo experienced a thrill of unease. His eyes were emerald green.

Sigid's voice at Feo's elbow made him jump.

'You recognise yourself, of course, just after inheriting the Wizardship.'

Feo's mind reeled. Now it all made sense. The sun and moon had indeed travelled backwards. And so had he - in time.

'You can move around freely. He can't see you.'

Automatically, Feo followed Sigid to stand behind the boy's shoulder. He was tracing the archaic script with one finger as he deciphered it. Feo leant forward and read the page. It was the light spell.

Memory engulfed him. He had been only a few weeks into his Wizardship, still mourning the loss of the uncle who had brought him up and studying every available moment to live up to his position.

Both the script and the language of the books were archaic and it had taken a huge effort to make sense of any of it. On this day, at last, he had felt he understood one spell.

Feo watched as the boy stood. His memory superimposed a vision of his older self in the cavern as the boy stretched out his cupped hands and intoned the words. But whereas in the vision, light blossomed between his fingertips, in the boy's fingers no light flowered.

The younger Feo sat down, his shoulders slumped. Half-remembered, half-observed, Feo felt his corroding despair. He turned to Sigid.

'Now you understand why I believed Magic was dead.'

'You felt no need. How could it work?'

'But I had no need. How could I feel one?'

'Ah! That is the first lesson of Wizardship.'

Feo's brow creased in puzzlement.

'You have heard the saying, "Do what thou wilt is the whole of the Law."?'

'Yes, but that is obvious madness. If everyone obeyed it, there would be chaos.'

Sigid raised his forefinger in denial. 'You are only seeing the outward meaning. There is an inward meaning also. The key to Wizardship is to train the will to need what you wish to accomplish.'

Feo's heart sank. 'How do I manage that?'

'Practise, dear boy, practise. You must do two impossible things before breakfast every day. At least.'

Sigid was chuckling as he took Feo's arm and led him back to the window.

'It's time we moved on, dear boy. Leave your younger self to his own problems.'

Feo turned his head to look at the dejected figure slumped over the desk. He pitied him. The boy didn't know that magic really could work. He didn't even know how long it would be before he found out.

This transition was different from the last. Feo could have told without the sun and moon that this time, he was travelling forward. The longer he spent in this disembodied state, the more his senses expanded. Those senses also told him that, after the first few moments, the window was no longer there. He was adrift without landmarks.

In addition, the medium itself had subtly changed. The formless grey mist was broken by flashes of colour, so short as to be barely discernible.

Feo had only just determined this when the flicker began again. As it slowed, Feo gradually became aware of his surroundings and by the time it stopped, he knew where he was. It was the room at the inn.

'In the name of Hoaga, the great one, the giver of Justice.'

'By the power of Zempel, the Commander, by the sword of Miktel, by the magic orb of Adana, may this work be done.'

Feo stared at his earlier self with fascination, the outstretched hands, the blazing eyes. The other figures in the room, Horsa and the innkeeper, seemed to orbit round the vortex of his anger.

'Need, dear boy, the need was here, all right. But the rest...' Sigid's expression was pained.

'The rest?' queried Feo absently, still staring at the scene.

'The control, dear boy! Totally lacking. You did achieve a result this time, but it wasn't exactly what you intended.'

'A pigeon isn't so much different from a fly,' said Feo with indignation.

Sigid actually winced. 'Where's the precision? A Hereditary Wizard must do just what he intends, no more and no less. And look at the aftermath.'

Feo turned back to the scene. His earlier self had finished the incantation and was swaying on his feet.

'Magic is certainly tiring...'

'The energy drain was ridiculous, dear boy! Don't you remember the later episode with the bandits? If there had been a few more of them, the exhaustion would have killed you.'

'Then what use is magic to me in fighting a dragon?'

'You shouldn't use that much personal power. You must learn to channel the natural energies, instead of using your own.'

'Just how am I supposed to do that?' said Feo, his ears burning.

Sigid looked at him sharply, then took his arm.

'Come with me, dear boy. We have a long way to go this time.'

The mist surrounded them again. Feo brooded over that last spell which Sigid had found so painful. It had been his first success. It wasn't such a bad attempt, was it?

He looked up. Wasn't it time the flicker started? The mist had wrapped them in its grey emptiness for a long time.

Feo was sure they should have arrived by now. A bubble of fear rose in his throat. If they were lost in this nothingness, there were no landmarks to find their way home. Turning, he looked at Sigid.

His uncle stood serenely beside him, his head thrown back and his eyes closed. A half-smile lay on his lips. Feo relaxed. Sigid had the appearance of a man who knew exactly what he was doing.

An indeterminate time later, the familiar flicker began. Feo could sense nothing round them; he was aware they had travelled backwards in time again, and thought they had travelled in space as well, but he had no idea where they were.

He found himself on top of a hill overlooking the sea. It was night, and a stormy one. The wind whistled past them, although their robes hung still. He turned to Sigid.

'You want to know where we are.' Sigid smiled. 'This is Bergon's Hill, at the southern tip of Cardevin. Below us are all the wizards of the island, led by Bergon himself.'

Feo caught his breath. 'You mean this is the night King Afram's fleet was sunk? But that happened three hundred years ago!'

'Three hundred and one, to be precise. This was the last occasion that such a gathering of wizards took place in Cardevin. They raised the storm which sank the ships.'

Feo looked out to sea. Could he see lights in the distance? He couldn't be sure. Then a great streak of lightening cut the sky. In its brilliant illumination, he saw for an instant the tossing ships at sea and the dark group below them on the hillside. The last moment of the flash showed the mast of the leading ship split from crow's nest to foot as the lightening struck.

'Watch the wizards.'

Feo was about to ask how he could do this in the dark when another flash lit the figures below. Their hands were raised, fingers twisted into strange shapes. As bolt after bolt hit the fleet, battering his ears with the crack of thunder, he watched the writhing gestures. He was certain there was a connection, but he couldn't decipher it.

'You don't yet understand? I'll show you.'

Sigid made a small gesture with his left forefinger and the wizards' hands trailed ribbons of cold flame. Feo watched, enthralled. He could see the power channelled through the many fingers and thrown at the ships. His own hands began to move in unconscious harmony. This was how it felt. It felt right.

'You've got it, dear boy. That's how you feed the energy into the spell. Not your own limited store, but the bottomless store of the whole natural world.'

Head swimming, Feo asked, 'Why did they need so many wizards, then?'

'One couldn't channel all that power. He'd burn out like a wisp of straw in a beacon fire.'

One by one, King Afram's ships were destroyed. The very last turned tail and fled for the horizon. It was split asunder by a final lightening bolt.

Silence fell. The wind abated and the clouds drew back, revealing a scattering of stars. Feo was aware of movement on the hillside, and the wizards were gone.

'It's time we left, dear boy. There's no more to see.'

Feo turned to Sigid. 'Can we go home now?'

'Just the place. I want a quiet talk with you and then you must get back to your body. Kirrin has looked after it well, but you have been away long enough.'

Feo was grateful for the interminable transition. He badly needed to order his mind. By the time they reached the familiar study, now empty of all other people, he was feeling more settled.

Sigid's talk was brief. Feo listened intently as he explained what he had shown Feo.

'So, dear boy, to sum it up, for a spell to work you must have need, control and channel the power.' Sigid paused and chuckled. 'And don't forget the impossible things before breakfast.'

Feo stood. 'Is it time to go back, now?'

'It is.'

'Will I see you again?'

'See me again? You might, dear boy. I shall be here and there, you know.' There was a sly twinkle in Sigid'd eye. 'Now prepare yourself for the return.'

Feo felt the pressure start to pull at the centre of his being. Before he knew it, he was looking down on the tower receding rapidly into the distance. The buffeting started, and the flashes of light. Just when Feo thought he could stand no more, he realised that they were subsiding, and he came to rest in the formless universe again.

He wasn't sure how long he stayed there. Time seemed to have no meaning. But then he began to drift downwards, and the drift quickened to a fall and the fall quickened until he was plunging towards the bottom.

The bottom of what? He had barely asked the question when he felt an almost physical thump.

Feo lay with his eyes shut. He wasn't sure if he hurt or not. He couldn't feel much of anything. Then he became aware of a nagging ache in the small of his back. His heels were sore, too, and his head thumped like a mountain full of dwarves.

A convulsive shiver shook him from head to toe. The damp chill of the surface he was lying on had penetrated to his very bones. Then someone started stabbing his chest with pins.

He dragged his eyelids open. A pair of emerald eyes was gazing into his own from a distance of six inches.

'Prrrraou?'

Kirrin was padding on his chest. He was back in the cavern.

Feo sat up shakily and Kirrin retreated to his waist. Bobbing with his unsteady motion, the light he had conjured rose to settle above his left shoulder. Kirrin jumped off and leapt to the edge of the grave, watching Feo as he stumbled out.

'You have returned.' The deep voice made Feo jump.

'I have indeed returned, Dominus.' Feo reluctantly moved to face his arbiters.

'Then you are ready to enter the ranks of Accepted Apprentices.'

Feo reeled. 'Dominus! I came here to become a true wizard!'

'Your feet are on the path, but the journey is longer than you know.'

'But I must be able to use the power now! Without it, I can do nothing.'

'You may use it, with our blessing, but you have much to learn before you become a Master. Did you meet your Mentor in the World Beside?'

Feo searched wildly for an answer. Mentor? The World Beside? What did Dominus mean? Then his mind cleared. He had been in the World, but not of it. He could touch nothing; he could not be seen. That was the World Beside. And, of course, Sigid was his Mentor.

'I did.'

'What is his name?'

'His name is Sigid.'

'Brothers and sisters, is Sigid acceptable?'

The many dark eyes regarded Feo and the mouths stretched to say, 'Aye.'

'Feodin Fiorson, you have requested entry to the Guild of Wizards.'

'I have.'

'You have passed your trial of worthiness.'

Feo swept his cloak over one shoulder. 'I have.'

'Feodin Fiorson, under pain of spending eternity as an excorporated head in the deepest cavern of this mountain, do you swear never to betray the secrets of this Guild to a mortal?'

Feo repressed a shudder and replied, 'I do so swear.'

'Feodin Fiorson, as a mortal you have died and as a wizard you have been reborn. Will you accept a new name from me?'

'I will.'

'You are still Feodin Fiorson to the common world, but henceforth, to your brothers in magic, you are Valdis. So Valdis; Apprentice Wizard, go forth.'

'Go forth, Valdis!' echoed the pallid mouths.

Feo took a step back and stopped.

'Dominus, what path do I take?'

Dominus looked at him, his eyes starting to close.

'There is no path,' he said.

Feo looked wildly round the cavern. On every ledge, in every alcove, there were heads. All had their eyes closed in pseudo-sleep.

Half-running, he raked the perimeter of the cavern, but there was no opening deeper than a few feet. He eyed up the entrance by which he had arrived, but it was much too high to reach, and there was nothing in the cavern he could move under it to stand on. It occurred to him that he could pile all the heads into a pyramid under the hole, but the thought of touching undead flesh was insupportable, and he concluded almost thankfully that even if he could reach the opening, it would be impossible to climb the slippery helix in the passage above.

He hunched his shoulders and returned to Dominus' niche. Even with its eyes closed, the head retained its aura of command, but the phosphorescent flesh was repellent. Feo shuddered and turned away.

Where was Kirrin? At least she was one natural thing in these monstrous caverns. Feo looked round. Kirrin was crouched beside the grave, eyes shut. Of course, she had stood vigil over his body while he was away. She must be tired. Even so, Feo thought she might have been worried by this predicament. After all, she was his familiar.

Kirrin wasn't worried. There must be a way out; she had just as much need of air and sun as he did. The longing rose in Feo to feel the wind across his face and to smell clean grass.

Longing? No. Need! He needed the open air. Feo stopped abruptly and looked up at Dominus.

'There really is no path,' he said. 'This is the last test, isn't it?'

Turning, he scooped up Kirrin. Then, standing straight with one arm outstretched, he allowed the need to be above ground to flood his being. Calling up his last memory of the sun, he fixed his position in his mind. He muttered a brief incantation, twisting his hand into a gesture which seemed right, and closed his eyes.

Feo felt a warmth on one cheek. He stood still, eyes tight closed, willing himself to be above the mountain again. Kirrin struggled out of his grasp and leapt down. Opening his eyes to see where she had gone, he was blinded by the sunlight.

He blinked and rubbed his eyes until he was able to see his surroundings. Before him was a steep slope falling away to the valley. On his left, a swollen scarlet sun was slipping towards the horizon. The air was clean and fresh and he breathed deeply, shuddering as he remembered the dank staleness of the lightless passages. Turning, he was faced by a sheer black cliff. It was the place he had entered the mountain, but he could see no sign of the opening. Turning again, he saw the cube of rock where Aisu had stood - and was still standing. She stepped down and, coming to him, clasped his hands.

'Welcome to life, Valdis, born of the mountain.'

'Valdis I may be, but Master Wizard I am not,' replied Feo with bitterness. 'I have travelled through the blackness of the death after death to have Dominus name me as Entered Apprentice.' He sank to the ground and buried his face in his hands. 'What am I to do?'

Justice Is Done

Aisu knelt beside him. 'Feo, you mustn't despair. Now that you have accomplished your trial under the mountain, you have a chance of success. I cannot tell you that the way will be easy, but you do have a chance.'

Feo raised his head, the setting sun flooding his face with living warmth. The memory of the caverns receded a notch and he shuddered once as he pushed the ghastly heads to the back of his mind. He couldn't give up now. Cardevin's very existence depended on him.Sigid would never forgive him if he abandoned it. He stood up, feeling a steel inside him that he had not felt before.

'I will go on to the end. Cardevin is depending on me and I can do no less.'

He felt a rush of affection for the little island which was his home. Its sleepy innocence deserved his defence, and he longed for a day when he could walk through the gate of his house and enjoy its peace again.

Aisu clasped his hands again. 'Well done! Remember, you know more than you think.'

She turned towards the track down to the valley. 'Come. We have preparations to make.'

The last sliver of sun was slipping below the horizon as they reached Aisu's house. Glowing in the ruby light, the carvings on the door seemed to have a life of their own. Feo had to look twice to be sure they were not moving.

Inside, the lamplight reflected from the dark panelling, the golden warmth embracing Feo after the pallid green under the mountain. Horsa and Shallon were sitting by the fire across the room, their heads bent together. Kimmi was at the big table finishing a bowl of stew. They jumped up as one when Feo and Aisu entered and Horsa started forward to grasp Feo's arms.

'You're back! We've been worried.' Horsa stopped and looked closely at Feo. 'You've changed. I'm not sure how, but you look different. What happened under the mountain?'

Feo shuddered. 'I don't want to talk about it now.' He looked down. 'Horsa, you're using your right arm!'

'Aisu's been working on it today.' Horsa pulled up his sleeve. A shadowy pink flush coloured most of the forearm, but that was the only trace of yesterday's terrible burn.

Feo turned to Aisu, a black cloud which had been pushed to one side lifting from his mind.

'Thank you!' he said simply.

Aisu smiled and led him to the table. 'We have plans to make, but first we shall eat.'

Feo sat near the blazing logs savouring the hot food. The warmth from without and within gradually dispersed the caverns' chill from his bones, and he started to think of the next day's tasks, oblivious of the chatter surrounding him. Gradually, he became aware that the voices were silent, the remains of the meal had been cleared and everyone was gathering for a conference. He drew his chair closer to the table and waited.

Aisu folded her hands and rested them on the table. Her dark eyes scanned the faces turned towards her before she began to speak.

'Well, children, now that Feo has completed his journey under the mountain, we must make some plans. You have a hard road to travel and you must be well prepared. The first advice I shall offer is that you should not use the road you travelled before.

'There is another route which approaches the dragon's lair from the back. It is not an easy path, and you will not be able to take the horses as far up the mountain. But it will be far more difficult for the dragon to find you. The road forks West from the route you used, just before you reach the foothills of the mountains.'

Shallon leaned forward. 'I know of that route, though I've never used it. Is the path up the mountain hard to follow?'

'The road runs through a village, up to the knees of the mountain itself. After that, you will need to follow the path on foot. I will draw you the route later.'

'We'll need to camp a night before we reach the mountains,' said Horsa, stroking his moustache. 'We must be fresh to face the dragon. Where would you advise we stop?'

'It would not be wise to camp too close to the village. It's very isolated and an armed party could cause unwelcome interest. I think you should halt a mile or two before it. The horses should reach there comfortably in a day. Shallon, how are the horses?'

'Well fed and raring to go.' Shallon ran a hand over her curls. 'I'd not have thought they'd recover so quickly, but that draught of yours worked wonders.'

'How are the supplies?'

Feo sat through the preliminaries, dreading the moment when he must speak. He jumped when Aisu said his name.

'Feo, you will need to protect the horses and packs when you leave them, so you have a task for tonight. You must visit your home and memorise one or two more spells.'

'But, Aisu,' stammered Feo, 'If I travel in the World Beside, I can't open any of the books. In any case, I have the most important ones with me.'

Aisu laughed. 'Feo, you don't have to physically open a book to read it in the World Beside. Just look at it and think about what you want and a shadow of the book will open before you. And I know the books you have with you. There are some spells you may need which are not in them.' She passed Feo a scrap of paper.

Feo scanned the list. How could he have left these out? He was quite unfit to be the Hereditary Wizard.

'You would be best to do it in your room,' continued Aisu. 'Make sure Kirrin looks after you. Everything else looks in good order to leave at dawn.'

Feo stood up, his heart thumping. 'I had best get started,' he said, 'but before I go I must say something. On our last attempt I made a terrible mistake.' He looked round his party at the table. 'I allowed you to come with me. It is only because of Aisu's help that it was not a disaster.'

'Feo,' Horsa broke in, 'You can't think we'd have let you go alone.'

'This time you must let me go by myself. No, don't protest. I swore I would never again take companions I couldn't protect. I hoped my journey under the mountain would give me the knowledge I needed, but I am confirmed only as Entered Apprentice and my magic is still unproven. It isn't enough.'

Aisu leant forward. 'Feo, I know you will all be in danger. This is a dangerous quest. But you must take your companions. You need them to succeed.'

'Aisu, I value your advice like no other, but I can't bear the responsibility of injuring or killing my friends. This time, I will not repeat my mistake.' Feo pushed his chair back and left the hall.

His heart was heavy as he trod the stairs to his room. It would be a lonely journey in the morning, and he wouldn't even think about what lay at the end.

Lying on his bed, he settled Kirrin on his chest and closed his eyes. The dizzying transition into darkness started almost immediately. Now that he knew what to expect, the buffeting didn't trouble him and sooner than he thought possible, he was slanting down to earth at his gate.

It was dark here, as it was at Aisu's house, and Feo hoped he wouldn't have to time-travel to daylight to see. He wasn't sure he could manage it.

He moved swiftly into the tower and glided up the stairs to the study. Inside, the shelved books and jars of strange powders were as he had left them when he packed his book bag for the journey. He half-expected to find Sigid in his chair, but the room was empty. Moving across to the desk where the open book lay, he realised that although it was too dark to see properly, he somehow knew where everything was. Encouraged, he laid his hand on the book.

The open page appeared under his hand, as clear as if the sun were at midday. He thought of another page and it was before him. Breathing a sigh of relief, he found the volumes he needed and set to work.

He was back in his room at Aisu's house in time to hear his companions come upstairs. Moving Kirrin to his pillow, he turned over and went to sleep.

* * *

The sun was at least two hours before rising when Feo woke himself. He dressed swiftly and shut Kirrin in the room before going downstairs. The log fire in the hall had collapsed to a heap of embers and the red glow was just enough to light Feo to the door. He let himself out and went round the house to the stables.

He found some empty saddlebags and filled them with parcels extracted from Shallon's careful packing. His sword he found in Horsa's baggage. Then, keeping to the grass beside the path, he led the horse silently round the house and a good way down the road before he dared mount and start on his lone journey.

It would have been so much easier if I could have transported to the mountain he thought, but then he shuddered. He'd never been to the far side of it, and the chances of transporting to a tomb in solid rock, or over the edge of a cliff were far too high. In any case, he couldn't have taken the horse with him, only what equipment he could carry.

By the time the sun rose, Feo was too far away to see the village. Green hills rolled on either side and the road wound between them, turning this way and that, but heading inexorably north. He glanced at the horizon before he continued. The sky was barred with ribbons of black cloud fringed with an angry red. For a moment, it felt as if the dragon were lurking there, waiting for Feo to arrive. He shuddered and moved on.

The leagues vanished swiftly under the horse's hooves, too swiftly for comfort. There was no-one abroad, only the crows cawing in the trees and a lone thurill which turned a somersault with fright when Feo came round the bend.

He missed the comforting warmth of Kirrin in his pocket, and he missed his companions. Horsa's steady strength, Shallon's cheerful competence and Kimmi's innocent chatter - he longed for them all and couldn't see how he could get through without them. He nearly turned back, but then he pictured them lying on the ground, maimed and seared by the dragon's blast and he was certain he must go on alone.

It was nearly midday before he reached the road which ran west. The grassy hills were behind him; here rocky bones broke through the thin soil and the trees had given up the struggle to survive. Even the rough bushes looked withered.

Feo paused and ate a hurried bite while his horse found a few blades of grass. Then he turned onto the western road and pushed on.

The horse's hooves clattered on the rocky surface, and Feo was forced to slow down and keep a sharp eye out for slippery patches. He didn't want to be left on the road with a broken leg in this deserted land. The road climbed gradually, curving back towards the north, and by mid afternoon Feo could see the first peaks of the mountains ahead. According to Aisu, there should be a village nearby and he began to watch for signs of cultivation. There was nothing.

Eventually, he spotted a cairn off the road to the right and dismounted to examine it. Lichen clung to the pile of small rocks supporting a single flat slab facing down the road he had travelled. On the slab was carved a curious sign, a square with two lines jutting up from the corners. Feo could make nothing of it.

He rode on, and a couple of bends along the road he spotted the first house.

It was very small and, being built of the same rock as the hills, melted into the landscape. As Feo drew closer, an air of desolation became apparent. He realised there was no roof, and one of the walls was crumbling. It was deserted.

Feo dismounted, glad to stretch his legs, and peered inside. He considered camping in the one dry corner, but the cottage wouldn't provide much shelter, and he hoped to find somewhere more inviting to stay before sunset. He went back to his horse and climbed on.

The steady climb flattened and Feo saw the first signs of farming on either side of the road. The fields were small and bounded by thin lines of stones. Among the crops on the left, a tattered scarecrow flapped in the chill wind, its turnip head carved into a twisted grin. Feo carried on, praying for some sign of habitation soon. The light was fading, and visions of log fires and steaming bowls of soup filled his mind.

Turning sharply to the left, the road passed between two more cairns and the first inhabited houses appeared.

Feo dismounted and knocked on the door of the nearest cottage. There was no light visible at the front, but the smoking chimney suggested warmth and food. There was a long pause before an old woman opened the door.

Feo doffed his hat. 'I am a traveller looking for food and lodging.' There was a snort behind him. 'And a stable for my horse.'

The old woman peered up into his face. She had small bright eyes and a bulbous nose which protruded oddly from the wrinkled skin.

'I don't take lodgers,' she said, 'but you can try Rogg's house, he sometimes lets a room. It's the third house from here. You'll know it by the tankard hanging outside.' She turned her back on him and shut the door.

Feo led the horse down the street. After a full day's riding, he was glad to stretch his legs. He thought the horse must be glad, too, to be free of such an indifferent rider.

Glancing round at the cottages, his heart sank. Despite the gathering gloom, few houses showed a light, and his longing for a roaring fire and hot food seemed unlikely to be fulfilled. He trudged on past the scattered dwellings, hoping that the third house would be more welcoming.

Rogg's door was wide open, the tankard over it hanging so low that Feo had to duck. It was very dark inside, the only light coming from a small and dirty window and two candles stuck onto a long trestle with their own wax. Four men were sitting round the table, each with a leather tankard before him.

Feo looked round, trying to adjust to the dim light. All the men were perched on three-legged stools except for the one at the end, who was sitting with an air of self-importance on a carved chair which must have been beautiful in its youth. Feo approached him.

'Good evening. Am I right in thinking you're Rogg?'

The man looked up. 'I am. What do you want of me?'

Feo's eyes, now more used to the light, caught a shadow of suspicion flitting across the flat face.

'I'm just a traveller, seeking a bed and food.'

'Well, sometimes I have room and sometimes I don't. Just a traveller, eh? That's a very fancy hat and cloak for a traveller.'

Feo glanced round the room. The standard garb seemed to be a ragged brown tunic and leggings. Every head in the place was turned his way and he realised the features shared as much similarity as the dress. It was the nose. He looked back at Rogg. He had it too - the same bulbous nose as the dame in the first house he had come to.

'The lady in the first house down the street sent me here,' he said warily. 'If you don't mind me asking, would you be related?'

Rogg looked at him with no diminution of suspicion. 'We're all related round here. Not many people in these parts.' He glanced involuntarily towards the north as he finished speaking.

'If you don't have room, can you direct me to someone who does,' said Feo, feeling exasperation start to well up inside.

'Now just hold a minute,' said Rogg, standing up. 'I'm not just the tavern keeper here. I'm the King's representative.' He puffed out his chest. 'I'm responsible for seeing that no undesirables come through here. And you look undesirable to me.' Thrusting his face close to Feo, he spat out, 'I think you're a magician!'

Feo stepped back a pace. 'What would be wrong with that?' he asked.

'A magician!' Everyone in the room pressed back against the walls, right hand with two fingers extended stretched towards Feo.

'You are a magician!' Rogg was triumphant. 'Tie him up!'

There was a deathly hush. The villagers edged a little closer to the door, their faces twisted with fear and hatred. Feo swept his glance across them, emerald eyes glittering in the candlelight.

'Which of you dare lay a finger on me?' He felt his cheeks flush with rising anger. 'Is this how you treat innocent travellers? Be content! I would not soil my garments by staying among you.' He made to turn to the door. Then he felt a pain like a knife in his head. Rolling over as he fell, the last thing he saw was a gangling figure with the village's bulbous nose and a large stick.

* * *

He woke with a pounding head, his cheek pressed to damp earth. After a moment, he forced his eyes open, but he could see nothing. He'd emerged from under the mountain; he couldn't be back there, could he? And anyway, this place smelt wrong. It had a miasma of last year's crops, mildew and beer.

Beer? The scene in the primitive tavern came into focus. The scared villagers, the innkeeper and the lad with the stick, who not only had the characteristic nose but also shared Rogg's flat face.

Feo tried to roll over and discovered he was tightly bound. His legs were tied at ankle and knee and his hands were pulled behind his back. Wriggling, he realised that not only were his hands tied back to back, but each finger was fastened to its twin. He was still trying to puzzle this out when he heard footsteps on a stair.

There was a bang as the door was thrown back and a torch thrust through it. The torch gave more smoke than light, but Feo's eyes, accustomed to the dark, sent a stab of pain through his aching head. He screwed them shut.

'Ho, magician, you awake yet?'

Feo cautiously opened his eyes a crack and found that they were adjusting.

'A fine state you've got yourself into, haven't you?' Rogg laughed. 'Weren't expecting my boy, Jer. Thought you were dealing with a bunch of bumpkins. Well, you know better now. Can't do much magic with your hands tied like that.'

Groaning, Feo realised the truth of this. With his hands immobile, he couldn't draw on the natural energies to fuel his spells.

'You won't have to worry about it long, anyway. Half an hour for the trial at first light, then zzztt.' Rogg drew his fingers across his throat.

The door banged again and Feo was left in the dark.

What was he to do? For a space, black despair overwhelmed him. He pictured the dawn trial, the sullen villagers gathered to see the show, the predetermined sentence, the slanting sunlight falling on his lifeless body.

How would they execute him? Would it be a rapid sword across the neck? Hanging? Or even burning at the stake? He shuddered.

His mind spun in panic. Gradually, it cleared, leaving behind one small pebble of determination. He would find a way out of this somehow.

His hands were abominably cramped and he tried to wriggle his fingers to ease them. It was impossible. They were too well bound. He lay back and tried to think of a way out. A picture of his study rose before his eyes. All those books of spells - there must be something in there to help him.

Kirrin wasn't with him to watch his body while he was away. He would have to be very careful to monitor its status. There was also the possibility that Rogg would return before he did. He could come back to his body and find it at the point of execution.

He pushed the thoughts away. There was no choice. He had to do it.

Manoeuvring into the least uncomfortable position he could find, he composed his body for a long trance.

Feo barely noticed the dizzy flight. Not knowing how long he had, he was rifling his memory for something that might be useful. When he reached his courtyard, he paused only for a rapid glance at the sky. Less than two hours till dawn! So little time to find what he needed.

Moments later, he was in the top of the tower scanning his library. There were so many books, some in archaic languages, some in ancient crabbed scripts. How was he to find what he needed in the time? He had hoped to find Sigid behind the desk, but there was no sign of him.

Grimly, Feo started his search. What he needed most was an unbinding spell. He couldn't find one.

There were spells for opening locks and for entombing things in the bowels of the earth. There were charms for finding lovers and for defence against a neighbour's malice. There were potions for protection against poison, healing wounds, sweetening sour milk and curing styes. Nowhere could he find anything to loose his own hands.

Feo paused and thought for a moment. It occurred to him that it could be useful to know what his friends were doing. Perhaps he could get some help from Aisu. No sooner had he thought than he glided through the window and was speeding over the sea.

He expected to arrive at Aisu's house, and when the headlong flight ceased and he realised he was close to the ground, he extended his senses to investigate it. There were no buildings nearby. Puzzled, he searched the ground for landmarks. He found nothing except a small group of sleeping bodies under a clump of trees.

He landed beside them and stooped to look at the nearest face. It was Shallon. Next to her was Horsa and Kimmi slept across their feet. He tried to shake Horsa but his hand passed straight through his shoulder. Even shouting in Horsa's ear brought no response. He stepped back, defeated.

Spreading his senses wider, he tried to find Aisu's house. It was nowhere near, but then he encountered something he recognised. It was the strange cairn outside the village. His friends were only a few miles away from it.

Glancing up, he was horrified to see the stars wheeling towards dawn. He couldn't linger. There was no time to find Aisu. Gliding upwards, he raced back to his study.

He continued the search, desperate for a shred of hope. Then he stumbled across it. It was a version of the transporting spell he had used to escape from the mountain.

He read it feverishly. It was simple enough to remember and would take him where he wanted to go, but it would leave him still bound and helpless. Without some way of untying himself, he would just slowly starve.

Supposing he transported back to Aisu? But the power needed was related to the distance. Without the ability to draw on the natural energies, he was certain that to travel that distance would kill him.

He could transport to his friends' camp, but he was uncertain he could survive that, either. It was too big a risk.

His head was spinning; he couldn't think straight. Through the whirling of fragmentary thought, one small clear phrase penetrated.

What about your body?

Feo panicked. He had forgotten that there was no Kirrin looking after his body. He had to return immediately.

The cellar was still dark and Feo was so cramped that he couldn't move. His face was slick with sweat, he was chilled to the bone and his heart pounded erratically. He realised he had only just got back in time.

Fighting to bring his heartbeat under control, he knew that he had little energy left to do anything.

The door crashed open and Rogg peered in, his nose grotesquely illuminated by the torch he thrust before him.

'Ho, Mister Magician. Still here, I see.' Rogg gave a hoarse chuckle. 'Too clever for you, us country bumpkins. Dawn's here, the goodmen are gathered and they all know what the verdict's to be.'

Feo knew he had no choice. Perilous or not, he had to do it. He transported.

Law Must Be Obeyed

Aisu's stableyard was grey and chill in the pre-dawn light. Bleached of all colour until the sun touched them, the walls cradled inky shadows at every corner. The horses moved restlessly in their stalls, still not settled from the disturbance of Feo's departure a couple of hours earlier.

A figure emerged from the back of the house, and the solid thump of the door closing echoed round the yard. Yawning and rubbing her curly head, Shallon entered the stable. She went from stall to stall, greeting each horse with a titbit and a muttered word. Then she stopped. The last stall was empty.

She checked for its saddle. That was missing, too. The saddlebags she had packed so carefully the night before were not as she had left them and two of the spares were missing also.

There were only two possibilities. Either some thief had crept in during the night and stolen exactly one horse and set of gear - or Feo had gone. Shallon headed for the house at the run.

Just outside the door, she nearly collided with Horsa, who was coming out at a similar speed.

'Have you seen Feo? Kirrin's in his room but there's no sign of him.'

'One of the horses is missing!'

'What else is gone?'

They raced back to the stable and checked the baggage.

'One parcel of food. One waterskin. Blankets.'

Horsa looked round the storeroom. 'Feo's book bag is missing.' He took one stride and opened another pack. 'Worse. His sword's missing - and that was in my pack.'

He sat back on his heels. 'There's no doubt. Feo's gone to face the dragon alone.'

Shallon's face was pale. 'I never dreamed he'd slip off like this.' She stood. 'We must tell Aisu.'

In the hall, a servant had raked the fire and a new log was blazing. Aisu came swiftly.

'Feo's gone? Has he taken Kirrin?'

Horsa shook his head.

'Then we must find him fast.' She turned to Shallon. 'Do you know how long he's been gone?'

'The empty stall's quite cold. it must be some time.'

'You must follow him without delay. I told him last night, he cannot succeed alone. I would like to scry for him, but you daren't stop.'

Ten minutes later, the party was thundering down the village street, without regard for Grem's dirty nightcap hanging out of a window. The screams of abuse trailed after them forlornly.

Dawn came and went unnoticed. They kept a sharp pace, fast enough to make good time but not so fast as to tire their mounts. Horsa felt as if they were crawling.

He glanced back at Kimmi and the two packhorses. Kimmi was dozing in the saddle, but Horsa reckoned he would manage to keep his seat. Then he turned back to Shallon, riding beside him. She gave him a quick smile and said, 'Don't worry. We'll catch up with Feo before he comes to any harm.'

before returning her eyes to the road ahead.

Somehow, Horsa believed her. He'd never met a woman like her before, utterly competent yet warm and loving as well. There was no-one he would rather have at his side on this desperate chase.

There was a wriggle in his top pocket and Kirrin's head poked out of the front of his cloak. Horsa gave her ears an absent scratch while he scanned the track for any signs of Feo's passing. There were none.

They paused at midday to stretch their legs and give the horses a short rest. The road was still enfolded in rolling hills. They were not yet nearing the area of the dragons' influence.

Shallon squatted and scratched a few lines in the dust.

'We're going to reach the fork in the road mid-afternoon. This is the way we took before.' She indicated the line stretching straight on until it curled round the bottom of the dragons' mountain. 'Will Feo have gone there or do you think he'll be heeding Aisu's warning and taking the back road?'

Horsa thought back to the previous night. 'He listened very carefully to Aisu. I don't think he'd risk running into a watching dragon. He'll take the other road.'

Shallon swept her twig over the left fork. 'This way, then. Out to the west and then turning up the back of the mountain.' She stood up and rubbed her boot over the marks. 'We'd better get moving.'

* * *

The shadows were lengthening as they approached the fork. Shallon reined in her horse, peering ahead.

'What's up?' Horsa drew up beside her.

'At the crossroad. Look, there are people.' Shallon pointed to a group of dusty figures clustered in front of a small brown tent at the centre of the junction.

Horsa shaded his eyes. 'Four or five by the look of it. And all in uniform. I wouldn't have expected them out here.'

'Nor I,' said Shallon, her lips compressed. 'It smells like trouble. And we can't back off - there's no other road.'

They rode slowly down to the junction, their horses' hooves clattering on the stony track.

'Halt! In the King's Name!'

A short figure in a well-brushed uniform coat blocked the way, one hand raised to stop them. Shallon dismounted.

'Your papers, please.'

Shallon handed over a small bundle of frayed parchment. The man leafed through them, pausing occasionally to examine one. Then he looked up.

'You have no entrance visas?'

'We need none. I'm a citizen of Fazimar Hayt and these are my cousins.' Shallon looked unconcerned.

The officer mopped a drip off the end of his nose with a spotless handkerchief and then looked Kimmi and Horsa up and down. 'You look enough like a Fazimari, but you,' he turned to Horsa. 'look more of an outlander to me. I've never seen clothes like that in Fazimar.'

'He's Fazimari, born and bred. He's a courier - travels abroad, so he has to dress to fit in there. He's found some wealthy patrons, though. Wealthy enough to fund a dragon hunt.' Shallon winked at the official.

'Ah, yes. The dragon permit. Is that where you're going?'

'We're meeting another member of our party up there,' Shallon indicated the left fork, 'and then we'll be off up the mountain.'

The officer produced his handkerchief again, looking doubtfully at the handful of parchment. 'I see you have the permit for the Upper Negus Reserve, but it's most unusual for Fazimaris to hunt dragon. Most unusual. I'll have to take a better look at these.'

Shallon pulled her horse a little closer. 'We need to get on to meet our companion. Else, we may miss him.'

The short man turned sharply on his heel. 'You'll have to wait and so will he. I need to examine these more closely.' He walked briskly over to the tent and vanished inside.

Horsa swung down beside Shallon. 'What's he doing in there? Can he stop us?'

'I think not. Not legally, anyway. I'd hoped he'd take a bribe, but he didn't twitch a whisker at the wealthy patrons.'

Horsa paced restlessly. 'I think I'd rather have a corrupt official. You're never sure what an honest one will do.'

'Steady. You're fretting the horses. We can't afford to seem too worried.'

With an effort, Horsa stood still. The sun inched across the sky and the three other officials moved around the area, casting suspicious glances in their direction. There was no movement from the tent.

Kimmi dismounted and stood by them. 'Are they going to let us through? Or should I go for help?' His eyes sparkled at the thought of a mad rescue ride.

Shallon laughed. 'No, Kimmi, I think he'll have to let us go.' Her face tightened again. 'But I'm getting worried about finding Feo. He's likely in some sort of trouble and he may need us now.'

Horsa took half a pace and stopped himself. At that moment the officer emerged from the tent, bearing the sheaf of parchment and a disgruntled expression.

'I can find nothing wrong with these,' he said, 'However, I have some questions to ask.'

'But we must move on,' burst out Horsa. 'We'll miss our friend.'

The officer drew himself up and tapped his uniform. 'I am the King's representative. While he is not present, I am to be treated as if I were the King. That is the law.' He pulled out a large sheet of text. 'Now, you are required answer these questions, under penalty of five year's hard labour in the lead mines!

'How often do you travel this road?'

Horsa bit his lip and turned away, fighting to control his anxiety. He barely heard Shallon's replies.

'Do you carry goods for sale in this province?

'Do you carry goods for shipment abroad?

'Have you ever been convicted for smuggling?'

The interminable questions continued until finally, the officer looked up from his paper, a stern expression on his face.

'I cannot fault your papers, so I will pass you through.'

Horsa breathed an almost audible sigh of relief and only checked a movement towards his horse when the officer continued.

'As the reserve officer for the Upper Negus has been removed from his post, I have assumed the authority to validate licences. Do you wish me to validate the Dragon Licence?'

Shallon nodded. 'Yes, indeed, Captain.'

The officer produced an ornate stamp from his pocket, breathed on it and pressed it to several sheets of the documents.

'I have validated your Dragon Licence, the Wyvern Sub-Licence and your Travel Pass.' He looked up and frowned sternly. 'You may go. But I must warn you that if I find, at any future time, you have transgressed the regulations applying to the King's highway, I will have no hesitation in restraining you all in preventive custody until I can obtain confirmation of your documents from the capital.'

Shallon swung into the saddle and passed the barrier at a sedate trot, Horsa and Kimmi pressing hard at her heels. As they turned up the fork, Horsa glanced up at the sky. The sun was a bare hour from setting.

The party pushed on hard, but the mountains were only a smudge on the horizon when the sun went down. As the last of the light faded, Shallon called a halt.

'It's too dark to ride. One of the horses will stumble and either break a leg or one of our necks.'

Horsa shook his head in despair. 'What are we going to do? We're hours behind Feo now. It'll take us most of tomorrow to catch him up.' He paused and then added, 'That's if we're even on the right track.'

'All is not lost.' Shallon rubbed her hand over her curls. 'He'll have had to stop somewhere for the night, and we've passed no villages. The moon rises in a couple of hours, and it's still half full. We'll have enough light to ride if we're careful. Till then, we'd better rest the horses and get what sleep we can.'

They tethered the horses under a clump of trees just off the road and, too exhausted to do more, ate a sketchy supper of cold supplies and rolled themselves in their blankets.

All too soon, Shallon and Horsa woke to the first gleam of light on the horizon. They shook Kimmi awake and packed up the spartan camp.

The moon rose, a huge copper-coloured half-circle, bleaching the foreground to colourless detail and casting sooty shadows across the land. They saddled the horses and rode on through the night. The deep shadows were deceptive, hiding still deeper holes, and they made slow progress. Horsa kept reminding himself that each step was one nearer to Feo. He wouldn't let himself consider the possibility they might have taken the wrong road.

The moon rose to its zenith and sank towards the western horizon. The road, which had been climbing and veering north, straightened out. Horsa could see the dark shape of Kimmi, asleep in the saddle, ahead of him and in front of him Shallon, patiently picking a way along the rough surface. Glancing to the right, he realised that he could see the horizon. The first faint light of dawn had appeared.

As the light grew, they travelled with greater confidence and by the time the sun rose, the tired horses had perked up and were moving at a gentle trot.

The dawn revealed a bleak land of low scrub and coarse grass. Everywhere, the grass was punctured by grey rock. Shallon called a halt for long enough to extract some food from the bags.

'We've seen no trace of Feo.' Horsa tugged his moustache, trying to suppress a gnawing worry that they had taken the wrong road.

'It's not likely on this ground and in the dark. We should be nearing a village. If Feo went this way he must have passed through it. We can ask the villagers and then we'll be sure we're on the right track.'

An hour's riding brought them in sight of a flock of sheep off the road to the left. There was no shepherd visible, but this small sign of habitation was reassuring. A few minutes later, Shallon dismounted to look at a cairn on the right. She came back looking grim.

'Feo may be in trouble.'

Horsa looked round the barren landscape, bewildered. 'Why do you think that?'

'That cairn marks the village boundary. This is a very isolated place and the villagers will be superstitious, especially living in the shadow of dragons.'

'We knew all that before we got here. Why do you think Feo's in trouble?'

'The rock on top of that cairn - it's carved with the sign against the evil eye. Feo wouldn't have disguised himself, would he?'

'No!' The gnawing worry filled Horsa's mind. 'No-one could mistake what he is and he wouldn't bother to hide it.'

'Then I think we'd better hurry.'

They rode on at a sharp trot, the fastest pace at which they felt sure of seeing any traces of Feo. Shallon scanned the way ahead, while Kimmi and Horsa watched the country to left and right of their track. Not a soul was in sight.

The road wound from side to side, twisting between the rocks as it climbed. On the left, the first house appeared, tumbledown and deserted. Horsa was conscious of a movement in his top pocket as Kirrin emerged. She looked him in the eye and mewed. Horsa stared, wondering what she wanted. Struggling to free herself from his cloak, she mewed again. Horsa jerked his horse to a halt.

'Stop!', he yelled, 'I think Feo's somewhere near!'

Kimmi and Shallon whipped round in the saddle.

'Where?'

Kimmi's sharp eyes lighted on the cottage. 'Over there - I saw a flash of colour!'

Peering intently, Horsa spotted a patch of orange through the empty window. Then he saw movement. Before Shallon had time to react, he spurred his horse forward and tumbled out of the saddle through the low doorway. Amid the rubble on the floor burned the phoenix plume of the Hereditary Wizard, and beside it lay a bound figure.

'Feo!'

Kirrin jumped down and sniffed anxiously at the body. Pulling a shoulder, Horsa peered at Feo's face. The eyelids trembled and lifted, revealing clouded green eyes. His skin was white and cold to the touch.

Firmly, Horsa was pushed to one side and Shallon knelt by Feo, drawing her knife. She slashed the cords which bound hand and ankle and Feo rolled onto his back with a sigh of relief. Kirrin leapt onto his chest and crouched almost nose to nose, purring, while Feo started to flex his fingers, working the blood back into them.

'I thought you were never going to find me,' he murmured after a moment.

'Are you all right?' Horsa was concerned about Feo's apparent exhaustion.

'I had to transport with my hands bound.'

Shallon produced a small flask and cup. 'Drink this.'

Feo spluttered over the fiery cordial, but Horsa was relieved to see that his eyes were now a clear emerald and his skin had a more natural tint.

'What happened to you?'

Feo sat up and continued to flex his hands. Kirrin settled on his knees while he told his story.

'That could be a problem,' said Shallon when he had finished. 'The only way up the mountain is through the village.'

'Wait a minute,' said Horsa, 'Couldn't you transport us at least across the village?'

Feo looked at his hands, which were now moving through a curious series of gestures.

'I can't transport more than myself and what I can carry. If that's the only road, we'll have to take it,' he said.

'Are you fit to ride?' asked Horsa, and then realised that Feo looked nearly normal.

Shallon looked sharply at Feo and said nothing for a moment. Then she rose to her feet.

'Our best chance is to race through the village before they get organised for a search. They'll be pretty cross at losing their best entertainment this year.'

Feo shuddered as he climbed to his feet.

'What do we do if they chase us?'

'They can't. They don't have any horses.'

'Yes, they do. Mine!'

Shallon moved out through the doorway. 'Then we'll have to take it as it comes.'

The second packhorse's load was redistributed among the other mounts and Feo climbed into the saddle. The enlarged party set off at a brisk trot, the grey stone of the road striking sparks from the horses' shoes. As soon as the first inhabited house appeared, they lifted the horses to a gallop along the village street, Feo's midnight blue cloak snapping in the wind of their passage. In the small area at the centre, the few villagers gathered round a large pile of wood fled, terrified to see the sorcerer who had been securely imprisoned last night riding free as air in the morning. Horsa saw the panic in their faces as Feo gave them an ironic salute.

Slackening speed as the road steepened, the party swept out of the village and started up the side of the mountain. As they topped a small rise, Horsa looked back towards the settlement. A small knot of villagers was boiling inside the entrance to Rogg's tavern. They were not yet bold enough to venture out, but something was going to happen soon.

He spurred his horse to the front and dropped a word in Shallon's ear. She shrugged.

'I don't see what they can do. The only horse they have is Feo's.'

They pushed on, putting distance between themselves and the angry villagers. The grey stone of the road gradually gave way to the ochre of the mountains, and the neat fields round the village were replaced by low scrub. At length, they reached a grassy clearing at the foot of the final escarpment and paused to rest the horses.

Shallon stood back, looking up the jagged yellow cliffs above them. 'This is where we leave the horses. They won't make it up this path.'

Horsa joined her. 'We'd better eat now, then. It's that much less to carry.'

They unsaddled the horses and tethered them in the thick grass under the cliff. Feo sat down on a boulder in deep thought. While Shallon made up packs, Horsa checked the weapons. The nicks and scratches from their last foray against the dragon had all been honed away at Aisu's house, and he squinted down the length of a gleaming blade with satisfaction. This time, it would be their turn.

Horsa whipped round, his hands shifting to a full grip on the hilt as he caught the sound of shod hooves on the path. Feo's horse appeared at the far end of the clearing, and on its back was Rogg.

Through the Back Door

While Shallon and Horsa were busy sorting the equipment, Feo ran through in his mind some of the spells he was going to need against the dragon. Without his book bag, he was frightened of forgetting.

He could see the velvet bag in his mind, still tied to his saddlebags. And where were his saddlebags? With his horse, in the tender care of the villagers. They'd probably burn them. At least it was better than letting them burn him.

Feo gave himself a mental shake. It was no use brooding about his capture. He'd escaped, and now it was time to move on. Wondering if they were ready to leave, he glanced round. Everyone was staring at the downward path. He turned, and there was Rogg.

Rising as if pulled by wires, Feo advanced on that bulbous nose. Before he had taken two steps, Rogg started edging the horse backwards, his hands shaking. The quaver in the tavern-owner's voice matched the one in his hands as he said, 'It's treason to attack the King's Representative!'

Feo stopped and eyed Rogg with rising disgust. 'Does the King know what's representing him here?'

Rogg's voice rose an octave. 'To insult the King's Representative is to insult the King himself!' He turned to Shallon and Horsa. 'Did you know that this man is an escaped criminal? You are required by law to deliver him into my custody at once!'

Shallon raised an eyebrow. 'Is that so?'

Flushed with indignation, Rogg spat out, 'That is indeed so! And if I don't get him, you will regret it!'

'Regret it? That sounds bad.' She turned to Horsa. 'Do you think we should give Feo to him?'

A smug smile spread across Rogg's face, bringing the nose into further prominence. 'As good citizens, I'm sure you are eager to uphold the Law. The penalties for thwarting the King's Representative are high.'

Feo regarded Rogg with distaste. 'I wasn't aware I'd been convicted of any crime. I was just a stranger passing through your village.'

'The King's Representative has the right - nay, the duty - to convict any undesirable in his district.'

'To convict of what?'

'Of being undesirable, of course!'

'And what makes someone undesirable?'

'I can tell as soon as I clap eyes on them - that's why I'm the King's Representative!'

Shallon stepped forward. 'As a responsible citizen, I will vouch for this man. He has committed no crime. I suggest you give up your claim on him and go back to your village.'

Rogg turned to her. 'I can't do that. I must take him back with me - and well bound, too. He won't escape again.'

Feo ran his eye over Rogg. The man was incredible. Then Rogg caught his look and turned pale. The horse crabbed to the side as he made the sign against the evil eye and he nearly fell off. Feo suppressed a laugh with difficulty. The man must be terrified of losing his status to have followed someone he obviously feared. Then Rogg's horse fidgeted sideways and Feo's eyes blazed. There, tied to the back of the saddle, was the velvet book bag.

Feo strode forward. 'Give me my books!' he demanded.

Backing the horse away, Rogg looked wildly round. 'Books? What books?' he stuttered.

Feo fixed him with a glittering eye. 'My magic books.'

Rogg fumbled round the back of the saddle, unable to tear his glance away from Feo's. Meanwhile, Shallon and Horsa were converging from either side. Just as Rogg found ties of the book bag, they reached him. Horsa removed him from the saddle with one quick jerk and Shallon caught the horse's reins.

Feo clutched his books to his chest, hardly able to believe he had them back. Rogg lay on the ground. With the point of Horsa's sword at this throat, he dared not move, and the cold gleam of the newly-honed steel was mesmerising.

'I should turn you into a toad!' Feo's face was red with anger. 'Then you'd have something to convict me of!'

Rogg barely dared to shiver.

'What are you going to do with him, Feo? We can't take him with us.' Horsa's sword pressed a trifle deeper into Rogg's throat.

'If we let him loose, he'll either try to follow us or steal the horses.'

'D-d-don't kill me!' Rogg's voice was a whisper. 'I'll promise not to do you any harm.'

Horsa looked at Feo. 'Would you trust him?'

'As far as the first bend in the path. Can you hold him a bit longer?' Feo sat down on a rock and extracted a small weathered volume from the book bag.

He was sure he'd seen something in there. Leafing over the pages, he scanned the ornate script - and there it was. His lips moved silently for a moment before he looked up and nodded at Horsa.

'You can release him now.'

Horsa withdrew the sword, but Rogg was too terrified to move until Horsa applied an ungentle boot to his posterior. Then he couldn't leave the clearing fast enough. The rattle of loose stones marked his precipitous passage.

Taking Horsa's sword, Feo traced a line across the mouth of the path at the point where it passed between two massive boulders. He raised the sword to a vertical salute and then swept it out to the side, feeling the warm surge of power start to come through as he chanted the words of a spell.

'By the sword of Miktel, sharp as this sword I hold,

'May this way be barred: as with rods of iron may it be barred.

'Let no living thing pass: neither human nor cattle nor scorpion.

'Let no evil pass this way: not wraith nor ghoul nor goblin.

'Let the way be closed till we come again: until we return with our trophy.

'Miktel, hear my words!

'By the power of Zampel, the Commander, may it be done!'

As Feo lowered the sword to rest, the air at the head of the path began to shimmer. The movement started slowly at ground level, but by the time it reached his head, it was moving fast and still accelerating.

Horsa came beside him and prodded the barrier with a cautious finger.

'It's hot!' he exclaimed. Then he added, 'Will it hold?'

'It'll hold longer than we need it,' said Feo confidently.

With a final glance to ensure his work was sound, he turned, and the pair made their way over to where Shallon was examining Feo's horse.

She looked up as they approached. 'The packs are ready,' she said, slapping the horse's rump to send him to graze. 'We'd better eat quickly and go.'

They took their meal sitting next to the pile of backpacks. Casting a glance round his little party, Feo wondered at their willingness to take part in such a perilous venture. Kimmi, of course, had all a boy's hunger for new experience and no sense of the danger, and Horsa had as much to lose as Feo if Cardevin was destroyed. But Shallon was risking her life for a little money and a cause which could mean little to her. Perhaps it was her growing attachment to Horsa which held her. He looked at Horsa. Was it possible that the most elusive bachelor in Cardevin had been caught at last?

Realising that the others had finished, Feo stuffed the rest of his food in his mouth and scrambled up to find his backpack.

As they started up the steep track, a deep rumble sounded in the distance. Shallon paused and looked upwards. Dark clouds were scudding across the sky and even the air seemed to be holding its breath.

'The weather's broken. We're going to have a hard climb.'

The wind rose gradually until gusts snapped any loose corners of fabric out behind them. Rain followed in driven sheets which searched out every crevice in their clothing. Feo pushed on upwards, his damp boots sliding on the loosened stones of the path. Kirrin had retreated deep within his cloak.

They paused early for the midday meal, sheltering under an inadequate overhang of rock. Sweeping horizontally round the corners, the drops searched with probing fingers for their prey. Even the waybread had absorbed the damp. Feo ate his share without appetite, watching the water run down the rock, making it look like oiled amber. Before they carried on, Shallon unwound the rope from her waist and tied them all in a line.

The way grew steeper as they went, and shortly after the halt the path petered out into a jumble of fallen rock, stained tarry dark with the storm. Shallon cast about for a way through, and eventually led them in a scramble over one side of the boulders. They followed her along a ledge where the sandy rim crumbled to a dizzying drop. At the end, the shelf narrowed until it vanished into the cliff face, but just before it became too small to provide a foothold, Shallon turned sharply sideways into a gap in the rock.

As they clambered up the crevice, they were momentarily sheltered from the gust-driven rain, and, freed of the need to battle against the weather, Feo realised how sodden they all were. Two paces ahead, Kimmi's brown cloak was black with water, its hem dripping a rivulet onto the loose stone. Glancing behind, he could see the water streaming off Horsa's hat brim. His own hat had lost the ability to deflect the rain and was channelling a steady stream down his neck. He shivered, thinking longingly of the roaring fire in Aisu's hall.

The end of the crevice was in sight and he anticipated their emergence without enthusiasm. The wind eddied in ahead, bearing the first promise of a renewed soaking. Feo sniffed. There was something else as well. Too tenuous to grasp, it evaporated as soon as it appeared. Feo puzzled over it as he pushed up the last few yards to the mouth of the crevice. The nearest he could get was the sickly odour of rotting meat. Then he emerged into the full force of the storm. He caught his breath.

Shallon had halted on an exposed apron of rock just outside the crevice. Before them stretched a narrow spine of rock linking the crevice to the main peak of the mountain. There was no other path. On every side the slope dropped away steeply, drifts of stone showing where the winter's avalanches had roared. Occasionally, the gusts of wind parted the curtain of rain enough to see impossible slopes diving straight for the valley floor.

Motioning them close to catch her voice before the wind tore it away, Shallon yelled 'We must take it very steadily over this. The path is better on the other side.'

She checked the ropes carefully before taking the first steps onto the rock spine. Kimmi followed, and then Feo, placing each boot with precision. The way was narrow and very slippery, and gusts of wind snatched at his body from all directions, struggling to hurl him down to the valley below.

As they passed the half-way mark, he took a deep breath. They were going to make it. Then he was overwhelmed by a stench of carrion. Plummeting from the peak ahead, a dark shadow screamed over their heads. Kimmi yelled and slipped. Feo grabbed automatically for the rope as it tautened and Kimmi's descent halted, suspending him six feet below the path. Bracing himself against the downward pull, Feo looked up to see the dark shape circling the peak. As it swooped down again, Feo muttered the half-remembered words of a repulsion spell. Heart pounding, he watched the swoop flatten before it reached them. In the few seconds it was overhead, he recognised it. It was a wyvern. There was no mistaking the black scales, shining with an oily iridescence, the cruel beak and the sinuous tail with its barbed tip.

They would have to kill it. A wyvern never yielded its prey once it had attacked.

He looked round. The wyvern was vanishing round the peak again. Kimmi was trying to scramble back up to the path, and Shallon was as occupied as Feo in helping him. That left Horsa.

Feo looked over his shoulder. Horsa had somehow managed to extract his sword. He waved it at Feo.

'Can you push it this way?'

Feo's heart sank. He wasn't sure he could exercise that fine a control. Forcing confidence, he looked at Horsa and nodded. He didn't have a choice.

The wyvern had already rounded the peak. Bracing himself against the drag of the rope, Feo muttered the spell again, making a couple of small changes. With a scream of anger, the wyvern veered away well behind them.

'A bit less next time!'

Feo delved frantically into memory and adjusted the pattern. The wyvern hadn't bothered to circle the peak. It was coming straight back from the other side. Tracking the approach, Feo timed his spell carefully. The wyvern came overhead and then banked off low over Horsa. He sliced at its belly and a spray of black drops hit the wind.

Screeching with outrage, it turned, talons reaching for Horsa's shoulders. With growing confidence, Feo muttered again and diverted it sideways. Horsa swung the heavy sword and sheered off one claw. Thick black blood coated the rocks below as the wyvern screwed round in a tight circle. It dived straight for Horsa, hooked beak seeking his throat. Feo nudged it and Horsa's blade thrust deep into its breast.

The heavy body plunged downwards, bouncing several times on the slope. Chased by a gust of wind, it vanished behind a buttress of rock far below.

Feo drew a deep breath, realising that if he hadn't been clinging to the rope, his hands would have been shaking uncontrollably. Steadying himself, he looked over to Shallon, who nodded to him and they dragged Kimmi to safety. The rest of the journey across the narrow spine passed in a daze as Feo fought to contain his shivering.

On the other side, a shaken party gathered in a shallow cave beneath an overhang of rock. Lying on the stony ground, they took stock. Somehow, no-one had been injured, although Kimmi still shook with a mixture of reaction and excitement.

Feo looked at Shallon's white face. 'How many more of those horrors are we likely to meet,' he asked bitterly.

'None, I hope,' she said, rubbing one hand over her curls. 'They shouldn't be round here at this time of year.'

Horsa was staring at his sword. The black blood which befouled it was evaporating into coils of thick smoke.

'Don't touch that,' said Shallon, alarmed by Horsa's instinctive move to wipe the weapon clean, 'It burns!'

He shuddered. 'If I'd known that, I'd have been more careful how I spitted it.' Bending down, he wiped the blade on a patch of clean sand.

Feo clambered to his feet, aware of Kirrin's small warmth wriggling in his pocket. 'It's time we moved.'

The rain had stopped, but the wind caught at them with stiff fingers as they emerged from shelter. Within a few minutes, Feo was chilled to the marrow. He pushed on against the almost solid air, steadied by the safety rope as his sodden boots slipped on the loose scree underfoot.

Ahead, Shallon and Kimmi led the way along the sloping shelf.

The ledge they travelled continued round the mountain some distance, jutting out from the rough brown rock face in a jumble of ochre rubble and dark puddles. Before they reached the massive boulder that masked the next bend, Shallon turned off and led them scrambling up a steep slope. If the wind hadn't been dragging at them constantly, the climb wouldn't have been difficult, but there didn't seem to be any path above. Feo wondered where they were going.

At that moment, Shallon twisted sideways and vanished into a hole. When Feo reached the opening, he found her and Kimmi waiting in the mouth of a tunnel.

Horsa pulled himself over the ledge and Shallon unhitched the rope, winding it round her waist. 'We won't need this for a bit,' she said.

Feo scanned the opening, puzzled. The rough arch at the outer rockface continued along a few feet of passage before opening out into a modest cave. Greyish daylight penetrated a few feet, revealing rough toolmarks in the rock where nature had been improved. 'What is this place?' he asked, 'and where are we going?' A wyvern would have had difficulty getting through the entrance, let alone a dragon.

'This is the tradesman's entrance to the dragon's lair,' said Shallon with a grin. 'It won't be expecting an attack from the rear.'

Horsa shuddered. 'Do you mean we have to go down there?' he said, pointing towards the sooty shadow at the back of the cave.

'We don't have to travel blind,' said Shallon, reaching into her pack. 'I brought a lantern.'

Holding the light high, Shallon led the way down the passage and through the cave. Pushed back by the lantern's light, the shadows parted to show a second arch leading into the rock. Feo followed Kimmi, his skin crawling as he remembered his journey under the mountain. At least this time he had the warm yellow glow of the lantern to follow.

After a few minutes, he tired of Horsa treading on his heels and delved into memory. A few muttered words produced a light balanced on his fingertip. The yellow of the lantern and the blue of the spell-fire conjured startling reflections from the rough tunnel walls, searching out specks of crystal and momentarily building them into fantastic creations before the lights moved on.

The passage wound down towards the heart of the mountain. The last pinprick of daylight had long vanished and the little party's world was bounded by the ambit of the two frail lights. Instinctively, they closed the gaps and travelled in tight formation.

After rounding a pair of sharp bends, Shallon stopped abruptly, raising her lantern high. The tunnel had opened out into a space so vast that its tiny light was lost, and they could only gauge the extent of the cavern by the echoes.

'This isn't the dragon's lair,' said Shallon in a soft voice. 'A college of wizards lived here in the great age of magic. They left and the dragon came. That's why the villagers are so fearful of sorcerers.'

Picking her way through the rubble on the floor, she continued, 'You may see relics of their occupation, but I wouldn't advise touching them.' She turned as Kimmi stumbled over a rock. 'Remember, although the entrances are too small for a dragon, sound travels. Keep the noise down.'

They all trod softly after that, and the pressure of the vast space destroyed any desire to speak. The raised lights gave tantalising glimpses of objects which might have been left by the wizards or might just have been oddly-shaped rocks. No-one was tempted to find out.

Shallon stopped again on the far side. 'We're very close to the dragon's lair now. You must be as quiet as possible.' After casting a short distance each way along the cavern walls, she located the exit. Feo turned his head as the rocky sides closed in on them and caught a last scintillating reflection bright enough to have shone from a diamond. He thought of all the knowledge the cavern must once have contained, and knew he would have to return one day.

A draught began to invade the still air, blowing direct on their faces. It carried the scents of open air and daylight, but some darker strands also, too faint to identify except that they were not pleasant. The tunnel was climbing now, and the longing for fresh air fought with apprehension of what lay between.

A light-coloured oval bloomed at head height. Shallon took a few more steps and doused the lantern. Feo hastily collapsed his spell-fire. As his eyes adjusted, he realised the end of the passage was in sight.

Holding their breath, the four tiptoed the last few yards and peered out of the narrow opening. Another cavern yawned before them, this time visibly vast, lit from two sources. One was the attenuated daylight seeping in from the cave mouth. The other was within. Curled on a mound of dull gold shards, its scales gleaming a phosphorescent green in the gloom, lay the dragon.

Let Sleeping Dragons Lie

Feo stared at the recumbent body, mesmerised. The huge eyes were veiled by smoky lids, the spiked tail-tip wrapped the nose, from one of whose nostrils a thin trail of vapour pulsed in time with the slow breathing.

A hand on his sleeve broke the spell and he followed the others back down the passage.

'We can't fight it in there.' Horsa tugged his moustache, looking worried. 'We'll get trapped against a wall and torched.'

'We wait?' said Feo, looking enquiringly at Shallon.

'Yes. It should wake just before dusk to hunt.'

'Then we have time to prepare.' Feo sat down with his book-bag and snapped a small spell-fire into being.

Horsa and Shallon had checked the weapons three times and were talking quietly, heads bent together, before Feo returned the last book to his bag. 'I've found what I need,' he said. 'Shallon, do you know how the land lies outside the cave?'

'There's a very wide ledge with the path going down at one side. It's fairly flat, good footing.'

'Are there any high parts, rocks or mounds I could stand on?'

'Yes, there are one or two places you could get a good view of the whole area.'

Feo's eyes glittered vivid emerald. 'Then this is how we'll do it.'

* * *

Time dragged in the gloomy tunnel, where there was no way to track the sun's descent. Feo sat with his eyes shut, running through his plans again and again looking for problems. He was vaguely aware of Kimmi fidgeting, but his concentration was too fierce to allow distraction. He had to get it right. This time, he could afford no mistakes.

A new sound caught his ear, a rustling, creaking noise. He opened his eyes to see Kimmi creeping back from the tunnel outlet, his face alight with excitement.

'The dragon's waking,' he hissed, 'and it's nearly sunset.'

The four of them crouched by the opening into the cave, watching the dragon heave its monstrous bulk off the golden pile. It swept its tail back and a few shards slid off the heap to tinkle on the floor. Wafting a nauseating gust from half-open wings, it lumbered outside and took off into the darkening sky.

Feo breathed out a breath he hadn't been aware he was holding.

'It's all right,' said Shallon softly, 'It'll take about a couple of hours to complete the night's hunting.'

Feo cautiously approached the gleaming pile of golden shards and laid his hand on it. It was warm. In the centre was a single whole ovoid. Shallon gripped his elbow.

'Scrub that time,' she said, 'She won't be away more than an hour. That's an egg.'

Outside, the light was fading. Grey shadows on grey ground hid obstacles which tripped the feet as they hurried through the preparations for battle. The ledge was very wide, as it had to be to accommodate the monster's landing. At one end, a narrow path, far too narrow for the dragon's bulk, hugged the cliff face on its way downwards.

Feo chose a mound of rocks as his post and built himself a solid standing-place on top. He positioned Kimmi with Kirrin behind, sheltered from the battleground by the mound itself. Horsa he placed to one side, shielded by a large boulder, with Shallon in support. He made sure that all three had a clear way to the slight security of the path. If all went wrong, he would hold the monster long enough for them to start on their way down to safety.

They waited. The light had nearly gone and the first star of evening glimmered straight above. A muffling silence blanketed the mountain-top. Running through the spells in his head, Feo forced down the cold lump which was trying to rise to his stomach.

The silence was broken. There was a hiss of rushing air and a great shadow passed between them and the star. With a clap of leathery wings, the dragon alighted in its ledge.

All at once, Feo's head was crystal-clear. This time, he, and Cardevin, would be the victors. As he gestured with one hand, a huge spellfire blossomed above their heads. It revealed the dragon rearing in surprise, exposing its dead-fish-white belly. The talons were ready to strike, the wicked head snaking to locate the target, but the eyelids were fluttering to protect distended pupils, blinded by the glare.

Horsa ran forward and planted a spear in the bulging flank. The dragon threw its head back, releasing an eldritch howl of pain. Its tail whipped round and Horsa jumped the jagged spikes on his way back to cover.

Raising himself to his full height, Feo intoned a few words and raised his left arm above his head. A fracture appeared in the air above him, spreading and growing until it delineated a dome separating the dragon from its attackers.

It was none too soon. As the fireshield was completed, the dragon's head lowered and a jet of white-hot flame clawed at the rounded surface.

Feo drew power with his right hand to feed the shield held with his left. This time, he must not falter. No-one could be lucky enough to have a third chance.

The energy coursed through him, resonating in his bones. The shield held. Abruptly, the fire cut. The dragon's mouth opened, bellowing its fury. Feo could see the red funnel of its throat, the razor-sharp yellow teeth. Then the jaws snapped shut as Horsa thrust another spear deep into its ribs. Kimmi dodged out far enough to let loose several darts at the dragon's flank and Shallon followed up with a rapid flight of arrows to its neck.

Swinging its great head from side to side, the dragon searched for its attacker. Seeing no-one on its injured side, it peered at Feo in puzzlement. The forked tongue flickered out to touch the green trickle of blood. Rearing up in outrage at the injury, the cruel talons raked the air, searching for a target.

'Feo!' Horsa was waving a spear behind his covering rock. 'Feo! I can't find its heart.'

Feo nodded. It was time to bring the next weapon into play.

Using a corner of his mind to hold the shield steady, Feo conjured up a yellowed page of writing. Muttering the complex formula, he gradually became aware of a brooding fury, straining against frustration for a target to annihilate. The spell had worked. He had made contact with the dragon's mind.

Slowly, he deepened and broadened the contact, until he could feel the hardness of the ground beneath the claws, the heat of the fire waiting to be released. Impulses of destruction, urges to slaughter, hatred of all other beings, all beat against his consciousness, battling to consume it.

Forcing away the desire to rend and kill, he explored the body. He found the ache of the healing injury in the wing-root from their last meeting. Then he located the more severe pain of the spear-thrusts.

Horsa's aim had been good, but not good enough. The dragon's heart was high in its chest, and both spears had missed it. Neither injury was mortal.

Feo withdrew until he could only feel the pressure of the beast's hatred. He felt as if he had been liberated from a cesspit. Locating Horsa's anxious face, he signalled him to aim higher.

Why wasn't Horsa moving in to attack? He was waving his spear all over the place. Feo sensed a shadow and instinctively ducked. The dragon's talons whistled past his face, followed by a searing jet of flame.

Feo held the shield. He felt the power-flow resonance through his body rise to a roar, but he kept the fireshield rock-solid. As the dragon withdrew, he became aware of the trickle of blood down his chest, but he didn't have time to think about it. Horsa had darted in for the kill.

The third spear flew high and true, straight for the heart. Sinking a little deeper into the beast's mind, Feo knew that this stroke was fatal.

Fatal, but not instant. Rearing up and clawing the air, the dragon swivelled its great eyes round, trying to locate its attackers. The spiked tip of its tail, sweeping a great arc, bowled Horsa over before he could reach his covering rock. He bounced off the side and managed to roll behind it.

A stream of arrows flew towards the dragon's head as Shallon and Kimmi backed him up. They lodged and hung, but couldn't penetrate deep enough to do serious damage. The olive tendrils writhed round its mouth and the great head lowered to blast out its adversaries with fire. This was what Horsa had been waiting for. He leapt out from cover and plunged his sword through the huge eye and deep into the brain.

Feo watched the chin drop into the dust. Horsa withdrew his sword and stood back, shaking the green blood from its blade.

Smoke began to trickle from the gaping nostrils and a new movement started behind the carcass. With horror, Feo remembered the dragon's second brain. The head was dead, but the tail had a pseudo-life of its own. The thick spiked length was convulsing in a violent arc towards Horsa and he was full in its path.

Feo dropped the fireshield and grabbed for power. The energy screamed through his body and shot from his finger in a searing stream. It crashed into the dragon's tail, hurling it backwards. Horsa whirled round and chopped. A final spurt of green gushed and the spiked end dropped limp to the ground.

They slowly gathered round the massive head, still not convinced it was over. A final thread of smoke drifted up from one scarlet nostril and dissipated in the chill night air.

Feo looked round his hunting-party. Dusty and battered as they were, they had achieved their goal; the dreadful monster lay dead at their feet. A wave of pride and affection welled up inside him.

'Well done!' he said. 'This was very well done.'

Shallon looked up, shaking her head. 'I never believed we'd do it,' she said. 'Three hundred years since the last dragon was slain! And then they had a small army.'

There was a silence before Feo spoke. 'If I had known that, I'm not sure I could have attempted it.' His heart thumped against his ribs as he thought of what could have happened.

Horsa shifted restlessly. 'I think I've seen enough for now. And the dragon stinks.'

The upwind corner of the ledge seemed the best place to gather the equipment. No-one wanted to enter the cave before they had to. Shallon made Feo sit while she cleaned the scores on his chest.

'Your tunic is past rescue,' she said as she finished, 'But at least you still look a wizard in that cloak.'

Feo stood up and pulled his knife from his belt. 'I may look like a wizard, but I have a butcher's job to do now.'

Shallon looked puzzled. 'Dragon meat isn't good to eat.'

'I don't want to eat it, but I need to get the dragonstone.'

'What is the dragonstone?'

Feo looked surprised. 'Didn't you know? Dragons have a lot of gallstones, which is why they're so bad-tempered. I need one good one to help me lift the curse.'

'Gallstones!' Shallon laughed. 'Who would have thought they were magical? Well, don't be too long. We need a hot meal before we start back. I want to get down to the horses by dawn.'

Feo pointed a finger at a pile of rocks and felt a trickle of energy flow down his arm. The stones crackled and started to glow.

'Will that serve to cook? I will be back to eat.'

He turned and walked towards the dragon, half exhilarated and half reluctant to approach the vast corpse. But the job must be completed.

Returning a time later smeared with green slime, he raised his burden for all to see. In his hands, he held a mass as big as his head, banded with colours and flashing an opalescent fire.

'I have the Dragonstone,' he said.

Illusion of Progress

Feo collapsed the spellfire to a more manageable size as they entered the cave. By instinct, they trod softly although they knew its tenant would not be back. At the rear, the golden pile gleamed, topped by the single ovoid which seemed to glow with an inner light.

They paused to look and the egg rocked.

Shallon stepped back and gasped, 'It's hatching!'

Horsa reached for his sword, but Feo stretched an arm to stop him.

'No!' he said, 'Watch.'

The egg rocked again, and then cracked from top to bottom. The two halves fell away and a tiny gold dragonet crawled out, spreading filmy wings to dry.

'You can't leave that here!,' said Horsa, shuddering.

'I don't intend to.' Feo picked it up and let it coil round his forearm.

'You're not taking it back to Cardevin!'

'Of course I am.' Feo drew himself up to his full height and swung his cloak over one shoulder. 'Don't you remember that the crest of the Hereditary Wizard is a dragon?'

'Of course, but it's going to be a ruddy big crest when it grows up! It'll gobble up the whole of Cardevin!'

Feo smiled. 'It won't grow any bigger. It's my familiar. And neither will Kirrin. She'll always fit in my pocket.'

Horsa tugged his moustache speechlessly as Kirrin emerged from Feo's pocket to investigate the newcomer. She sniffed twice at it and then returned to the pocket to continue her nap.

'I hope you know what you're doing,' growled Horsa, and stumped towards the passage.

They dropped down the sloping tunnel towards the Wizards' Cavern, Shallon's lantern at the fore and Feo's spellfire lighting the rear. The cool night air blew from behind them, tainted with the scents of battle, dragon blood and fire. As they entered the cavern and the lights cast fantastic shadows round them, Feo slowed, feeling a tug to linger and explore.

Shallon turned. 'Come on, Feo. We need to get through the village before it wakes.'

Her voice echoed round the vast space, its sounds oddly transmuted as they rebounded. Instead of growing softer and softer, they increased to a roar before fading.

'On... Feo... ON... FEO... ON... FEO... ON... FEO... ON... ON... On... On... on...'

Feo shook himself and hurried to catch up. As he reached the centre of the cavern, he caught the last echo, soft as a whisper.

'On, Feodin, on, well done, well done.'

The tiny dragon on his wrist raised its head for a moment, then buried it in Feo's sleeve.

They emerged from the mountain to find a clear sky with a fine crescent moon. Looking up, Feo could see the Hunter chasing the Gryphon picked out in stars as brilliant as King Druvillian's diamonds.

Pausing a few minutes in the entrance, the party roped up for the journey down the slope, round the ledge and back across the wyvern's ridge. As Feo expanded the spellfire to light the way, he saw Kimmi glance along their path and give a shudder.

'The wyverns will be abed,' said Shallon, 'But be careful where you put your feet; the light's deceiving.'

They slithered down the steep slope, dislodging showers of rock which bounced off the ledge below and vanished into impenetrable blackness. Feo breathed a sigh of relief when they reached the level ground of the ledge. It would be too cruel if the group which had survived a battle with a dragon unscathed were to perish on a barren mountain.

Although the night was fine, the ground was still wet underfoot and the going was treacherous. When they reached the narrow spine where they had killed the wyvern, Shallon paused a long time assessing the path.

'Feo, can you send the spellfire along the spine? I want to see what the footing's like.'

Feo sent it slowly along, pausing over the spot where Kimmi had slipped.

'I think we'll be all right. Watch that spot three quarters across. It looks as if there's some loose stone.'

They inched across the ridge, trying to penetrate the inky shadows cast by the spellfire. Shallon's foot slipped just before the doubtful spot and Feo heard Horsa draw in a horrified breath, but she was prepared and caught herself.

On the other side, the crevice where the path continued was as black as a dragon's heart. They paused to remove the ropes and struggled down, slipping and sliding on the water-loosened gravel.

The ledge at the bottom was a relief. It was too dark to see the drop and the surface was sound. They were able to speed up and Shallon's glances at the height of the setting moon grew fewer. But soon enough they were off it and into the jumble of boulders left by a rockfall. These were a nightmare, huge pools of bottomless shadow disguising holes just the right size to trap a foot. By the time they reached the proper path, not one of them was without bruises and scrapes.

'That's the worst of it,' said Shallon cheerfully. 'The rest's just an easy walk.'

It wasn't, but it was a lot quicker going and they reached the clearing a couple of hours before dawn.

One of the horses trotted over to greet them, and Shallon stroked its nose as she cast an eye over the area. 'Six horses and the packs just as we left them. I'd say your barrier worked, Feo.'

'Hot food,' muttered Horsa, 'A warm bed.'

'Hot food, yes,' said Shallon, overhearing him, 'But no sleep until we're through the village. You wouldn't want to meet the villagers again - they've had time to prepare themselves.'

Feo and Horsa gathered wood for a fire while the other two opened the packs and found food and the cooking pot. A few muttered words from Feo soon produced a cheerful blaze despite the dampness of the wood and they all gathered round it, drawn by the warmth and homeliness after the long trek down the dark mountain.

It wasn't until Feo sat down that he realised how tired he was. He pulled his boots off and rubbed his feet. They were so cold he couldn't feel them. Horsa was sitting beside Shallon, holding his hands to the fire and Kimmi bent over the cooking pot, stirring as if he thought it would make it cook faster.

Hot food and a blazing fire restored all of them. The cold had seeped out of Feo's bones and his feet were his own again. He unwound the dragonet from his wrist and fed it scraps of meat until it would take no more. Looking into the golden eyes, he murmured, 'What's your name? Tsiri, Tsiri, that's it.' He let the dragonet curl back round his wrist and wriggle under his cuff to sleep.

He sat back against a rock and stared at the sky. The crescent moon hung a finger's breadth above the horizon, waiting to drop down for a day's rest. He straightened with a start.

'How long is it to the New Moon?' he asked.

Shallon glanced at the sky. 'Should be five days from now.'

'Five days! One day to get back to Fazimar City, three days on the ship, one day to lift the curse...' Feo looked horrified. 'We can't afford any hold-ups, not one.'

'Don't worry, Feo.' Horsa leaned back and stretched. 'We've just killed a dragon. We can do anything!'

'We should make it,' said Shallon, 'Provided, that is, you don't go off on any jaunts by yourself!'

Feo coughed and looked down. The memories of his solo trips were not happy.

Grinning, Shallon added, 'We'll be fine. Make the most of the fire, though. We move in fifteen minutes.'

They entered the outskirts of the village with the first rays of the sun. The vast shadow of the mountain was slowly withdrawing, allowing the dingy stone houses to acquire a patina of pink. As they reached the centre of the hamlet, Horsa pointed.

'Look, over there. It's Rogg!'

In the dusty triangle a lonely figure sat, his hands and feet fastened in the stocks. Behind him was an untidy heap of wood, roughly kicked away from the post which had been its centre. Feo pulled out the Dragonstone and held it high overhead, its opalescent bands glinting in the dawn light. Rogg turned his head and cringed, trying to hide behind the rough wood of his imprisonment.

Luck stayed with them for the morning. The weather was fine, the road was good and they made excellent time to the fork where they had turned to go behind the mountain.

'We'll stop to eat on the other road,' said Shallon. 'We should have a clear ride to Fazimar City now.'

They rounded the last bend before the road joined the main highway to the city.

'Why are there soldiers there?' asked Feo.

Horsa whipped round. 'The checkpoint! They're still here? This is a disaster. They're bound to arrest us this time!'

'Isn't there any way round?' asked Kimmi.

'No,' said Shallon, 'And they've seen us now.

Two of the guards had turned their attention to the smaller road and were pointing up it talking furiously. Then one of them ran to the tent and came back with the officer.

Behind them, a disembodied eye appeared. Looking concerned, it blinked several times and then vanished with a soft plop.

By the time Feo's party reached the junction, the officer was planted in the middle of the road with his hand outstretched.

'Halt, in the King's name!'

Shallon stopped in front of him.

'Good morning, Captain. What can we do for you?'

'Papers, please!'

Shallon pulled out the wad of well-thumbed parchment. The captain took them, mopping his nose with a handkerchief held in his other hand.

'You have no entrance visas.'

'As I told you last time, we don't need any. We're all Fazimari citizens.'

The Captain cast an eye over Horsa and Kimmi and then fixed his gaze on Feo.

'I haven't seen you before. Where do you come from?'

Feo opened his mouth, wondering what to say. One wrong word and Cardevin was doomed.

Shallon broke in smoothly. 'He's a cousin of mine.'

'He doesn't look Fazimari to me. I've never seen clothes like that anywhere.'

'Like my other cousin, he's also worked abroad for years, trading exotic cargos. He dresses to impress his customers.'

Mopping his nose again, the Captain thumbed through the parchment. Feo could hear him muttering, 'Dragon hunts? Dragon Hunts! Most un-Fazimari.' Then he looked up.

'Did you kill your dragon?'

'Yes,' said Shallon.

'Then where are its ears?'

Horsa's mount side-stepped nervously, responding to its rider's tension.

'Its ears?' said Shallon.

'Its ears. All dragon hunters are required to display the dragon's ears as proof they have killed one.'

'There's never been a regulation like that!'

Horsa muttered to Feo, 'This is trouble.'

'Can't we bribe him? We've got to get moving!'

'No chance. He's an honest official'

Feo looked at the Captain, his heart sinking.

'The regulation was passed two days ago. Where are the ears?'

'Back on the mountain,' snapped Shallon. 'And what would you have done if I'd said we hadn't killed a dragon?'

'I'd have sent you back to get one,' replied the Captain severely. 'A licence is a contract. You must fulfil it.'

'Well, we killed our dragon and we haven't got its ears. What are you going to do?'

'If you don't want to go back and get them, I'll have to detain you while I send to Fazimar City for instructions. This is most irregular.'

'But we must be back in Fazimar City tonight. We can't afford any delay. My cousin's stars predict disaster if he isn't there.'

'I can't help that. The King's business takes precedence!'

Kimmi sidled over to Feo and whispered, 'If I set fire to the tent, do you think we can get past them?'

'On no account,' hissed Feo. 'I'll deal with this.'

Feo gathered his cloak round him and groped through his tiredness for the need to convince the soldiers. Then, uttering a few words under his breath, he walked his horse over to stand beside Shallon's and fixed the Captain with a very bright emerald eye.

'Captain, I know you are a most conscientious man, whose only desire is to carry out the King's wishes.'

The Captain drew himself up and straightened his cloak. 'Indeed, I have the honour to be one of the King's servants. My duty is to perform his wishes.'

Feo bent down closer to the Captain and lowered his voice so the troops couldn't hear. 'There is to be no word of this to anyone. Anyone, you understand?' All the time Feo was talking, his hands, hidden in a fold of his cloak, were working through a set of magical gestures, laying a compulsion on the Captain. 'I am a Special Envoy for the King to the Upper Negus Reserve. I am tasked by him to slay a dragon and return instanter with my report.'

The Captain's eyes were fixed on Feo's face, a slight glaze filming their usual steely blue.

Feo continued, 'Of course, I will be reporting on my experiences with various people on the journey.' Feo shook his head. 'The King will be most displeased at some of the treatment we've had.'

As the Captain stared at Feo, a slight expression of unease penetrated the glazed features.

'Now you, my dear Captain, have been the soul of propriety and courtesy. You wouldn't obstruct a King's Envoy.'

The Captain's face brightened. 'Yes, Sir!' His expression clouded momentarily. 'I mean, no, Sir!'

Feo sat back in his saddle. 'Captain, it's time we were about the King's business. Our papers, please.'

'Your papers! Of course, Sir!' The officer dived into his pocket and pulled out his stamp. 'I'll mark them to show you passed this temporary waystation.' He dived into his pocket again before realising he held the documents in his other hand. Breathing on the stamp to moisten the ink, he added the print to the earlier ones and looked up to beam at Feo.

'There you are, Sir. All in proper order.'

'Thank you, Captain.' Feo held out his hand.

'Sir!' The Captain saluted and handed back the wad of parchment. Then he turned to his men, who were standing, pikes at the ready to secure prisoners.

'Sergeant!'

'Sir!' The soldier with a red pennant on his pike stepped forward.

'Fall the troops in.'

'Sir!'

Feo watched Shallon's face with amusement as the troops lined up along the side of the road and the Captain marched smartly to position in front of them.

As the party trotted down the road to Fazimar City, the Captain shouted, 'Ten...Shun!' The soldiers drew themselves up in stiff formation, pikes shouldered, and as Feo passed, the Captain and troops gave him an immaculate salute.

The day continued fine and they made good time until they were within a few miles of the City walls. Then Kimmi nudged his horse up alongside Shallon's and said, 'What's that? Is there a fire?'

In the distance the road was smudged across by a brown cloud. Shallon sniffed and said, 'Not fire - worse. It's the market carts leaving the city. We'll have to draw off the road.'

Feo looked at her in horror. 'We can't do that! It'll take hours!'

'We can't do anything else. They'll block the whole road.'

'Feo, can't you do anything about it?' Horsa looked at him hopefully.

'I can't control all those people and animals. It would take all the wizards of the continent to do that!'

Kimmi edged his horse alongside. 'If you were the King's Envoy, they'd move for you then, wouldn't they? Just like the soldiers.'

Horsa looked at him, bereft of words. Then he thumped him on the back. 'That's brilliant, Kimmi. Feo, can you do it?'

'I think so.' He turned to Shallon. 'What does an official King's Envoy look like?'

'He wears a red uniform trimmed with gold and sable.'

Feo's hands were moving busily and through a shimmering mist his blue cloak transformed into a red coat frogged with gold.

'More fur round the neck... and braid on the sleeves... Trousers, black with a gold stripe... a little broader... Square fur hat... That's perfect.'

'What about his attendants?'

'An outrider with pennant...'

'Kimmi, cut a long stick from the bushes.'

Kimmi came back tying a rag to a six foot branch.

'Red uniform, black braid... Pennant, red, black leopard couchant. Swordbearer...'

'That's me,' said Horsa, drawing his sword and hefting it upright.

'Red coat, black braid... Trousers, black, red braid... Hat, fur, flat... Guard... We've not really got enough for that - he should have two or three - Red coat, black trousers, red braid, pillbox hat...'

Feo looked round his party, amazed at his own work. A small military detachment looked back at him, even their bearing changed to match their dress.

Horsa paced towards Feo, his sword firmly vertical before a slightly worried expression. 'How long can you keep up the illusion?'

Feo straightened his back in the saddle. 'As long as we need,' he replied.

They pulled into neat formation, Kimmi with the pennant a few horse-lengths in advance, Horsa with his sword followed by Feo with Shallon guarding the rear. Breaking into a smart trot, they approached the dust-cloud.

'Make way, make way for the King's Representative. Move aside for the Royal Party!'

The first cart swerved off the road well before they reached it, the driver pulling frantically on the reins. The second and third were a short distance behind and bounced over the verge, shedding limp cabbage leaves as they went. There was a gap before the next group of carts, and Feo could see the ripples of disturbance in the flow as the news was passed back. By the time they reached them, the road was clearing. A couple of miles later, they passed the last cart without ever having broken their trot.

They pulled up just down the road under the shade of a large oak. Muttering a few words, Feo dissolved the illusion, and the vivid colours of their uniforms, which were already a little faded, trickled away, leaving them in their travel-stained clothes.

'Wouldn't it have been better to keep the uniforms until we're in Fazimar City?' asked Horsa, brushing the cart-dust from his tunic.

'Too dangerous,' said Shallon. 'Too many people to ask questions there.'

'Will we reach the gate before they lock it for the night?'

'I hope so.' Shallon rubbed her hand over her curls, looking doubtful. 'And we may have trouble getting past the guards. They'll want to see our papers.'

'We'd better get going then. We can eat while we ride.'

They set out at a steady pace. Feo glanced at the sun.

'Can't we go any faster?' he muttered to Horsa.

'The horses wouldn't take it,' said Horsa, patting the dusty neck in front of him, 'They've done a lot of hard travelling.'

By the time they came within sight of the gate, Shallon was casting anxious glances at the sun, which was dipping low to the horizon. Feo shaded his eyes and peered into the shadows of the arch. Two figures sat, one each side of the gate, pikes leant against the arch. As he watched, one stood and picked up his pike.

'They're shutting the gate!' yelled Shallon, kicking her horse into a gallop.

Feo thundered behind her, watching the guards in the gate with desperation. The second was still sitting, but the first was already fumbling with the open gate. They weren't going to make it.

It was too far to shout and in any case the guards couldn't have missed them, racing down the road in a whirlwind of dust. Feo stared at the distance separating them from the gate. They couldn't lose at this stage, not after all they'd been through. If only something would delay the guards, just for a few minutes.

His horse stumbled and Feo nearly shot over his head. He was an idiot! Of course he could delay the guards!

The dozing sentry raised his head as his companion stopped pulling at the gate and pointed at him angrily. Obviously, the first guard wanted some help. Feo muttered an incantation and twisted his fingers. He watched in satisfaction as the second guard's head dropped back on his chest. The first started forward as Feo muttered again, then halted, turned and vanished at a shambling trot behind the gatehouse. Two minutes later, Feo's party thundered through the arch and turned sharp left. The slumbering guard never stirred.

As they halted outside the inn, Shallon asked Feo, 'How did you do it?'

Feo looked innocent. 'Do what?'

'The gate guards, of course!'

'Ah!' Feo shook the dust off his phoenix-feather hat. 'The sitting guard was easy. He was so sleepy he only needed a little encouragement. The other was a little harder until he realised his bladder wouldn't wait.'

Shallon looked sideways at him and grinned. 'No rainbow toads this time, then?'

'I never like to repeat myself,' said Feo severely. He paused. 'Besides, I'm not quite sure how I did that.'

* * *

The innkeeper was delighted to see Kimmi. He'd been managing the horses himself since he'd fired the ostler for being blind drunk while the guests were waiting for their mounts. He offered Kimmi the job.

'I'll miss you all,' said Kimmi wistfully to Feo, 'But you can't fight dragons all the time, can you?'

Feo shuddered, remembering the black-encrusted claws and the odour of decay. 'No, you can't.'

'You will take me if you go on another hunt?'

'Of course I will.' Feo smiled, vowing silently that he would never undertake anything so perilous again.

Shallon returned from a visit to the Golden Conch, near the harbour, with good news. She'd booked passage for them on the Amagadis, a ship sailing on the first tide in the morning. She found Feo engrossed in his books, Kirrin beside him on the table.

'I'd have thought you'd have been drinking a tankard by the fire after the last week,' she said.

Feo looked up. 'Your job is finished,' he said, 'But mine is only half-done. If I don't fit the ritual exactly to the curse, then Cardevin will implode.' He rubbed his eyes and added, 'Or if it's nearly right, I might implode.'

'And Horsa?' asked Shallon, a trifle anxiously.

'He won't implode. And I expect he's drinking a tankard at the moment.'

Horsa had just finished his tankard and was ordering another when Shallon found him in the common room.

'Make that two,' he called to the serving wench.

Shallon sat down opposite him and they looked at each other a little sadly.

'I've booked your passage,' said Shallon. 'The ship sails in the morning.'

'What will you do when we're gone?'

Shallon shrugged. 'Guide people round the game reserves. Escort travellers to Memeron.'

'No dragon hunts?'

She laughed. 'We don't get many of those.'

'I will be back, you know.' Horsa saw Shallon's face brighten.

'You will?'

'Soon. But I'll have to help Feo first. He needs me. When Cardevin is safe, I'll come.' He leant over the table and took Shallon's hands.

She gripped them and said softly, 'I'll be looking out for you.'

Horsa released her and stood up. 'I must go and look for Feo now. Everything rests on him.' He walked to the door, knowing that the warmth which spread through him was not from the wine.

Feo read long into the night, Kirrin dozing beside him. When Horsa shook him awake at dawn, his head was still spinning with incantations and formulae.

'Come on, Feo, we need to leave.'

'Why so early? The tide doesn't turn until midmorning.'

'We've got to visit all the port offices to be cleared aboard, remember?'

* * *

Feo and Horsa strode down the stone corridor, their heavy boots thumping on the flags. Feo's midnight-blue cloak swept his heels and the phoenix-plume, which was the badge of the Hereditary Wizards of Cardevin, drooped from his hat. Horsa wore the plain brown tunic and trousers of the traveller.

A few yards down, they found the heavy wooden door labelled "Keeper of the King's Game". They knocked.

There was a long pause before a voice said 'Enter'. Crouched behind a dark desk was the wildly-bearded figure of Snorkin.

'I'm Snorkin.' He paused. ' Keeper of the King's Game. What are you here for?'

Feo stepped forward and presented the Keeper with a sheet of parchment. 'One Dragon Licence, duly signed by our guide. We have killed one dragon and one Wyvern.'

Snorkin took the licence and fumbled for his spectacles. Peering at the document, he tutted. 'Dear me. We can't have this, you know. You had a sub-licence for two Wyverns and you only killed one. I'm afraid there will be a small fine for that. Shall we say, thirty doublards?'

Feo fixed Snorkin with a glittering emerald gaze. 'Thirty doublards,' he said dangerously.

A strange look came over Snorkin's face. His features all blurred for a moment, and then rearranged themselves into an ingratiating smile.

'Oh, not quite as much as that,' he said, 'but you are certainly entitled to a refund. I work it out as...' he screwed his forehead up for a moment, 'eighteen doublards, I believe.' He reached into the purse at his waist and counted eighteen bright coins onto the desk.

Feo swept them up and dropped them into his pocket.

'That's a very fetching armlet you have,' remarked Snorkin. 'I don't think I've ever seen one quite like it.'

Feo rapidly pulled his cloak round him. Snorkin would remember nothing of this meeting, but if the officials in the docks saw the dragonet, there would be trouble.

They left Snorkin shaking his head in bemusement and strode down the corridor.

'I hope we have as little trouble with the port officials,' remarked Horsa.

'We will,' said Feo, 'We will!'

Behind them, a disembodied eye appeared, hanging just below the ceiling. It blinked and stared after them malevolently as they passed out of the passage into the busy port area.

Saving the Vinefruit

'Papers?' The bored official held out his hand for Feo's bundle of frayed parchment. He turned them over distastefully. 'Not very clean, are they?' He peered at the last sheet. 'I'm not sure I can read this.'

'They're all in order,' said Feo, curbing his impatience. 'And you'd expect them to be a bit worn. They've been on a dragon hunt.'

'A dragon hunt! Did you kill your dragon?'

'Yes.'

'Have you got its ears?'

Feo suppressed a groan. 'No, that regulation came in after we set out on the hunt.'

'But not after you killed the dragon?'

'No,' Feo admitted.

'Then as soon as you became aware of the new regulation, you should have taken steps to obtain its ears.'

'But the Captain of the Guard at the checkpoint agreed that we were not subject to the new regulation.'

'Regardless of what the Captain of the Guard said, I must have the dragon's ears to validate your exit papers.'

'But I haven't got the ears and I need to embark before my ship sails.'

The official leafed through the papers again, casting sideways glances at his nearest colleagues. One was busy examining a case of wooden puzzles for contraband, ranging the pieces all along his desk, while the other was stamping a foot-high pile of documents for an exporter of dried thistleberries.

'If you won't produce the ears I will have to impose a fine.'

'A fine!' Feo felt his cheeks flush with anger.

'Twenty-five doublards.'

Feo drew himself up to his full height and fixed the official with a stormy eye. 'Twenty-five doublards!'

The official flinched a trifle and said, 'Well, since it's your first offence, let's say eighteen doublards.'

Feo reached into his moneybag and counted out eighteen doublards in stony silence. The official rapidly swept them off the desk and into the depths of his tunic. Then he affixed a large seal to the top document and scrawled his name beneath.

As they walked towards the exit of the crowded building, Horsa muttered, 'Why didn't you magic him?'

'Too much audience,' muttered Feo back. 'Too likely to attract attention. We can't afford any more delays.'

Outside, brilliant sunshine splintered off the water with a painful intensity. The pair halted, assaulted by this and the mingled odours of dried foodstuffs, spices and the effluent of the ships' bilges.

'Where's the Amagadis?' asked Horsa.

'She should be at the south end of the quay, according to Shallon.'

They looked both ways, then turned away from the crowded line of ships by the port buildings, bustling with dockers heaving sacks on their shoulders. The other end of the quay was quieter, holding ships with their hatches battened, ready to sail, and several gaps where ships had left on the last tide.

Feo walked down to the first ship, Horsa following, and peered at the name on the stern. Just above the back of Horsa's head, the disembodied eye appeared. It looked displeased. After staring at Feo for a moment, it blinked twice and vanished with a soft plop.

Horsa turned to the half-heard sound. A gust of wind whipped Feo's cloak out sideways and he stumbled towards the water's edge. Horsa turned back and grabbed his arm just in time to save him falling into the noisome harbour water.

'Where did that come from? There's barely enough breeze to take the ships out.'

'I thought I heard something,' said Horsa, 'but when I looked, there was nothing.'

Feo scanned the quay, but there was no-one within several ships of them.

'Must have been a freak,' he said dismissively, and they walked down to find the Amagadis.

Their ship was the last in the line and they reached it to find the captain nearly dancing with impatience at the top of the gangplank.

'Feodin Fiorson? Come aboard! With this light wind, we've only a few minutes to catch the tide.'

As soon as the gangplank was raised, the sails were hoisted and the Amagadis made for the harbour mouth. Feo checked the baggage in the small cabin and settled with several books open before him. Kirrin settled down with one paw on his books while the dragonet investigated the inkwell. When Horsa returned from the deck, he was busy making notes.

'Good thing the sea's so calm,' Horsa said, pointing to the inkwell. 'Captain Pollik says the voyage won't be fast, but we should make Cardevin in three days.'

Feo grunted, finishing a diagram with a small flourish. 'That should just give enough time to set up the ritual.'

'Have you completed it yet?'

'Nearly. We perform it on the highest peak of Cardevin at moonrise. I'll need several items I have at home, together with the dragonstone. I should have the form of the ritual complete by this afternoon.'

Feo worked on through the day, emerging on the deck a little before sunset. He and Horsa leant on the stern rail, watching the sun sink into a fiery sea. The wind was fresh on Feo's face and he relished the salty breeze after long hours in a stuffy cabin.

Next morning, he woke early, sure that something was amiss. The motion of the ship had changed. It was rolling slightly from side to side with a queasy corkscrewing action.

Pulling on some clothes, he stumbled up to the deck. There he found Captain Pollik in agitated conversation with his helmsman. Overhead, the sails flapped loosely with the motion of the ship.

'But the wind is out there. You can see it.' Captain Pollik waved his hand to the side.

'It may be out there, Cap'n, but it's not here. And we can't get to it.'

Feo peered over the side. The sea was heaving with an oily swell. As his gaze travelled outwards, he saw a sharp boundary on the water. Beyond it, the waves tossed and sparkled, their tops frayed in the breeze. Within it was only that smooth-surfaced heave.

Walking round the ship, he traced the perimeter. As far as he could see, it formed a true circle with the ship in the middle.

Feo returned to the cabin, deep in thought, and shook Horsa awake.

'What's wrong?' Horsa rubbed his eyes.

'We're becalmed.'

'How long does Captain Pollik think before we get some wind?'

'No, no, you don't understand. It isn't natural.'

'What do you mean?'

'Come and look for yourself.' Feo dragged Horsa up to the deck and walked him round the ship. Leaning over the stern rail, they stared out over the oily surface where the wake of the ship should be.

'I've never seen anything like it,' said Horsa, stroking his moustache. 'But if we don't get some wind soon, we'll never make Cardevin in time.'

'I'm going to see if I can sort this out. We can't afford any delay.' Feo turned abruptly and headed for the cabin.

When Horsa put his head round the door half an hour later, Feo was immersed in his books, Kirrin curled up on a corner of the table and the dragonet poised on an open volume. He went away silently and came back a little later with Feo's breakfast.

'I think I've worked out how to tackle this,' said Feo, looking up. 'It's obviously the Sultan and he'll have several wizards holding this calm.' He stood up and paced round the cabin.

'I can't collapse the calm; there's too much force against me and in any case it would alert them immediately and they'd just think of something worse.'

'Then what can you do?' said Horsa. 'We've got to find some wind somehow.'

'I'm going to cleave the calm right up the middle. That will let the breeze reach the ship and on the way it will draw in some extra energy from the magical calms each side. That will give us more wind and will keep the Sultan's lot busy feeding their spells.'

'Won't they realise what's happening?'

'I think it'll take a while. They'll think I'm trying to collapse the calm and they'll know it's still there.'

'Meanwhile, we'll be making fast time. Feo, that's a good solution. Can you make it work?'

Feo swept his cloak over one shoulder and picked up his notes. 'Of course I can make it work. I am the Hereditary Wizard of Cardevin!'

They emerged on the deck and headed for the stern. Captain Pollik was still standing beside his helmsman, but he'd given up shouting at him and they were both staring dispiritedly forward at the limp sails.

Spreading his arms wide so that his cloak hung like a piece of ocean at midnight, Feo began his incantation.

'Azeron, Queen of the sea, Lady of the deeps,

'Nooth, Lord of the Tritons, mighty warrior of the oceans,

'Lend me your aid; for with your help all may be accomplished.

'Let that which is one become two; yea, let the one be cleaved,

'Let - '

'Hoi!' Captain Pollik's voice echoed over the afterdeck. 'Hoi, you! What do you think you're doing?'

Feo turned, his arms dropping. A leaden lump hit his stomach and his hands were shaking.

'Doing? I'm getting the wind back.'

'What do you mean, getting the wind back.' The Captain stamped across the deck and his voice rose to a roar. 'You're one of those bejiggered magicians, aren't you? Fakers, the whole pack of you!'

Feo drew himself up to his full height and stared down his nose at the Captain. 'I am the Hereditary Wizard of Cardevin and the post has been in my family for five hundred years.' He dropped his voice to a menacing growl. 'And I will prove I am not a fake.'

Captain Pollik's face was bright red and he was spluttering, bereft of words. Horsa stepped quickly between them.

'Captain Pollik, I know you are a man with heavy responsibilities, but we need to get to Cardevin quickly. I'm sure you too have to get your cargo into port in good time.'

The colour seeped out of the Captain's face. He muttered shakily, 'The Balderan Vinefruit - it will be ruined. And so will I!'

227

'My friend here isn't exactly making magic. You can see the unnatural way the wind is avoiding us.' Horsa waved a hand at the oily swell. 'That's due to a spell. All Feo is doing is to counteract it.'

'Counteract it?' repeated Pollik, looking a trifle dazed.

'Then we get to Cardevin in time and you get your Balderan Vinefruit to port in good condition.'

The Captain stared at his seaboots for a minute. Then he looked up and said heavily, 'I don't have much choice, do I? Do your worst!' He turned away and then turned back to say, 'But if you wreck my ship, I'll... I'll keelhaul you!'

Feo turned back to the stern rail and resumed his chanting, amazed at how easily Horsa had handled the angry Captain. He could do it - but only with the help of magic.

As he continued, the boundary of the calm developed coloured fringes. They grew, concentrating on the area directly behind the ship. He reached the end and the colours clumped together for a moment, then split into two adjacent lines. These moved further apart and for'ard, until they swept along the length of the ship's hull, and Feo and Horsa felt the cool breeze on their faces for the first time that day.

On his way back to the cabin, Feo gave the Captain a slight bow and touched his hat. Pollik looked at him as if he were a strange denizen of the ocean deeps, stranded on the ship where he had no business being. Then he turned and shouted orders to trim the sails and set course, burying his confusion under a mass of activity.

True to Feo's prediction, the wind seemed to gather strength from the enclosing calm and they put a goodly number of sea miles behind them that day. By midday,

Captain Pollik was thawing. By sunset, he was positively mellow and invited Feo and Horsa to join him for dinner.

Lamplight gleamed off dark wood, silver glowed on a milk-white cloth and each perfectly-cooked dish was succeeded by another. Captain Pollik obviously enjoyed his food and made good use of his travels to procure the best. He was also fond of wine. As the last dish was removed and the table cleared, Feo leant back in his chair and felt a warm glow of satiety and liberal amounts of alcohol.

'So you're really a magician,' asked Pollik, swirling his after-dinner Aquavera round its glass.

'I'm the Hereditary Wizard of Cardevin,' replied Feo, making as much of a bow as he could seated at the table.

'And you brought the wind back.'

'Indeed,' said Feo, careful not to mention that he was indirectly responsible for the calm.

'Saved my vinefruit,' said the Captain, taking a long drink. 'Saved my reputation.'

'The least I could do,' murmured Feo.

Captain Pollik stared into his glass for a moment. 'Why would someone becalm my ship? They couldn't want to spoil the vinefruit, could they?'

'Er... No!' said Feo.

Pollik shot him a glance. 'They were trying to stop you, weren't they?'

'Er...' He tried to think of something to say. If Captain Pollik thought he was bringing trouble to the Amagadis, things could get very difficult.

'Lousy landlubbers!' Feo jumped as Captain Pollik slammed his hand down on the table.

'How dare they attack my ship! We'll get you safe to Cardevin, don't you worry.'

Feo breathed an inward sigh of relief. It was going to be all right.

* * *

A pounding headache threatened to burst out of his skull as he turned over. Cracking an eyelid to peer at the porthole, Feo realised it was still dark. He groaned and rubbed his face. What was he doing awake at this ungodly hour?

He felt a slight weight materialise on his chest and he groaned again. It was Kirrin. Why was she waking him so early. And after the evening before. Captain Pollik's hospitality had been more than generous and they had stumbled to bed by the light of the moon with every intention of sleeping until midday.

Kirrin kneaded his chest with barely-sheathed claws. Reluctantly, Feo realised he was not going to get to sleep again. He might as well go on deck and try to clear his head. Climbing the companionway, he felt Kirrin wriggle in his pocket. Evidently she was sleepless too.

He leant on the stern rail, letting the breeze blow the hair off his forehead. It was possible, he thought, he might feel alive sometime today. Perhaps late in the afternoon.

The eastern horizon was paling and Feo gazed at it, waiting for the first sliver of sun. But black clouds were boiling up from nowhere and faster than the world could roll they grouped over that lightening sky and then launched themselves outward.

Feo stared in surprise. He'd never seen clouds behave like this. He looked round wildly and realised that the cloven calm had vanished. Then he realised he'd been stupidly optimistic thinking he'd get a clear run to Cardevin. The Sultan had struck again.

Already he could feel a slight chop in the waves and Captain Pollik erupted on deck, a greatcoat clutched round him. He took one look to the east and yelled at his sailors to reef the sails.

The clouds roiled as they raced towards the Amagadis. Purple streaked the black as they broke and rejoined and then a bolt of vivid blue arrowed into the sea. An ear-splitting crack echoed across the ocean and the air was filled with the dry smell of ozone. Feo watched with a thumping heart while the white breakers streaked towards the ship. They hit with the first gust of gale and the Amagadis heeled hard over.

Feo clung desperately to the stern rail, certain the ship was going to turn turtle and drag them all to the bottom of the sea. But slowly, very slowly, she righted herself and they were running under bare masts. Beneath him, the foaming wake spread outwards and he gripped the rail to steady himself, his cloak cracking behind him in the gale.

A tousled figure lurched beside him to the rail. Horsa's face was white with worry.

'What's up, Feo? Pollik expected a clear run.'

'This isn't natural.' Feo pointed to the black cap of cloud poised over the ship.

'The Sultan again!'

'What else?'

The intensity of the storm was increasing. Even with no sail set, the Amagadis was bucking and heaving in the violent seas. Captain Pollik and two of his men were struggling to control the rebellious wheel and keep the ship running before the gale.

'We can't go on like this.' As Horsa spoke, the motion of the ship grew wilder and she started to dip her bow into the sea, sending sheets of icy water over the deck.

'I can't control this,' said Feo in despair. 'There's too much power involved.'

'You've got to do something or we'll be dining with the Tritons tonight.'

Feo stared out over the waves, which were now breaking above the sides of the ship. Was this to be the end of it all? After all they had overcome, would he and Horsa be floating at the bottom of the sea, their hair rippling with the currents, while Cardevin vanished forever? He shuddered. This wasn't the way he wanted to die, not in this cold salt water, full of weed and debris churned up by the storm.

He jumped as a wave towered over the ship's rail and broke around his feet. The deck was awash. If the Amagadis took on much more water, she would sink. He had to keep the sea out. He turned, suddenly clear in his mind. Keep the water out. That was all that mattered.

'Azeron, Queen of the sea, Lady of the Deeps,

'Bura, Lord of the Storm, friend to all mariners,

'Preserve the Amagadis, named for your child,

'Called after your daughter, Lady of the dancing waves,'

He tossed into the sea a piece of cork from a net stowed at the ship's side. It bobbed up and down on the water, skidding down the glassy side of a wave and shooting up to the crest of the next.

'As this fragment of Amagadis, so the whole.

'Let the ship and all she carries, the vessel and her cargo, live and lifeless,

'Let them float like this fragment, let them cling to the surface between your two realms,

'Let them cling to both, eschewing neither.

'So may balance be kept, so may harmony be achieved.

'Azeron, Bura, mighty pair! So may it be!.'

As Feo dropped his arms he could feel a difference in the Amagadis' motion. The heavy waterlogged feel had gone. Waves were no longer crashing onto the decks. When he peered over the side, he could see streams of water falling into the sea from the bilge pumps, which were at last making headway.

Round the waterline, the sea sat in a glassy curve, as if it were pressed back by an invisible bubble. Feo tossed another piece of cork over the side. It travelled a short distance and bounced back to land at his feet.

There was a movement in his pocket and a moment later Kirrin popped her head out from the cloak. She looked round and sniffed with an air of satisfaction.

'What's happening?' Captain Pollik came stamping over in his heavy seaboots, a bewildered expression on his face. 'Amagadis... She feels wrong.'

Behind him, the bemused helmsman was controlling the wheel with one finger.

Horsa stepped forward. 'Captain, your ship is now safe. It's unsinkable.'

Pollik managed to look startled and doubtful at the same time.

Swinging his cloak back, Feo tossed another piece of cork overboard. It landed back on Captain Pollik's toes. 'See. The ship and everything on it are protected. There's nothing to fear.' He paused. Pollik's face was turning a strange colour. Underlying the windburn was a spreading tinge of green.

'Captain, are you all right?' Feo stepped towards him as Pollik turned and headed for the companionway fast.

Realising that Horsa was unusually quiet, Feo took a look at him. He was rather pale. Feo swept a glance round the deck. The only sailor in sight was the helmsman and he had an uneasy look about him, although he was still controlling the wheel with one finger as the Amagadis bounded along. Then Feo noticed a growing feeling of discomfort in his stomach.

He and Horsa exchanged one glance and then both followed Captain Pollik below.

Feo ventured on deck for some fresh air about midday. It was still deserted apart from the long-suffering helmsman. His stomach was slowly accustoming itself to the strange motion of the ship and as he leant on the stern rail, he really began to believe that they would reach Cardevin safely.

Behind the ship, the glassy bubble flattened the water, but on the outside of the invisible shield, a wide foaming wake mingled with the tossing waves. At the side, the wild sea was sectioned by the bubble, its dark heart revealed next to the hull while ragged foam crashed fruitlessly high overhead.

Wrapping his cloak round him, Feo let the storm whip the hair back from his face, chilling his features and scouring the last remnants of sickness from his system. As his mind cleared, his thoughts turned to the final part of his task - the complex ritual which would lift the curse.

He ran through the various stages mentally - the laying-out of the diagrams, the purification of the working area, the invocation of the correct powers, the performance of the final ceremony which would shatter the Sultan's curse.

It was all detailed in his notebook, all the signs and sigils, the candles, fires and incense, the verses that must be chanted and the names which must be called. But was it right? Had he missed anything in the long hours of research? The consequences of a mistake could be dire, he knew full well. A mispronounced name, a botched gesture, could wreck the whole thing. Then Cardevin would be irrevocably doomed and as for he himself, his own fate could be anything from simple oblivion to an eternity of tormented wandering through a hostile astral universe. He shuddered and admitted to himself, very quietly, that he was afraid.

Horsa appeared on deck a little later, the colour slowly returning to his face in the fierce wind. Feeling some comfort in the familiar presence, Feo let his mind go blank for a while. He jumped when Horsa spoke.

'Nearly home now. And only the last stage of the task to complete.'

'The last stage - and the most difficult of all.' Feo's face was set. 'Horsa, what if I get it wrong?'

Horsa swung round to face him. 'Feo, we've travelled to an unfriendly country, threaded through a maze of hostile officials, bamboozled the King's servants, slain a dragon and smuggled out a kitten and a dragonet.' He glanced at the golden head of the lizard drowsing on Feo's wrist. 'We are not going to fail now.'

'I'm only an apprentice wizard!' Feo laughed bitterly. 'Suppose I make a mistake?'

'You won't. You can't.' Horsa eyed him over, his face adamant. 'We won't reach Cardevin until morning. Come below and I'll help you check the ritual. It's too cold up here anyway.'

By the time they had looked over all Feo's work, it was well into the night. The sounds of carousing which had barely caught their attention earlier had long died away. Feo lay staring at the cabin ceiling, a little less uneasy about the morrow but still unable to sleep. Eventually, soothed by Kirrin's sleepy purr, he dozed off.

He woke to a shout of 'Land Ahoy!' and a beam of sun falling across his face. Horsa was not in the cabin. Scrambling onto the deck, Feo found him at the bows, peering at the horizon.

'I can't see land yet, but the lookout says it's there.'

'How long before we dock?'

'Pollik says in the afternoon.'

Feo looked up. The sails had been set sometime since last night, and the canvas bowed against a clear blue sky. The storm had vanished as if it had never been. He lifted his hands and spoke a short verse. Collapsing in on itself, the protective bubble dissolved and salt spray stung his face. The Amagadis gave a jolt and resumed her normal swoop through the waves.

'That's better!' Captain Pollik appeared and clapped Feo on the shoulder. 'Feels like my ship again. Not that I'm not very grateful for your help,' he added hastily. 'Would have lost my vinefruit without it.' Feo noticed a strong odour of rum and realised that the Captain had been a member of last night's party.

'Pleased to be of service,' he said, giving a small bow. 'We owe it to you that we'll reach Cardevin in time.'

'Welcome on my ship any time,' said Pollik. 'Just send me word.' He paused and thought for a moment, frowning. 'But I'd rather you weren't arguing with this Sultan fella next time.' He beamed at both of them and moved slightly unsteadily towards the stern.

The day wore on, too slowly for Feo's anxiety to reach Cardevin and start on his preparations and yet too fast for his apprehension. About noon, a shadow appeared on the horizon. Gradually the peaks of Cardevin etched their familiar shape on the sky.

They tied up in port later that afternoon. The Harbourmaster came on board to inspect the Amagadis' papers with the Fazimari Agent while Feo and Horsa sat on a coil of rope, awaiting clearance to go ashore. Along the quay, dockers tramped, heavy sacks over their shoulders, loading the other two ships which were in port.

'Ahoy!' Horsa had jumped to his feet and was waving furiously to attract the attention of a young man who was strolling beside the ships. 'Ahoy! Stefan! Tell King Olave we're back!'

Stefan jumped and turned round. 'Horsa! And Feo! He'd given up hope. I'll talk to you later.' He vanished into the warren of dockside streets at a dead run.

As the Harbourmaster left the ship a short time later, a group of people appeared from the town. Their vivid brocades contrasted sharply with the dusty workwear of the dockers. Feo leant over the rail and peered at them. A glint of gold in the centre of the group caught his eye and he recognised King Olave wearing his circlet and his purple robes. On one side of him stood the Commander of the King's Armies, his scarlet uniform resplendent in the afternoon sun, and he was flanked on the other by his Chief Minister.

'Ahoy, the Amagadis!' Stefan, the King's First Page, was approaching the ship.

'Ahoy! Who goes there?' replied the sailor on watch.

'King Olave and attendants. May we come on board?'

'Not without Harbour Clearance.'

'Your passengers, Feodin and Horsa, will they come ashore to greet King Olave?'

'No-one leaves this ship until the Harbourmaster and the Agent agree clearance.'

'When will that be?'

The sailor shrugged. 'Our Fazimari Agent hasn't agreed to sign the papers off yet.'

'Stefan!' Horsa leant over the rail. 'We'll talk to the King from here. There are preparations which can be started while we're waiting for clearance.'

The royal party reached the ship's side and stopped. Olave stepped forward and tilted his head back, his already short stature foreshortened by the angle.

'Feo! It's good to see you back. Have you brought the dragonstone?' The King peered anxiously upwards.

Feo bowed as elegantly as he could from the strange angle. 'Your Majesty. We have the dragonstone.'

King Olave's face broke into a broad smile. 'I knew you'd do it!'

'I wish we had known,' muttered Feo under his breath.

The Commander of the King's Armies stepped forward. 'I believe there are some preparations we can make.'

Horsa joined the discussion of what needed to be brought from the Hereditary Wizard's house, where it was to be taken and how many mules would be required to carry it. Soon, messengers were riding in all directions.

All the details settled, the royal party departed and Feo and Horsa sat on the coil of rope. Feo could see Horsa looking sideways at him and knew his pallor was betraying his fear. There was only one more step to lift the curse - but that was the most critical of them all.

The Great Reworking

A bustle along the quay finally signalled the return of the Harbourmaster with the Fazimari Agent in tow. Feo and Horsa stood up, anxious to disembark. A few minutes later, Captain Pollik came on deck, the roll in his gait a little more pronounced than usual.

'S'time to go ashore. Just got our clearance. Set you ashore, then we catch the evening tide.'

'I can't thank you enough for your help, Captain Pollik.' Horsa shook the Captain's hand vigorously. 'We've arrived in time. Now we just have to do our bit.' He glared at Feo, who was feeling slightly offended at the offhand dismissal of his monumental task.

'S'no problem. Without your help I'd have lost my vinefruit. All of it.' He shook his head solemnly. 'Very valuable stuff, vinefruit.'

'Indeed. We hope to meet you again, next time you're in port here.'

Feo and Horsa descended to the quay, followed by their bags. Stefan appeared from nowhere and led the way through the narrow streets.

'Have you all the items?' asked Feo.

'We've everything on your list. It's all packed on mules and waiting in the King's mews.'

'You haven't forgotten the incense? Or the chalk?'

'Everything's there, just as you asked.'

Feo didn't reply, but concentrated on putting one foot before the other, each pace bringing him one step nearer to the final ritual. They were already climbing slightly and the salt smell of the harbour was dropping below them.

Two twisting roads later, they reached the back entrance to the palace and the King's mews.

Passing under the arch and the big clock, they entered the cobbled court, where the loaded mules were milling round fretfully. Feo passed among them, checking as well as he could that what he needed was there. As the grooms strapped the bags on the last mule, King Olave and his ministers arrived.

'Is all ready? Then we'll leave now.' Olave and his attendants passed under the clock tower and turned up the hill. As the last mule followed them out of the yard, the air twisted behind it and an eye blinked into being. It stared after the group with cold malice and then imploded with a faint pop.

Feo strode up the hill, keeping pace with the mule carrying his book bag. He ran through his preparations again, mentally checking each action and word. He could find no fault. Raising his eyes as they rounded the first bend of the winding road, he saw one of the mule drovers look away hurriedly, hiding his fearful expression. Feo was puzzled. Surely the man wasn't afraid of him. Then he realised that he was afraid of the forces Feo handled. This was the hour of the Hereditary Wizard, this was his arena and no-one else could do his work. Feo settled his hat at an angle and went up with a new spring in his step. He would not fail them.

As they rose up the side of the hill, the trees which had surrounded the palace gradually gave way to rough grass and low scrub. Beneath them, Cardevin's harbour and town lay like a model, painted blue sea beyond the shoreline, painted red roofs at all angles in the town. Only the movement of people in the streets insisted that it was real.

The path grew steeper and narrower as it coiled round the hill. Mules and people moved into single file, grunting with the effort of breasting the slope.

Feo, following the mule with his books, glanced to his left. The track ended abruptly at the steep drop down to the trees and Feo thought he could see traces of old avalanches half-hidden in the vegetation far below. He glanced nervously up the slope above him several times, but the rock was solid and static in the evening sun. Turning his gaze towards his feet, he concentrated on putting one foot before the other.

As they rounded the next bend, he felt movement in his pocket and Kirrin wriggled her head free of his cloak. She sniffed the air looking uneasy, her nostrils twitching in search of something she couldn't find. Then she wriggled further out of the pocket and mewed. Feo looked at her and then in the direction she was staring. At the same moment he heard a rattle of loose stone.

'Avalanche!' Feo yelled as he slapped the precious book-mule on the rump to make it jump clear. He leapt himself and felt the impact of a few small stones as the body of the rockfall thundered behind him.

Coughing in the residual dust, he looked round apprehensively. The avalanche had swept over the track and down into the valley, save for a handful of loose rocks. Standing on the other side of its path were the last drover and mule. Of the mule between, there was no sign. Feo peered down with caution. The animal and its invaluable pack must be buried under tons of rock several hundred feet below. There would be no chance of recovering either.

A hand gripped his elbow and he turned to find Horsa.

'Feo, what happened?'

'One of the mules is lost,' said Feo in despair, 'and I don't know what it was carrying.'

'I'll find out. We can send someone to replace it.'

He was back a few minutes later. 'It was carrying all the incense and most of the cedarwood. Why didn't they have the sense to divide the loads!'

'The incense! And cedarwood! I must have aromatics to burn!' Feo's mind spun as he tried to encompass the disaster and find a route round it.

'We could send someone back for more,' offered Horsa without conviction.

Feo shook his head impatiently. 'They were to have packed all my incense and there's no-one else on Cardevin likely to have any. And who do you know who burns cedarwood fires?'

By now, the rest of the party had jostled round the mules and were staring at the detritus. Several were casting nervous glances at the now-static slope above. The tail-end drover had unfrozen and was throwing the rocks from the path over the edge. Feo clasped his hands behind his back and thought furiously. This was his operation and there was no-one who could help him. He longed for some advice from Sigid, but there was no time spare to contact him.

He tossed up one idea after another and discarded them all. It was no use looking for resin trees to make incense; they only grew in the East - the realm of the Sultan. No-one in Cardevin would have any - it was only used by magicians and in the temples of the mainland. There were no other magicians on Cardevin. Cedarwood - he was certain he'd need more than was left. He needed good fires at each corner of his diagram to protect his ritual.

Unconscious of what he was doing, he paced round the confined area of the track. A hand caught his shoulder and he realised he had strayed dangerously close to the edge. He stepped back and noticed a tiny sprig of green clinging to the brink. His mind swerved onto another tack. Herbs! They were aromatic, too. And powerful. And this was just the right sort of country to find them.

It wasn't quite as simple as that, of course. He didn't think the powers he was going to invoke would respond to simple herbs. They were used to feeding on the rich scent of incense. But there were other entities who would respond to the call. The only trouble was they wouldn't be drawn by the same ritual.

His head spun. He would have to recast the whole thing. While he was trudging up a treacherous hill path. And redesign all the sigils and symbols. And reconstruct all the invocations.

It was a monstrous task, but he had no choice. He had gone too far now to give up.

As he followed the book-mule up the narrow track a blizzard of thoughts whirled through Feo's head. He sorted through them doggedly, aware at the periphery of his mind of the presence of Horsa beside him, ready to send for his requests - or prevent him from stepping off the path.

Thyme, borage, cestula, scrub-wood, the stream of requests passed from Feo to Horsa and on to the impromptu gang of runners. When the plodding mule-team reached the summit, there were already signs of activity.

Feo's gaze swept over the hilltop. The precipitous path had emerged onto a smooth plateau. It was so level that Feo wondered if the top of the hill had been sliced off by a forgotten generation of sorcerers. Near the mouth of the path were a number of piles of greenery. The largest was more brown than green and was the scrub-wood, the heap growing larger by the minute as scurrying bodies added armfuls. Beside it, someone had thoughtfully spread a cloak to hold the small heaps of herbs. Feo dropped to his knees and started sorting.

'More cestula!'

'We've got enough borage now.'

'Can someone find a little trefoil?'

Now he moved to the scrub-wood and sorted it into two piles, aromatic and ordinary. Both would be useful, but in different places. Finally, he sat back on his heels.

'I think we have enough.'

Turning, he found that Horsa had placed his book-bag behind him. He delved to the bottom and pulled out a small book bound in time-stained parchment. Flicking its pages furiously, he began jotting in his notebook.

The sun dropped lower and lower. As it touched the horizon, he shut the book and stood up.

'I've finished. Now we begin the Working.' He looked round the sky. 'About an hour to moonrise. It will have to be enough.'

Feo walked to the side of the plateau where the mule packs had been spread and the contents laid out on the short turf. Opening a parcel, he shook out a bundle of white cloth encrusted with silver embroidery and carefully laid it down beside him. He removed his hat and cloak and brushed the dust of hard travel off his clothes. Then he picked up a small flask and poured scented liquid over his hands. Donning the white robe and resuming his cloak and hat, he raked his gaze round the plateau. Every eye was on him. A taut silence clamped the air.

'Let us begin.' Feo swept his cloak back over his shoulder and picked up a large bag of ground chalk and an iron tripod.

'The first thing to do,' he remarked, 'is to lay out the diagram.'

He strode to the centre of the area and stood the tripod on the ground. A sense of calm descended on him after the frantic activity of the last few hours. He had planned everything to the best of his ability. Now, all that remained was to play his part accurately. Muttering a short prayer, he located the East and started to pace out his pattern, trickling a thin stream of chalk as he went. It grew rapidly from the basic star to a series of interlocking figures, the chalk lines glowing almost luminous in the fading light. Finally, he completed it with a double circle and stepped back to check his work. He was pleased. He could find no error.

Next, he inserted the sigils one by one, taking care that each was clear and correctly oriented. He knew the entities he was trying to employ would not respond unless properly called.

The pattern was now eye-wrenching in its complexity. But still there were spaces in it. Feo enlisted the help of the onlookers to build small fires in these, of aromatic wood at the corners and ordinary wood before each sigil. Now there was only the clear space surrounding the tripod.

Feo cast an anxious eye over the sky. Might Hoaga grant him enough time to finish! He breathed a soft sigh of relief; there was still a little time before moonrise.

Sorting the herbs, he placed each one in a different-coloured pouch and dropped them in his pockets. He picked up a bunch of cestula and circled the diagram sunwise, brushing the perimeter with the cestula and chanting the charms to drive all evil influences from his work. Then he ordered the fires to be lit. The groundwork was complete. The structure was laid. Now, it was time to activate the magical machine.

The leaping flames cast distorted shadows over the whole plateau. Men who were standing still and straight bred wraiths which danced grotesquely at their feet. Feo himself had countless shadows twisting round him as he stood beside his circle. Stretching his senses, he could feel a low vibration, almost a hum, emanating from the diagram. Even now, before the rituals had bound and awakened it, he felt its potential power. And all this energy must be controlled and channelled by him. Pushing fear down deep enough so it could not distract him, he moved to the first sigil.

Feo raised his hands, the silver on his robe sparkling in the flickering light, and chanted.

'Spirits of the forest and the valley, come close and attend.

'Nymphs of the rivers, hear my plea.

'Satyrs of the hills, aid my task.

'I am here to right a wrong.

'I am here to lift a curse,

'A curse that was most wrongfully set.

'Aid me in my work, help me in my task.'

He paused and spread his arms, the cloak flapping in midnight blue wings behind him.

'Nathos, satyr of the Cardevin hills, attend and guide my hands.'

Feo made a complex gesture and cast a pinch of herbs from a red pouch onto the fire. The flames leapt unnaturally high, casting a pink light over his face and sending out clouds of resinous smoke. A new note joined the vibrations he could feel in his head.

Feo progressed to the next sigil.

'Ximini, nymph of the Great River, attend and support my words.'

This time, the herbs came from a yellow pouch and the clouds of smoke bore an odour of salt and clean air. Another note joined the first, forming an incomplete harmony.

One by one, Feo visited each sigil. The clouds of smoke rose, filling the air above the pattern, twining in tortuous shapes and flooding the whole hilltop with dizzying scents. And in his head, the notes mingled, finally making a chord.

He returned to his packages and extracted a parcel wrapped in green cloth. Followed by Horsa, who was bearing the bag of chalk and a willow broom, he moved to the North edge of the diagram. There he stood for a few moments, head thrown back and eyes closed, feeling the currents of power that swirled round him. The ritual was well begun, but he still had much to do.

Kirrin struggled out of his pocket and perched on his shoulder, her eyes glittering all shades of green in the eerie light. He rubbed her head, the resultant current of support steadying him. Then he held the package up before his chest and paced forward. Horsa kept level with him on his right.

As they reached the start of the pattern, Horsa applied the broom and swept a narrow path through the lines. Careful not to tread on any part of the diagram, they made slow progress towards the centre. Feo kept the package before him and repeated a short verse beneath his breath.

They were nearly half way to the centre when a feeling of apprehension descended on Feo. It became difficult to move forward. He felt as if he were trying to push his way across a vat of honey. Kirrin stood up on his shoulder and he could see from the corner of his eye that she was puffed out to twice her normal size. Then he realised that the smoke, which had been twisting round the area in close coils, was eddying wildly. He kept repeating his spell because it was too dangerous to stop, but they were hardly making any progress now. Risking a quick glance at the sky, Feo discovered that a dense black cloud was hovering over the hill.

He didn't know what to do. The thoughts whirled round in his head so fast he could barely catch them. He couldn't pause in what he was doing to deal with this new problem; the diagram was broken to allow them access and he must hold the breach until he could repair it, or uncontrollable forces would be loosed to the outside. Yet this cloud, which he was sure was the source of the impediment, must be dealt with, or they would not be able to reach the centre and complete his ritual. He could see Horsa looking sideways at him and took a deep breath. There must be a solution. There must.

The forces held by the pattern were pushing at him. He could feel his grip on them slipping as his mind churned round the menace of the cloud. He couldn't deal with both at once. He would lose control and his essence would be forced from his body by the colossal powers and sent spinning round a hostile universe.

His face was rubbed by something soft and a small noise caught his ear. He realised his hands were shaking so badly that he was in danger of dropping his package. Kirrin made another sound and he had a sudden picture of her on his shoulder. She was sitting bolt upright and he could see lines of power gathered in her mouth. They came from the diagram. 'Kirrin!' he breathed, 'Can you do it?'

Kirrin uttered a 'mrreow'.

Rapidly rearranging the complex connections in his mind, Feo felt the pressure pass from his hands. He straightened and looked again at the cloud.

'Kirrin?' murmured Horsa.

Feo nodded. He leant his cheek against warm fur for a moment and prayed that Kirrin would be able to maintain the block on the breach while he dealt with the Sultan's attack.

Drawing himself up to his full height, he held the package aloft. His voice boomed over the plateau.

'By Azeron, Lady of the Deeps, by Nooth, Lord of the Tritons, Ahmed, you shall not halt us.' Feo allowed the need to destroy this threat to rage through his body.

'May your evil depart: it cannot touch us.

'May your threat disperse: it cannot harm us.

'May your opposition cease: it cannot stop us.

'May Nooth, may Azeron make it so.

'I command you, desist, or the waters that cradle Cardevin will devour you!'

He brandished the green package above his head. The black cloud broke up into a group of cloudlets that swirled round in a way no natural storm would behave. The aromatic smoke billowed outwards and then gathered once more in protective coils round the pattern.

At the same moment, something gave. As if a smothering blanket had been removed, they felt the way forward clear. Kirrin sat down on Feo's shoulder again and resumed her scrutiny of the ritual. They moved towards the centre once more.

Horsa brushed clear their path through the last circle and Feo felt a rush of ice-cold air batter at his face. He forced it back, pulling another strand of control into his grasp, and paced to the centre where the iron tripod was waiting. Holding his package aloft, he allowed its wrappings to fall away. The Dragonstone's opalescent bands flashed in the multicoloured firelight and then seemed to light with a fire of their own. Feo could feel the latent power throbbing within it, barely contained by the encompassing pattern. He laid it gently on the tripod. The smoke bent inwards and twisted into a rope above their heads.

Stepping slowly backwards, Feo returned to Horsa. He took the bag of chalk and closed the circle when they had passed through. Now they must repair the rest of the pattern before the last part of the ritual raised its full power.

Feo glanced up to see if the cloud had finally dispersed. His ears were assaulted by a mighty roar, as if the thunder were screaming 'NOOOooo...'

The black cloud had gathered once more, and now was streaked with purple light. Boiling overhead, it emitted a spear of searing lightening which plunged towards them. The smoke rolled up and the lightening exploded in a torrent of brilliant sparks.

The crack of thunder hit their ears with deafening intensity. Then a curtain of rain descended.

Within seconds they were drenched. Worse, the rain was attacking the chalk lines. In his mind, Feo could see all his work washed away, the forces he had gathered so carefully dispersed and causing havoc in their uncontrolled passage to oblivion.

'Hurry,' he said to Horsa, his voice hoarse with tension 'We must complete this before it's destroyed.'

They moved outwards, Feo repairing the lines and Horsa now using the willow broom to tidy the patches. The rain pelted them like stones, but the lines of the pattern were surprisingly resilient. Although the forces which bound them were not yet complete, they still offered some resistance to the water. Feo began to hope they might make it.

Step by step, they fought their way out. Despite the downpour and the gale which drove it, they made progress. Line after line was completed, and then, when they felt they could bear no more, they couldn't find the next line.

Feo stood. There must be more. But there wasn't. Suddenly triumphant, he raised his arms.

'THE PATTERN IS COMPLETE!'

The fires flared fifty feet high, straining to reach the cloud. The smoke followed, shooting up in columns which were almost solid, passing the flames and piercing the roiling black. The cloud crumbled, torn apart by the blast. Its fragments vanished to the four points of the compass.

As the fires dropped back, Feo surveyed his diagram. Whole and undamaged, the fragile lines were glowing with an inner life. And in his mind, the strands of control lay ordered, awaiting his manipulation.

He returned to his station in the North. Stretching his arms out to each side, he began the final incantation.

'Nathos, Ximini, Carakis, Therion, Barad

'Verama zerani u'malich'

The fires at each sigil flared and dropped in turn. As the last one soared, the rest rose to join it and all settled into a steady pulsation.

Feo paused, the folds of his velvet cloak snatching blue highlights from the flames as it swayed in harmony. Already he could feel the faint tickle of the manifesting power.

'Nathos, aruch arba'ah vemeteinu.'

The first fire shot to twice its height, dominating the scene.

'Ximini, aruch arba'ah vemeteinu.'

The second fire joined the first. The plateau was filled with orange light, staining the twisting smoke so it itself looked aflame against the dark sky.

One by one, Feo called the entities to attend. As each arrived, he could feel the balance of forces shift, until finally he felt almost as if he were floating, supported on all sides. The coloured fires roared brilliantly at each corner of the pattern, combining to flood the whole area with vivid white light. The smoke curled in ordered twists round each fire. Scanning the whole diagram, he could find no fault. All his powers were present.

Feo took a deep breath and raised his arms again. This was the critical moment when he linked all the energies and must control them. Behind him radiated from his feet five different coloured shadows. Before him pulsed five sorcerous fires, their forces under the tenuous restraint of Feo's pattern. He drew all his faculties together for the final unleashing.

'Nathos, Ximini, Carakis, Therion, Barad,
'Mecharak!'

The fires leapt and started to bend towards the centre of the diagram. Feo felt a surge of power run through him.

'Paliti!'

The fires curved downward towards the ground, like the fingers of a giant hand closing. Smoke billowed and then wreathed round the fires, protecting their clean line. Feo felt himself at the centre of the web of forces, part of them, yet also guiding them where they had to go.

'Darod!'

The flow of power became almost unbearable as the fires homed on the centre of the diagram. Then they touched the Dragonstone. Its bands flashed unbearably bright and Feo fought to control the raging torrents of energy released. His whole body resonated with the screaming forces as he channelled them to the centre. The Dragonstone flared brighter and brighter under the tormenting fingers of fire. Feo swept his arms round and forced the smoke to weave a protective cage round the middle. He felt the forces respond to his control and then the light from the Dragonstone exploded upward into the sky. The smoke forced it into a tight column, but at the top the fire burst out in a dome of sparks which encompassed the whole island of Cardevin.

Feo hung on desperately, pushing the immense power into its necessary path. He felt a slight check in the flow as it met the sultan's curse before the irresistible force swept it away and then it was running free, cleansing Cardevin of all malign forces.

Feo Cast Adrift

Feo was tumbling through the void. It was dark, dark as the caves of Askelar. There were no features in the darkness and he could only tell he was tumbling by the slight queasiness in his stomach.

Something caught the corner of his eye and he turned his head to look at it. There was nothing there. He tried to turn round, but without references, he couldn't tell if he'd succeeded or not. Lying back, he allowed himself to drift, mind blank, senses asleep.

He didn't know how long he stayed like that. As there was no light in the void, there also seemed to be no time. But finally, after a minute or a lifetime, he discerned something in the distance.

It was only a speck. It passed through his field of vision so swiftly he wasn't even sure it was there. The next time he saw it he managed to turn his head and track it for a little. It was real, it was there.

Feo tried to straighten himself up to halt his motion. With a reference point it was different and after a few minutes' struggle, he had managed to halt his tumbling and orient himself to face the light.

Although it was so tiny that it seemed to have position but no size, Feo was sure it was getting larger. He stared at it for several minutes without detecting any difference, but the certainty remained. Closing his eyes, he tried to blank his mind again, but it was impossible. The void was no longer formless. The tiny point of light had given it a shape.

Where was he? The question echoed through his head. Following quietly in its footsteps was the next question. How did he get out of here?

He opened his eyes and looked round. There was still only the one speck in the blackness. He leaned forward, his attention caught. Surely the point was closer. Or bigger. Or both?

Not daring to move, he watched. Although still tiny, the speck had definite dimensions now. He was positive it was getting closer. For a moment he panicked as he thought he might be falling into a lonely sun, but he didn't think it looked bright enough for that and he resumed his watch. Gradually, the point filled more and more of his field of vision, until he could start to detect some detail on it, a slight patterning of lighter and darker areas.

The closer it approached him, the more clearly he could see the dappling. The light had assumed the warm amber colour of an inviting room and he thought longingly of soft chairs and crackling fires. He was starting to think he would be able to touch it soon, when a dreadful thought occurred. What if he whirled past, too far away even to touch the warmth? He twisted, trying to make sure he would reach the light and it started to jink about in the void. He almost panicked again, and then he realised it was moving to meet him.

It grew closer and closer, now plainly visible as a spherical bubble of normality in this sterile wilderness. The shadows started to take form and Feo realised there was a human figure in the sphere. It was silhouetted against the light and Feo could see no detail.

The sphere was yards away, and then feet, and then Feo was touching it and the figure in it reached out a hand to him. Feo grasped it and was pulled into the light.

'Feo, dear boy, You're frozen! Come and sit by the fire.'

'Uncle Sigid!' Feo looked round wildly, but there was no trace of the void or the bubble he had entered. He was standing in a pleasant room with a wall of books behind him and a blazing hearth in front. 'Where am I?'

Sigid chuckled. 'It's just a little place of mine where no-one disturbs me. Now come by the fire.'

Feo realised he was shivering. He allowed himself to be seated by the fire and a hot drink was pushed into his hands.

When Feo had absorbed most of his drink and his hands had stopped shaking, Sigid leant back in his seat and remarked, 'That was quite a show, wasn't it?'

Feo looked up, startled. As the void had been formless, so it seemed to hold neither time nor memory. Until this moment, he had totally forgotten what he had been doing before.

'The ritual! Did it work?' he asked anxiously.

'Of course, dear boy, it was a complete success. After that magnificent, that... that stupendous ritual, Cardevin will be free of all evil for many years to come.' He chuckled. 'And Ahmed has a bloody nose!'

Feo looked puzzled.

'When you removed the curse, it rebounded back to its source. Ahmed and his wizards were able to neutralise the worst of the force, but their magic is burnt out for a very long time. They'll be fully occupied fighting off their neighbours with ordinary weapons. Ahmed will be lucky if he's still Sultan in six month's time.'

Sitting back, Feo let a warm content spread through his body. He had completed his task. They had won and Cardevin was safe.

'Of course,' said Sigid, looking at him severely, 'You should have been able to get yourself out of the void.'

'The void?' said Feo, a wave of sleep rolling over him, 'But how?'

'By need, dear boy, by need. You should know that by now. After all, you used it to get out of the caverns under the mountain. You mustn't allow the void to possess you. It is formless and timeless and if you just drift, eventually you will dissolve into it. No-one could save you then.'

Feo shuddered, wondering how many lost souls were already diffused through that black nothingness, their last coherent thoughts fading into oblivion. Then a sudden thought alarmed him. Why was he here?

'Sigid, am I dead?'

Sigid looked startled. 'Dead? No, no, after the strain of that immense piece of magic, your body is exhausted, so you came here.' He beamed at Feo. 'It was just a little bit over the top, you know.'

'I used the Grimoire of Arbesius and the Spell-Book of Nagi Isher,' said Feo indignantly, 'and ...'

'Yes, dear boy, I know, but we'll discuss that later. Now I think Kirrin is getting a little anxious about you. It's time you went back.'

The heat of the fire was fading and the room seemed to be growing hazy. Sigid's voice diminished into the distance. Feo could feel something hard pressing into his back and he was cold again. His clothes were drenched and he was freezing, all except a fiery heat trickling into his mouth.

'Mrrriaou?'

'Feo, are you all right?'

It was surprisingly hard to sit up, but someone helped him. Kirrin insisted on sitting on his shoulder, her soft fur a small spot of warmth against his neck. Horsa was putting away a small leather flask and urging him to get up, while the King and most of his party were gathered round looking white and shaken.

Feo struggled to his feet and surveyed the plateau. The fires had all gone out and the only light was from the narrow crescent of the new moon. Like an import from a strange land, the lines of his great pattern shone dimly with reflected light. The Dragonstone sat on its tripod, its fires quenched, and over everything lingered a haze of aromatic smoke, blurring outlines and softening the starkness of the burnt turf.

'Come on, Feo. You can ride one of the mules back down.'

Wrapped in a dry cloak and swaying with the plodding of the mule, Feo dreamed of the hot food and blazing hearth which were waiting for them at the palace. Then he realised that he wasn't cold right through at all. In the centre of his being that core of warm content still glowed. Cardevin was safe.

* * *

In the north of Fazimar a day or so later, Shallon and Aisu sat at the dark wood table in Aisu's house. Their chairs were pulled up to a blazing log fire and a pitcher of hot spiced wine stood on the hearth.

'Feo should have lifted the curse by now,' Shallon said. She looked a little pale. 'I wish I knew if he succeeded.'

'And when Horsa is coming back,' said Aisu, smiling.

'If Feo has succeeded, Horsa will be back soon.' Shallon blushed.

'We'll look and make sure all's well,' said Aisu.

She brought out a frosted mirror and a small brazier from the cupboard and set them on the table. The aromatic smoke rose and hung in wreaths about their heads. Aisu beckoned Shallon forward, and they both peered into the glass.

Shallon gasped and then turned red. A tiny image of Horsa was talking to a very pretty girl with flowing blond hair. Smiling a goodbye, he turned and walked away, and then Shallon saw he had a pack slung over his shoulder. He went up the gangplank to a ship. Shallon could just read the name - it was "Amagadis". She leant back, her hands shaking.

'For a moment, I thought... But he's on his way. Three days...'

Aisu smiled. 'All's well in Cardevin, then. The new moon was yesterday, so Feo has lifted the curse.'

* * *

Shallon stood on the quayside, waiting for the Amagadis to be towed into dock. She could see Horsa on the deck, but he hadn't spotted her yet among the piles of cargo and bustling crowds of dock workers and visitors. The ship kissed the quay, and two men in blue tunics caught the ropes and made her fast.

The gangplank was lowered, and at last Shallon managed to catch Horsa's eye. His face lit up. He waved, and she took an involuntary step forward, her heart starting to race. She'd not quite been able to believe he'd come back until this moment. A minute later, she was caught in a fierce embrace. Their lips met, and a warm glow started in the pit of her stomach and spread through her body. He was really here!

* * *

Feo paced up the centre of the Great Hall beside the Lord Chamberlain. Sunlight streamed in through the high windows, striking azure highlights from his cloak and sparking flame and gold from the phoenix feather in his hat. On either side, the nobles of Cardevin rose from their seats at the banqueting tables to honour him.

Reaching the high table, he swept off his hat and made a low bow to King Olave. The King rose and escorted Feo to the seat at his right hand, before turning to the body of the hall.

'Nobles of Cardevin, our esteemed Hereditary Wizard has saved this country from a terrible fate. He fought a dragon in a strange country...'

Feo sat, acknowledging the plaudits from the assembled nobles with a modest nod of his head. Then he froze. Olave wouldn't mention his stay in prison and his capture by bandits. Would he?

It was a long speech, and Feo only realised it was finished just in time to rise to his feet as King Olave turned to him. He bowed his head as Olave removed a heavy gold chain from his own neck and placed it round Feo's. Then he turned to face the hall.

'King Olave, Nobles of Cardevin, it has been my honour to add to the roll of history one more time when the Hereditary Wizard has been the saviour of his country...'

* * *

Where the river met the sea, the Hereditary Wizard's stone tower clung to the cliff. The sun shone, striking blazing colours from the opalescent stone on the tower-top. A couple of figures bustled round the house, trimming the garden and carrying baskets of food.

In the courtyard, a small black kitten with no hair of white played with a straw, and curled on one gatepost was a tiny golden dragon.

About The Author

Lynn is an engineer who believes in magic.

Her work has not changed her fascination with the supernatural. She has been an avid reader of Fantasy and Science Fiction since her schooldays and has a fascinating collection of books on Magic, Witchcraft and ESP.

About fifteen years ago, she decided to satisfy a long-held wish and start writing fiction. Since then, she has written numerous short stories, one completed novel, The Dragonstone, and three part-novels (one for the National Novel Writing Month in 2011).

Find out more at
www.ghostlypublishing.co.uk

And connect with me on Facebook at:
www.facebook.com/GhostlyPublishing

Coming Soon:

Jimmy Threepwood
and the
Veil of Darkness

Even heroes do bad things, but there's something really unfortunate about being selected to join the forces of evil and become one of the four horsemen of the apocalypse.

When Jimmy Threepwood is collected to face his dark destiny and destroy the world with his supernatural powers, he needs to make a choice...

What lengths will he go to for the sake of revenge?

Priced £7.99 from Ghostly Publishing Online and in all good bookshops

The End is Nigh!

18th of October 2012

Lightning Source UK Ltd.
Milton Keynes UK
UKOW042019240313

208083UK00001B/4/P